Michael D. William Jr. has been writing gay African American stories for close to 30 years. To his credit, he has copyrighted 3 books this particular manuscript is the first for available commercial viewing and the first of the trilogy. The main specialty of what the author writes is characters that are nonconformist anti-hero types.

I would like to thank members of my family and a select few friends I've had over the years who have encouraged me with my writing to never give up. And I'd also like to dedicate this book to my English teachers, because without you I wouldn't have been able to improve my style of writing.

Michael D. Williams

PALE TWISTED FOREST

AUSTIN MACAULEY PUBLISHERS™

LONDON • CAMBRIDGE • NEW YORK • SHARJAH

Ordering Information
Quantity sales: Special discounts are available on quantity purchases by corporations, associations, and others. For details, contact the publisher at the address below.

Publisher's Cataloging-in-Publication data
Williams, Michael D.
Pale Twisted Forest

ISBN 9798889106531 (Paperback)
ISBN 9798889106548 (ePub e-book)

Library of Congress Control Number: 2023922495

www.austinmacauley.com/us

First Published 2024
Austin Macauley Publishers LLC
40 Wall Street, 33rd Floor, Suite 3302
New York, NY 10005
USA

mail-usa@austinmacauley.com
+1 (646) 5125767

I would like to acknowledge Austin Macauley Publishing for taking a chance on me and giving me my first real introduction to the public. And I'd like to acknowledge the other publishers and literary agents who reviewed my work and helped me to find my way to Austin Macauley Publishers.

Introduction

This is a story pertaining to a unique individual who's descended from an African American couple who fled the horrors of Jim Crow South, which took place in the early 20th century. Their journey takes them to Russia shortly after the beginning of communism. Unfortunately, they are imprisoned in a cold gulag where they both spend a miserable two years. After they are released, the couple struggles to find work in a foreign unforgiving land. But being black in the Soviet Union was in some ways worse than being born black in the old American South.

Eventually, the couple, Jonah and Martha Fisk, finds work with a mid-level government official named Korcoff Vamitri as a janitor and maid. As time passed, Russian became the Fisks' second tongue. Under the guidance of Vamitri, the Fisks learn many things, particularly about how the Russian government work and how knowing too many secrets can get you killed or give you great power. Luckily, this proved to be the latter for Korcoff and the Fisks and some of the people Korcoff answered to.

Sadly, for Korcoff, one of his secrets could more than likely get him shot by Stalin himself personally. It was already strange to most of his colleagues that he was unmarried, so some does suspect the truth. Fortunately, in a dark way, Jonah Fisk has the same secret, which he keeps from Martha for a time at least. So Korcoff and Jonah become reluctant allies despite Korcoff's obvious racism.

However, sometimes any kind of so-called fault a man might have, whether it's physical or emotional can be passed onto your children unintentionally. Which is what happens in a roundabout way. A character trait Jonah shared with one of his sons who becomes one of the very rare black agents for the KGB.

Surprisingly, Peter Fisk serves the state well, mainly from his post in Africa. Due to the color of Peter's skin, no one ever suspects he was a spy for

Russia or that he preferred other men over women. But because of his Soviet training, he is able to seduce a female recruit and father a daughter by this recruit who would become his wife. A woman who happens to be of afro-Greek descent herself.

Their daughter whom they names Natleaha grows up to be one of the best and seductive assassins for the Soviets during the Cold War. Natleaha's bisexuality makes it easy for her to get close to any target, male or female. Her exotic inner racial beauty is her greatest weapon. Unfortunately, despite her formidable skills, they doesn't prevent her from being assaulted. During a raid on a drug gang's headquarters, a large man catches her by surprise.

The assailant brutally rapes her before she manages to snap his neck while he was on top of her. Sadly, the rape leaves her pregnant, so she cuts off all ties to the KGB. She plans to abort the baby, but her parents talk her into having it.

When she gives birth, Natleaha gets the shock of her life when the baby boy she gives birth to was ivory white with kinky bright blond hair. Clearly, she doesn't want the baby but Peter, her father, reminds her of their family's unorthodox traits and lifestyle, which was passed down to all of them. Natleaha however was unmoved and still wants nothing to do with the baby.

Only giving the boy a name, Ivan T, a cruel joke of sorts, naming him after Ivan the Terrible, the worst Czar of recorded Russian history. This turns into a cruel reminder by nearly everyone, especially by other children as he grew up. After dumping Ivan on her parents' doorstep, Natleaha disappears. Locating his mother would be one of Ivan's obsessions. As suspected because of his skin tone, Ivan is an outcast and terribly ridiculed as a child.

With his grandfather as his only caring relative, Ivan grows up kind of bitter, but not evil. Yet he has a slight urge of a killing streak he inherited from his absentee mother. At a young age, Ivan knows besides his white skin that he had what most people call abnormal feelings for other boys his age and older.

After the fall of Communism in Russia, Peter decides to spend more time caring for his grandson, since his wife wasn't up to the task. In grammar through high school, Ivan excels. Even though he was an albino, Ivan grows to be a tall muscular, handsome young man. It isn't even a surprise to Peter when his grandson come out to him, mainly because of his own sexual inclinations.

However, he does not like Ivan's tendency to offer himself to older men or that he prefers hanging out with members of the growing Russian Bratva. Ivan couldn't explain it, but some of these tattooed handsome men appeals to him. Before Peter realizes what is happening, his grandson quit his nearly complete FSB training to join a very brutal mafioso organization.

Though his new superiors did not approve of his sexuality, they considered Ivan a promising soldier. With his fighting skills, Ivan quickly becomes an efficient enforcer and killer for the Bratva. The men in charge tell Ivan that he can have all the men and boys he wants as long as he obeys their rules without question, Ivan agrees.

As the events proceed with the Fisk family, an enemy lurks around the corner determined to destroy them all. With warnings from the distant past coming back, the family attempts to amass the means to retaliate before tragedy shakes them all to the core.

Chapter 1

In the middle of the Atlantic Ocean, the year is 1931 and a young black couple is on a cargo ship fleeing the oppressive horrors of the deep South, as well as the devasting effects of the financial misery called the Great Depression. Weeks before, they leave the state of Alabama Jonah and Martha Fisk realize they were not safe in their small town of Beachwood, just 30 miles away from the city of Montgomery.

The lynching of a close friend of Jonah's for stealing jewelry from a wealthy man's house is what mainly prompted their decision to leave. The town's people would constantly hear rumors from visiting Northerners about how it was more liberal for different races in Soviet Russia. So, they scrimped and saved everything from the menial jobs they both had to buy passage on a ship destined for Russia.

Aside from the obvious reasons of wanting to leave America, Jonah had other reasons, ones he thought he would never share with his beautiful wife.

Shortly before their journey, Jonah and Martha secretly traveled to L. A. California to buy Russian translating books from a Communist cell operating out of California. The Fisks needed the books desperately if they were going to communicate with the people in the Soviet Union. During the long journey, Martha and Jonah had various thoughts going through their minds.

"Does she know?" Jonah asked himself as the ship that he and his wife was on moved through the waters of the ocean.

"Five years, I maintain my love for Martha. I knew even before we left Beachwood that she would follow me anywhere. But it just happened."

"When me and Willie met, I knew that no good would come of it, but he was so beautiful, the prettiest colored man I'd ever seen. I wanted to fight it, but I couldn't help it. The urge just came back sumthin' fierce."

"You just haveta bury it now," like Jonah's Grandma told him when he was a teenager. "It ain't natural cause people won't understand, especially other colored folks. They'd think the devil done got in you for sure," she'd say.

"Sure, there were slip-ups here and therefore I met Martha, but they were mainly wit' white boys cause dey were easy to play wit' dat way. Then I met Martha when I was twenty. She was the first girl I'd been wit, but then four years in it, I met Willie. He was a nineteen-year-old boy whose family had jus' moved into town and he managed to get a job at the town grocery store, which everybody thought was weird since only white folks were allowed to shop there. But I didn't care. All I knew was that Willie brought back the feelings I'd buried deep down. And he liked me in the same way too. At first were jus' friends and the like, but then months into our friendship Willie jus kissed me one day when we were down by the pond under a tree for shade. From that point on, we were joined at the hip. I was sure nobody in town knew what we were really up to, except maybe Grandma.

It was well-hidden and I still laid with Martha proper like. I found out Willie wasn't truthful wit' me about who he was seein'. He told me I was the only one sides his own girlfriend, but it was a big fat ass lie! This lie got him killed and almost me too. He was bein' kept by one of the well to do white men in town. The married middle-aged man was the one who helped Willie git dat job at dat store come to find out. And he didn't like findin' out his pretty high yella' boy was rubbin' against a dark monkey. So, he made up a story about Willie stealin' from his wife. Grandma got wind of it and hid me outta town fo' months. Still the jealous white man wasn't satisfied wit' only lynching Willie. I think Martha still thought I was a man who friends wit' a thief and nuthin' else," Jonah silently and fully recalls.

Martha just watches her husband sleep on a cot abroad the ship. She was glad to be going far away from Beachwood. There were certain things her husband didn't know she knew. For instance, the white man, Jonah's friend Willie was messing with came by her house while her husband was in hiding.

When he couldn't find Jonah there, he decided to tell Martha everything out of spite.

"Yo' husband is a pansy ya' nigga bitch!" he said to her with a snarl.

"What are you talkin' bout?" Martha angrily asked in response. "Dat coon of yours was messin' wit' my Willie! But he's my property and yo' low husband won't be messin' wit nobody from now on! And if I ever see ya' man round here again, he's dead!" the white man yells before storming out of her house. From that moment on, the rest of their time in Beachwood was spent practically in hiding. But Martha still had secrets of her own.

"I think I'm wit' child, but I don't know if it's yours," Martha says softly out loud so she doesn't wake up Jonah.

Nearly from the moment Martha and Jonah met, Martha had been carrying on a passionate affair with his oldest uncle, which happened to be Jonah's grandma's first child. Martha had used special tea the last two times she accidently got pregnant. In the beginning, Martha tried to resist the uncle, but she was no match for Jonah's uncle Otis's seductive charms.

"You need a real strong man, not dat half mixed up boy my nephew is," he told her in a sweet devilish voice.

And before she knew it, Martha was flat on her back in his bed. Despite his age, he was a better lover than his nephew. Otis touched her body in all the right places. Jonah had his moments and was more tender, but Otis was more animalistic and passionate. The last Martha and Otis were together was three months before her and her husband left the country. When Otis found out from his mother that Martha was leaving with Jonah, he was furious. Probably for weeks, Martha managed not to sleep with Otis. So, he confronted her about it when he knew Jonah wasn't home.

"What chu gonna leave fo'? It's my nephew's problems dat's got 'em in dis fix not chu," Otis said tenderly to Martha.

"He's my husband, I don't wanna see 'em die. I love 'em and I know dat don't mean much to you, but I do."

Martha was surprised at herself right then because despite everything, she meant it. Deep down in her heart, she realized Otis really didn't love her. She was just a pretty toy for him to play with, something to prove his aging prowess.

"Jonah can never love ya fully, sumthin' will always git half of his heart."

Martha knew what Otis meant, but she didn't care, half of love from a man was better than no love in her mind. Growing up an orphan, Martha knew what it was like to have no love.

Leaving behind his family was difficult for Jonah, Martha was aware of that, but it had to be done. That angry rich white man wanted Jonah's neck to crack at the end of a rope for taking his boy from him. He would never be safe in the South, neither would Martha by association. So, after a tearful goodbye to his grandmother, Jonah took a train with Martha to a seaport by the Mississippi river, then another train to California. From there, they rode the large cargo ship bound for Eastern Europe. All in all, the journey took a week. Finally, the couple reached the port of St. Petersburg. Thankfully, Jonah and Martha didn't have much, just five change of clothes.

"Where are you from?" an officer stationed at the port asks the Fisks after they've stepped off the long boarding plank. The officer mostly knew the answer to his own question, due to the fact he had a copy of the ship's itinerary. And he also asked them in English with a thick Russian accent, of course. But the Fisks were none the wiser, so Jonah answered for him and his wife.

"We are from America, but we can speak some Russian," Jonah answers in proper English without his deep Southern drawl.

"Really, is that right? What is your business here? Why have you come?" the officer asks sternly.

He couldn't believe Americans would come here, especially as tourist not nowadays, white, black or otherwise.

"We wish to become citizens. We heard that the Communists give better equality than where we're from," Jonah says to the officer confidently.

But the man still wasn't buying it, if anything he was growing more suspicious. The duty officer had read and heard about what was going on in America then. They could barely afford to feed themselves, let alone go traveling on a whim to other places for citizenship. Average Americans are lazy and scared, but not that scared.

They're spies! Spies trying to help establish a network here to destabilize our new strong government.

But these two monkeys won't, the man slyly thinks to himself. However, the officer is trained to mask his thoughts by showing false mannerisms and words out of his mouth, which unfortunately for the Fisks he does now.

"Oh, of course, Russia is always welcoming to people who wish to happily help our lovely country. Wait over here while I call a driver to take you and your lovely wife to a hotel where we house our guests," the officer says with a convincing smile.

Unaware, the Fisks go stand by the man's booth station. Continuing to smile at the Fisks, the officer radios the secret police who quickly drive to the port and arrest the Fisks. Jonah and Martha can't even manage to get a word in edgewise before they're forcibly shoved into the back of the police car. They weren't even allowed to get their clothes. Instead, their luggage is left by the port station.

From that moment, the Fisks knew they weren't going to a hotel, but someplace different altogether. Instead, as they painfully suspected, they are taken to a KGB interrogation building. Martha and Jonah are each put into a different dimly lit room with an iron chair. For months, each day, the Fisks are beaten and barely fed and asked the same questions.

"Who are you really? Who do you work for in your government? What is America's plans for our country?"

The interrogators would always ask and demand during each brutal secession. Eventually, the Russians realized they could only torture Martha so much because she was pregnant. And they figured whatever color the baby was, it could be used for the State. So, she was shipped off to a low-level gulag where they made uniforms for the soldiers and police.

Jonah however wasn't as fortunate. Seeing as how he looked strong, he was tortured for several more months until the KGB decided he should be sent to the gulag in Siberia. It would be his home for the next two years.

Eventually, after the Russians were completely satisfied the Fisks weren't spies, they let them go. Martha was the first to be released, seeing how the gulag guards weren't trained to care for women with children. Martha wandered the streets of Kazan where the gulag she worked at for a month with her small torso. All she could do was beg for food in the freezing weather because no one would hire a black outcast with a baby. The only thing she could do was beg and steal blankets out of the trash and sleep in allies with her baby.

After a month of this hell, Jonah was able to find her, which under the circumstances wasn't too hard because how many homeless black women with a baby were there wandering around the country. The main goal now that they were back together was to find food, shelter and work. Since the Fisks probably would have a near impossible time finding work in the less important cities in Russia, they needed to get to a main city. What little they knew of the country they decided to make their way.

To Moscow. And the person who helped them wrote down the address of one of the building they should go to for work. When they got off the train, Martha asked a woman which way was the building they needed to go to in broken Russian. Following a verbal struggle, the Fisks were able to find out which direction to go in.

At the end of an hour and a half walk, they were in the front of a blue brick four story office building. A black iron gate circles around to the back to the front of it with guards stationed at the sides of it and one in a booth in front of the entrance.

"Who are you?" the guard in the booth demands with his rifle. Once again, Jonah speaks for himself and his wife.

"We are here for work. We heard that Mr. Korcoff Vamitri is looking for workers to clean the building he works in."

"Does he? I didn't hear of this," the guard says.

Just then Jonah notices that the guard is strikingly handsome and the other guards nearby have slightly dark good looks too. Once he noticed this, Jonah wonders if Korcoff is what he suspects he is.

He can't be, not here, Jonah thinks. But then he recalls back in Kazan how the woman who gave them the address to this building was looking him over like a slab of beef.

He couldn't figure out why since he discovered mostly white Russians don't like black people. But what Jonah didn't realize was that two years he spent in Siberia working and lifting, eating nearly raw meat and vegetable gruel, was that he grew into s striking figure himself. Black or white, he was a muscular and handsome.

Taking a chance, Jonah added some emphasis on his next words.

"We were personally recommended for work here." And Jonah looks deep into the guard's eyes as he says this. After a moment, the guard starts to catch the hidden meaning of Jonah's words.

Martha on the other hand is puzzled.

"Jonah what is—" she begins to say, but he stops her.

"Shh, trust me, I know what I'm doin," he whispers to her to calm her nerves and the toddler by her side.

If anything, the time Jonah spent being tortured and slaving away in the gulag was that his grandmother was half right. You can bury it for a while, but only for a while, but some men can't. He learned that in Siberia. Since then, he's had a special talent of seeing other men who don't know how to hide it.

"I will see if Mr. Vamitri can see you," the guard at the station informs the Fisks.

Spending a few seconds talking on the radio, the Russian was hard for Jonah and Martha to follow. The guard then tells them an office clerk will come out to meet them and escort them to Korcoff Vamitri's office.

Minutes later, a young blonde woman comes to the gate.

"If you both will follow me please. And make sure your child doesn't touch anything," the clerk informs them sternly.

The Fisks follow the clerk up a driveway path and into the main entrance of the building. There are other office workers inside the building, but Martha and Jonah don't really notice them as they walk by to an elevator at the end of a long hallway. They get on the elevator and the clerk pushes a button for the elevator to go up to the top floor of the building.

When they reach their destination, the clerk motions for Martha to have a seat against the wall with her son. But when Jonah goes to join his family in sitting the clerk stops him.

"No, you come with me, Mr. Vamitri will see you now," she tells Jonah.

So, he shrugs and follows her. They walk down another hall. This one is a little shorter than the last. Reaching a door with bumpy glass in the middle in the shape of a long square trimmed in wood. The clerk then knocks on the door.

"Come in," someone on the other end answers in deep male voice in Russian.

The clerk opens the door and walks in with Jonah. A dark-haired balding, broad shouldered, kind of heavyset man wearing glasses is sitting behind a desk reading files.

"That will be all, Mrs. Eva."

"Yes Mr. Vamitri," the clerk answers as she walks out closing the door behind her. Without looking up from the files, Korcoff addresses Jonah.

"You can have a seat and tell me why you are here." For the moment, Jonah obeys and sits.

"I heard you were looking for workers and me and my family need work."

"Really, what else did this woman tell you Mr. Fisk?"

How did he know my name? And how the hell did he know it was a woman who told him about Korcoff? Jonah wonders in shock. Korcoff then looks at Jonah in the eyes for the first time as he continues to talk.

"Yes, I know who you are Jonah Fisk. You, your wife and son are vagrants, drains on the State. You seek to come into my office and as you Americans say, shake me down. Fool, you are nothing but a low-grade monkey bum, a filthy mutt."

It was taking all of his self-control not to get up out of the chair and smash this racist's fat face in, but Jonah kept his cool. There was more at stake for his family and he wasn't going back to the streets if he could help it.

"I'm not asking for a handout, I'm looking for a chance to work for the State, but me and my family need jobs to do that."

"Family? The boy's probably not even yours."

Where the fuck did that come from? Jonah wondered.

"My son is not your concern Mr. Vamitri."

"Ah, but he is. We all are concerns for Mother Russia, to be used as the State sees fit. Can you accept that? I doubt if you can. Work for the State? You don't know what that even means. To give your life for a cause greater than you, to sacrifice your personal feelings and desires for little reward, so that the greater cause can succeed. How can you accept that? You came from nothing, you've never had to build something for a greater cause."

He was mostly right, thought Jonah. But he did know what it was like to be used. Used by that rich white man back in Beachwood and the gulags in Siberia. But Jonah did know he was on borrowed time and the only way to live in the here and now was to survive in a system that would chew him up and spit him out at the slightest misstep.

"You're right. I don't know about what concerns the State and how they see everyone in this country, but I do know what it's like to be used by the State. I learned that in Siberia as you well know. And I can learn better how to give my life for the State. You can teach me. You're open to the possibility of teaching me or else you wouldn't have agreed to see me, let alone talk to me in English."

Jonah's last words got Korcoff's attention.

"You surround yourself with fit men to guard you, but they don't know what it is to sacrifice, not really. But I already do and I've only been here for a few years. Teach me, mold me, let me show you I can work for this State as you have."

Korcoff gets up from his chair and walks over to Jonah. He notices Korcoff is a lot taller than he thought. He leans down and puts his hands Jonah's shoulders, speaking directly into his ear, he says subtly.

"Not you, your son."

"What?"

"Your favored son, the one you cherish most. You and your wife can work here as cleaners of the offices and toilets to earn your shelter until your dying days. But your favored son your most cherished child will be trained to work for the State. And if the child is like their parents, then so much the better."

This is not what Jonah meant. He had hoped him and his wife would work for Korcoff and unfortunately probably his children too, but only until they could earn enough to return to America in time when things would probably get better. Jonah knew that more than likely him and Martha would never go to America soon. Like it or not, this would be home for them. But Korcoff wanted a blood dynasty started that would not only be loyal to the State, but to him.

Fighting and dying for a country that does and would probably always hate them. Jonah could try to gain control of Korcoff and find a way to get out of the pact he wants Jonah to make. But that was out of the question, Korcoff knew more about Jonah and his family than he knew about him and he was better at shielding himself from having people see what he really was. He'd been doing it a lot longer too. Jonah didn't have the strength to do so anymore, which probably what mostly influenced his answer to Korcoff.

"Alright. I'll agree to work for you and my child and grandchild will be trained to work for the State."

"Splendid, you and your wife cans start work tomorrow. I'll arrange for someone to watch your son as you both work and in years' time your other child can be trained under my guidance."

"I understand," Jonah woefully acknowledges.

Korcoff then looks deep into Jonah's eyes and puts his hand under his chin. "Don't worry, not all of what will be asked of you will be unpleasant." By Korcoff's tone, Jonah knew exactly what he meant. Afterwards, Jonah is barely able to drag himself out of Korcoff's office.

It almost seems Jonah is about to walk past Martha when he's leaving Korcoff's office.

"What did he say?" Martha urges.

"We start work tomorrow," Jonah flatly responds. After a slight detour on her part to her superior's office for instructions, the clerk quickly catches up to the slow walking Fisks.

"This way please," the clerk instructs.

It then dawns on Jonah and Martha that they forgot they have no place to sleep. So, the clerk was probably going to take them where they would be staying while they worked there. Of course, this was true on their part, the clerk was instructed to take the Fisks to a private room. The room they're brought to seems large enough, even when three cots are added to it later on.

The next day comes and the Fisks are given their tasks to do in the building. Compared to what they had to do when they first arrived in Russia, their present jobs are not that hard to them. Weeks pass and Jonah still hasn't told Martha about the agreement he made with Korcoff. Only that Korcoff agreed to hire them as a janitor and maid. Year pass and the Fisks witness the Soviets become involved in another World War.

First, as the one of the main instigators close ally, then after a deadly betrayal a ruthless enemy. During these years and before their arrival, the Fisks hear that their home country has had only one president, while Russia has had two. As his son Marvin grows older, Jonah can see what Korcoff meant about what he said about Marvin. Thankfully he's not old enough to fight in the war, but he is old enough to work at the Fisks adopted home.

The Fisks also discover that Dictator Stalin is not too concerned with the safety and comfort of his people, but he does leave you alone if you work and contribute to the State, Stalin's State. Korcoff is useful to the State despite the hushed rumors. And the dictator knows about what Korcoff uses as toys. But as long as Korcoff or even Jonah don't raise Stalin's suspicions further about them, they can continue to live.

"How long did it go on between you and Uncle Otis?" Jonah asks his wife one day in their new three-bedroom apartment.

"What?" Martha asks back.

She hadn't thought about Otis in years, save for the obvious reminder. Things had been tense between them ever since Jonah got a letter from his father about his grandmother dying. In Jonah's mind, she was the only one who understood him. And now that understanding and love was dying. So now Jonah has decided to air out all the dirty laundry between him and Martha.

"You heard me. How long?" he further demands.

"Why do you want to bring this up now?" Martha counters.

Fortunately, Marvin isn't at home to witness his parents arguing, even though he's old enough to suspect the truth.

"I don't want any more lies between us. Now did this happen because of Willie?"

"No before yo' uncle made me feel good," Martha calmly says.

Jonah then shook his head.

"Yeah. I heard from other women Uncle Otis has a way of doing that. I kinda had a feelin' back home, he was up to something wit' chu."

Despite his calm exterior, Jonah is upset about this because he's stuck raising his uncle's kid and he's speaking to his wife in their old American South drawl.

"'Yal musta' had a good laugh at my expense while you was rollin' round naked wit each other."

"No, it wasn't like dat, it was jus lust. Yo Grandma knew bout us, but she didn't want you hurt in spite of everything we both knew bout chu. So, I stayed cause I loved you, I still do. What about what you've done? What you still doin!" Martha accuses.

Jonah knew exactly what Martha was talking about. She did know about Willie without him telling her and she probably has guessed about him and Korcoff.

So it's all out now, fine let it be out now, he thinks.

"I figured it out when you looked at dat guard in dat way you looked at Willie."

"So, you know all of me Martha, but I know you too. Ya hear me? I know you! Dat baby you carrying probably not mine?"

"Oh, yes, it's yours Jonah! You may hate Marvin, but you won't not love dis child! I'll kill you if you try it! I don't care what chu are, cause you're the only other black face, so you know how I feel! Whether I like it or not, you're gonna have to be enough fo' me! And if you think bout leavin' me or other, I'll kill us both! You know I will, Jonah."

Martha's words hit Jonah square in the gut. He knew his wife meant it. Unlike her, he occasionally had other diversions, but he was now all she had. For emotional support, intimacy and love. So, he lets the argument go and goes into another room to cool off.

Weeks later, Jonah is allowed by the Russian government to go to the funeral of his grandmother, but Martha and Marvin have to stay behind as insurance in case he thinks about not returning.

Those days her husband was away were unbearable for Martha, but to her surprise he came back.

He did love her, at least part of him did. More months down the road after the end of the second World War, Martha gives birth to another son. Jonah and Martha decide on the name Peter. Three years later, Martha has another boy named Eric. Jonah loves his two sons deeply, but in time, he notices something Familiar in Peter.

As the country enters the 1950s, Stalin grows more paranoid by the day and things become stricter. Thankfully, Jonah, Korcoff and others like them have artfully learned how to ride under Stalin's radar. Eventually, Stalin's own paranoia costs him his own life. Marvin by then has come of age in this strict world. He realizes that Jonah isn't his real father.

At twenty-one, he feels closed off from his younger brothers. Marvin can't stand the way Jonah showers his attention and affection on Eric and Peter. The only loving support he gets is from his mother. Feeling no full love at home, Marvin decides to join the Soviet Army. Jonah doesn't care either way, but Martha is against it.

"Why would you do that? The army is no place for people like us, especially here," Martha reasons with her son.

"I'm sorry mama, but there's nothing else for me here, except being a janitor like Jonah. Who knows? Maybe, after basic training. I'll be stationed someplace where it isn't so bad for blacks."

"No place is better for blacks baby. And probably not for a long time."

"I'm going to the army mama," Marvin repeats before he walks out the door to go to the enlistment building. Martha cries uncontrollably for days afterwards. Jonah tries to console her, but it doesn't work.

At the completion of his basic training, Marvin is stationed in Berlin in Germany. Through the years, he manages to phone messages and letters to his mother to let her know where he was stationed at and that he was fine. Jonah doesn't even try to hide the fact he doesn't care anymore from his wife.

Marvin could be dead for all he cared.

Chapter 2

Moscow 1963, Peter Fisk is a handsome figure at only seventeen. Excellent grades in school, does good in whatever athletics he puts his mind to. Although he has deep intelligence and cunning at such a young age, his heart is set upon becoming a ballet dancer. Many times, Peter has begged his parents for money to go to the ballet in the city.

"Are you sure there's not another reason you wanna be a dancer son?" his father would always ask Peter in a suspicious underlining tone.

Jonah already sees it in Peter's eyes of what he'll become if he lets it. Martha is sadly aware of Peter's unusual nature also. But she yet doesn't know the price he'll have to pay for his father.

On a drizzling day like many others, Korcoff calls Jonah into his office.

"Your son is quite impressive, you must be very proud. What are your plans for him?" Korcoff asks.

Jonah at first is taken aback because his boss is speaking to him in English, which was strange to Jonah when Korcoff knew he could speak almost perfect Russian a little after the first time they met.

"Yes, me and Martha are proud of Peter. He wants to be a dancer someday soon," Jonah answers back in Russian to remind Korcoff that he can.

"No, no let us speak in English, this is an important day and I would discuss this day in your native tongue."

"Whatever you want," Jonah replies quietly.

"Good, good, so you say your son wants to be a dancer. I guess that makes sense in way, since he likes to keep company with them from what I hear. You love and care for him a great deal, don't you? Yes, you do. I see it in your eyes. Your other son holds no real interest to you but Peter give you pride."

Korcoff was right, Jonah loved Eric too, but he didn't dote on him like he does with Peter. Eric's mother doesn't even seem too overly interested in him not like she was with Marvin.

Korcoff saw this in Jonah before he even asked him. All of this talk, the meeting in Korcoff's office and casual questions were just for show. Jonah and Korcoff both knew what was going to happen to Peter now. Korcoff just wanted the pleasure of reminding his reluctant pet nigger of it.

"We're in an arms race with the Americans. One of us wants to beat the other to space, our leaders have practically said as much. To win this race and this cold war we need soldiers and territory to help us win. The Americans believe this as well as we do. Your son has shown talents that could be used to help us do this."

"What kind of talents?" Jonah asks wanting Korcoff to explain it better. "He's intelligent, cunning, subtly graceful and ruggedly beautiful. Properly trained, Peter could fit in virtually anywhere in the world, go places where an average agent of Mother Russia could not go."

Jonah was seeing the big picture better now. Not only did Korcoff want agents loyal to the State, but he and Russia wanted sleepers, sleepers that could blend in within lower income neighborhoods and underdeveloped countries. Sure, they could plant spies in higher government or the military, but with agents in the lower slums where they cannot go, the upper spies would have even more information to help Russia topple a government.

Although not many black people from the rest of the world would willingly come to Russia and many of the few that did have nearly died from the tortures of the gulags. But Korcoff Vamitri found a rare source. It walked through his front door nearly twenty years ago. A rare limited source that mostly Korcoff has control of.

Jonah partially zones out during the rest of what Korcoff is saying. He definitely gets the point that his son has no choice about whether he wanted to report for intense training ahead of him or not. The Fisks have no choice, but Jonah kept having to be reminded of that.

To say this was a blow out fight would put it mildly. "Whatta mean I have'ta go away fo' training!" Peter yells using the slang he's heard his parents use.

"It's necessary! You have to go."

"But why? Da State already took Marvin from us! You and mama gonna let 'em take Eric too?"

"It won't be forever."

Jonah knew he was lying but he made a promise to himself that he would not lose track of Peter and practically forget him and Martha did with Marvin. Meanwhile, Martha is silent through the whole argument. Instead, she just sits in a chair holding her face in her hands.

"You know they're not that many opportunities for people like us, especially here in this country. You've heard about what it's like in America for black people, it's doubly so here. Whatever chance they give you, you have to grab it with both hands and hold on tight."

"But I don't wanna go, I already have a life here wit someone."

"I know Peter, I know."

Of course, Jonah realizes his young son is not a virgin. All the times Peter went to the ballet by himself and taking hours to come home long after the shows were over. He may have been black, but Peter was still very handsome. It would make sense that he would catch somebody's eye. But Peter's father knew where ever the Soviet Union would send him, he would never be in want of companionship. Jonah puts his hands on Peter's shoulders in an attempt to calm down.

"Whoever you're with now will understand because they were born here in this country just like you. They know how things are here. I'm sure you won't have to explain it too much to them. Whatever tests the State throws at you, you'll excel at it and pass. Be three times as better than the white recruits you'll be training with. Where ever they send you or whatever they make you do, remember you do have family who love you and you're never ever really alone no matter how you feel."

Once that's said by his father, Peter felt a little angry about leaving his family and his life.

After saying goodbye and explaining to his friend why he was leaving, Peter doesn't feel so bad. And discovered his father was right, they did understand. A week later, Peter reports to one of the State facilities in Chelyabinsk for the beginning of his training. At first, he spends a year learning physical combat and the use of various weapons. Later on, down the road he trains in Cuba and parts of the Middle East in espionage and seduction.

The Soviets use instructors, videos and live physical volunteers to help hone the cadets seductions techniques. Peter was slow and clumsy at first with this part of the training but he eventually got the hang of it. While he was in the Middle East, one of his instructors sent Peter in an area out in the desert where there were hills. It was rumored that there were a small band of insurgents hiding in the hills.

Peter wandered around near their camp and was captured. Using what little linguistic skill he had, Peter pretended to be a lost man from a village nearby. Before the insurgents could verify his story, other Soviet soldiers who were following Peter from a distance attacked the small band and wiped them out. It was darkly perfect. Peter didn't look like any Russian soldier the insurgents ever seen.

Following another year, the Soviets believed Peter was ready for field work. Proving himself to be a dangerous man armed or unarmed and fluent in six languages, two of them Zimbabwe and Ugandan African dialects. And this didn't count his parents native English or of course the Russian he already spoke before his training. Months before he was to leave for his first assignment, Peter grew close to another recruit from Cuba. She was a strikingly beautiful Afro Cuban Greek.

Despite his own tastes, Peter found the woman named Clearessa intoxicating, but she wasn't interested in him at all. For weeks, he pursued her, yet she rebuffed him at every turn. Clearessa preferred the white cadets over Peter.

However, despite being five years older and more experienced than Pete, she fell victim to his hot-blooded inherited Fisk cunning mixed with his learned seduction techniques. And part of her was attracted to him, but she just wouldn't admit it. One night, it happened, Peter and Clearessa were both taken away by passion. Afterwards on his way to Spain for his first assignment, all Peter could think about was Clearessa's naked coke bottle shaped body.

It would be years before Peter would see her gain. Though he would have other lovers and assignments around the world, Clearessa stood out among them. Though he traveled constantly, Peter found ways to contact his family, especially during the stays on an assignment. Still, he couldn't stop thinking about Clearessa. Also, as the years went by, Peter was getting better and better as a spy, but the Soviets and Vamitri wanted more like him.

They demanded that he marry and father children. Of course, there was the obvious problem with that demand, but the Soviets didn't care. They wanted Peter to find a black woman to marry. The Russians could have sent him to America to live and spy in an urban slum or Britain or France. But they decided on stationing Peter in Uganda, a country in Africa.

Russia figured if there were any situations that be used to their benefit or resources to take advantage of they'd already have a man on the ground and maybe eventually a wife for their agent to help move things along.

"How can I stay here? There's nothing to report," Peter complains to his father over the phone.

Though he's black and speak the language, Peter feels out of place. It's been six years since he's seen his parents. Jonah is still surprised that Peter is no longer speaking to him in the Southern slang he grew up with.

"Don't worry, they have never kept you in a place permanently and I'm sure they won't now," his father reassures him.

On the upside, during one of his trips to Cuba, Peter saw his brother Marvin again, who was a Major in the army now. It had been some years since he'd seen his older brother, so at first Peter didn't recognize Marvin when he saw him, he looked much older than he thought. But Peter still thought it was good to see Marvin.

When Peter asks Marvin had he spoken to their parents, Marvin's only reply was, "That situation is done with, drop it." Which Peter reluctantly does. But he did manage to talk his brother into taking a picture with him.

Afterwards, Peter mails the photo back to Russia to his parents. When Jonah sees the photo, he nearly rips it apart when he sees Marvin is almost the spitting image of his uncle Otis. Martha manages to grab the picture out his hands before he does.

"I don't think I can make a home here. This place is so different from the other places I've been. Where ever else I've been I could blend in, but here is not so easy," Peter continues to say into the phone at a large tourist hotel.

He looks out the window and see thin framed very dark complected woman with a wrapped bright colored green dress. She has on a tan scarf wrapped around her head and she's carrying a large basket on top of her head. She has on stitched saddles that barely cover her feet. Peter doesn't know what to make of her or many of the other people like her.

Weirdly, Peter could go to the white United Kingdom citizens he saw on his way to Uganda but when he reached Uganda, he could barely say three words to these people without stammering.

"You're over reacting, Peter. Where you are is no different than any other place you've had to work or scout for Russia. The people there you just have to take a little longer to get used to."

After saying those words, Jonah suspects what his son is feeling. He's heard the rumors about the countries in Africa and how they feel about people like him and his son. And he's sure Peter has heard the rumors too, which is probably the main source of his anxiety. And the fact that he's not as unique as he was in Russia or even Britain, Spain or France doesn't help either.

For the first time in his life, Peter is in a situation he can't spy his way out of, so to speak. The phone conversation continues between father and son for another half an hour until Peter says to has to go.

Leaving the hotel, Peter hops into the jeep he owns from the salary given to him by the Soviets. The roads back to the village his shack and radio are at are very bumpy and uneven, mainly dirt.

The terrain of Uganda is so unlike anything Peter has ever seen. With the exotic trees and wildlife, he's never seen or read about. One of the few things about Uganda that Peter likes is the people don't make him feel like an outsider despite the way he feels. To them, Peter is just another African living in their village. Unfortunately, he did have to kill a man who asked too many questions.

Mainly about where he suddenly came from and how he was so knowledgeable about Europe and America, but knew little about Africa. Peter was careful to make the man's death look like an accident. He infected the villager with rare disease he secretly kept in a vile for other purposes. When the man grew ill, Peter offered to take him to a hospital miles away. Before they left, Peter messed with the seat belt so it wouldn't fasten.

The villager was so sick, weak and delirious he didn't even notice. On the route to the hospital, Peter drove close to a cliff on the edge of a bumpy road, purposely going over the most bumps and large rocks on the road. Due to the motion of the jeep, the man fell out of the jeep over a cliff falling down on the jagged rocks way down below.

Afterwards, Peter showed great remorse to the man's wife and children when he told them his version of what happened. After that, Peter didn't have to eliminate anyone else in the village.

Sometimes, the Russians would have Peter travel to other parts of Africa to see what was going on. Whenever Peter went to parts of Africa where he wasn't familiar with the dialect, he'd find a white nationalist who always happen to be there that spoke English. This tactic always seemed to help him get by. It seemed that the Soviets preferred to keep Peter in the continent for a while, only traveling out to the Middle East some more times, but his main stay was now Uganda.

Peter did have another close call with a Nigerian who was a member of a group of guerrilla fighters who's main base of operations were located on the outskirts of the Congo. The Nigerian was radical to say the least, rough and thuggish. For Peter, it was a good diversion to appease what people would call his unusual appetites. But during the time they spent together, the Nigerian wanted Peter to fight for his group's cause.

When Peter refused, the Nigerian threatened to expose their relationship, which would've gotten them both killed. So, Peter slipped away under the cover of night without the guerrilla fighters knowing. And they couldn't track him because he always used various aliases whenever he was in a different country. And also, he knew how to slightly alter his appearance. Peter decided after that ordeal to keep to himself no matter how lonely he got.

It's 1972 on another hot day in the Zophrim village in Uganda.

"Umm, what time is it?" Peter says to himself in a drowsy voice as he sits from his pallet.

As he pours cold water from a bucket on his face and bare chest, Peter hears the noises of the people outside coming to life in the morning sun. Peter has a breakfast of hard bread and fried eggs over a hot plate. When he's finished, he goes outside. So far, Peter hasn't any word of new assignments through his hidden radio or from his handler who's stationed in Cape Town.

"Yep, no encoded messages for weeks," Peter gladly says to himself.

Peter then chooses to take a walk to pass the rare downtime. Given the heat he goes shirtless, wearing only pants and his army hiking boots. Peter also carries a canteen of water to quench his thirst. Given his training and stamina, it's no surprise that he walks miles from the village.

In a short while, he's far from where man dwells, only seeing animals now. In the trees, Peter sees several chimpanzees pulling on branches above them. Further down out in the open, he sees a rhinoceros grazing on dirt grass. Even further on, he witnesses a family of giraffe walking toward some tall thorny trees probably to eat the leaves off of.

Peter is not even frightened when he witnesses an antelope being chased and then eaten by a leopard.

Elephants marching to the closet stream, lions eyeing all other animals from a distance ready to strike.

They don't even appear to notice Peter, let alone be frightened by him. This is the type of behavior poachers count on and Peter count on and Peter is aware of this. But fortunately today, there are none hunting for rare animals. For once, Peter appears happy to be here, but he knows it won't last. It never does, although for some reason, the KGB have him stay in the continent.

Although things seem good, aside from the poachers and other game hunters. Political unrest is looming everywhere in Africa and Peter knows it's only a matter of time before things explode. While Peter is leaning against a boulder staring into space, he hears some shouting from a distance.

"Mr. Masumbi. Mr. Masumbi!" they're yelling.

Peter turns to the direction of the voice and spots a boy from the village with his arms up waving at him.

"Mr. Masumbi, Mr. Masumbi!" the boy continues to shout.

It's the name Peter has been using since coming to Uganda, so he walks toward the boy.

When he's closer, he responds to the boy, "Yes, what is it?" Peter casually demands.

"There are visitors who have come looking for you," the boy answers while he's catching his breath.

Peter knows it could only be somebody from the KGB, but they wouldn't come in person, let alone more than one person. They would always radio him or have his handler send and encoded message by mail. This personal visit was very unusual to say the least to Peter.

"Alright, let's go," he tells the boy before they started back to the village.

When Peter and the boy return, Peter notices another jeep besides his, which is parked near a shack three huts down from his.

"They are waiting for you at your place," the boy explains to Peter.

"Thank you," Peter says right before him and the boy part ways.

Peter was intrigued by the personal visit. To him, it must've been very important to prompt a face to face. When he reaches his shack at the door, he hears what sounds like a man and a woman talking in Russian. When he opens the door, Peter's heart almost stops from shock. Standing there is the woman he thought he would never see again.

It was Clearessa standing there, still beautiful and shapely. Off in the corner, Peter notices a pretty little girl with long dark hair playing with a doll. The girl is tan colored and she looks up at Peter and he sees his mother's eyes looking back at him. He's so distracted by Clearessa and the discovery that he's a father that he doesn't even notice the sort of fat old white man sitting in a chair. That is until he speaks.

"Hello Peter. It's so nice to finally meet you in person. I've monitored your career with great interest. Your parents Jonah and Martha are very proud of you," the man says with a broad smile.

The man's words don't shock, he was aware the KGB knew all about their agents and their families. He only had eyes for Clearessa and the little girl she brought with her. Even the man sees Peter is not paying too much attention to him he still continues to talk.

"Where are my manners? My name is Korcoff Vamitri, I'm a very old friend of your father's."

"What does the State want of me now?" Peter sternly asks as he turns his attention to Korcoff.

"I am here to congratulate you both on you upcoming wedding," Korcoff answers. Peter is stun, but he glances over at Clearessa and her face shows no expression, it's totally blank.

"What do you mean? What wedding?" Peter nervously asks.

He realized he would eventually have to get married to keep up appearances, but he thought it would be a sham marriage with someone he didn't care about with no children. In one of their conversations over the phone, his father did tell him in a roundabout way about the dark gift of their family that even his great-grandmother knew about. But now it appears that the decision of fathering a child has been taken out of his hands.

By the way, Korcoff is looking at him like he definitely knows all about that aspect of the Fisk Family. So quickly understanding him and Clearessa have no say in the matter given they both work for, Peter readily accepts his fate.

"When are we to be married?" Peter calmly asks.

"You and your new family are to fly back to Russia and have a lavish ceremony there. Then you are to honeymoon for a week in St. Petersburg," Korcoff gladly announces Peter looks deeply at Clearessa whom stays silent and then he looks again at his daughter with sad eyes.

"Her name is Natleaha if you're wondering," Clearessa says finally speaking.

My dearest Natleaha. I'm so sorry for the fate I've doomed you to, Peter woefully thinks to himself.

All present find places to sleep in the shack. By daybreak, they all leave the village in the two jeeps. Once they all reach the airport after the long journey, no one is surprised to find four first class plane tickets waiting for them at the check in desk. At the assigned wedding, Peter's parents are present along with his brothers Marvin and Eric.

At the wedding Peter meets Clearessa's father, a twice widower, a gruff, burly Cuban with a grim scowl. He, of course, gave her away. The two of them were married in the main orthodox of the religion of Russia in a church of the State's choosing. After the ceremony, the newly married couple went on their honeymoon in St. Petersburg while Natleaha remained in the care of her grandparents.

Aside from the circumstances that reunited them, Peter couldn't keep his hands off Clearessa. His engorged penis penetrated her with such force that it startled her. Though she's had other lovers besides Peter, she's made sure to take precautions to not to get pregnant again. During the first two nights of their honeymoon, Peter ravishes her, making their bodies entwine with each other in passionate sweat despite the cold outside.

"I love you. I love you," he says as he holds her in his arms.

Clearessa barely says four words during their time together on their honeymoon. Following their honeymoon, the couple receives their orders to return to Africa with Natleaha. But this time, they're stationed in Cape Town closer to Peter's handler.

One day, as the couple is walking outside around the neighborhood with their daughter, Clearessa hands Peter a piece of paper with typed names of places and map locations.

"What's this?" Peter asks looking at the list.

"It's a list of remote places you can amuse yourself from time to time while we're married," Clearessa bluntly answers.

He didn't know what she meant until he discovered what the remote places were. They were locations of remote African tribes that mostly walked around nude, painting their beautiful bodies in bright painted colors, adorning themselves with genital piercings. In some of the tribes, the men would wear on their heads lions manes, shaving off their body hair with white strips largely etched on their legs and thighs.

The men would perform all sorts of sexual fertility rites and passages of manhood. Witnessing these events made Peter enflamed. The uninhibited nature of these people was something to behold. With this gift, Peter never lost his love and passion for his wife and she knew it.

Though she was a small child, Natleaha already showed signs of a murderous streak. She liked playing with dolls and toys as some girls her age do, but she could not keep a pet. Whenever anyone in her family would give her one, something terrible would always happen. Within months, she supposedly accidently drowned three hamsters, threw a cat in front of a moving car, claiming she thought it could fly over the car. And then she beat a boy a few years older than her with pole because he tried to kiss her.

"You cannot do things like that Natleaha, innocent people and animals do not deserve to be hurt!"

Peter would severely scold her. Even when he'd spank her with a thick belt, she was indifferent, showing little remorse for a child her age.

"What did you expect, just like the rest of your family! Naturally, she would have unnatural impulses," Clearessa would say about her own daughter. Peter and his father Jonah feared what Natleaha might become as she got older. But on the bright side, she was an only child.

Her parents flat out refused to have any more children while she was in their care. It seemed with each newer generation, the Fisks were more dangerous than the last.

"What is my granddaughter becoming?" Jonah fearfully wondered in his old age. Peter was cunning and seductive, capable of killing when he had to. Marvin may take after his real father and probably has his own set of demons.

Jonah wasn't sure and he really didn't care. His youngest son Eric seemed content with his life as a medical examiner trainee do to a country exchange program he was lucky to be a part of, which granted Eric a trip to America. He dealt with death every day, but it didn't seem to bring out abnormal impulses in him.

The agreement Jonah made with Korcoff was becoming a moot point with every passing year. Jonah was getting old, but Korcoff was older still. The State could have Natleaha when she was older, her parents had decided. They figured maybe the KGB could control her. But the one lesson her mother drilled into Natleaha was, don't ever have children of your own, for if you do, they might be the death of you. And her family knew, even as dangerous as she was growing up to be, no telling what type of monster she might birth herself.

Chapter 3

1982 in occupied Berlin on the liberal side of the wall. Natleaha has reached sixteen and she is celebrating with some friends by practice shooting on some rats in an alley with a.32 caliber handgun she stole off a border guard she is secretly sleeping with.

"This is the life! Killing vermin!" she shouts as she drinks from a bottle of Jack Daniels.

"What should we do now?" one of her friends ask in a hazy voice in German.

Natleaha answers back, "Anything we want, the night is young and we got more rats to kill!" she screams.

Natleaha has been in Berlin for a year now, since her uncle Marvin who is now stationed here had agreed to take her off her parents' hands. He knew she was a nightmare, but strangely enough he had ways to keep her under control, namely filling her with tales of being an assassin. Of doing whatever you want in the world as long as you killed for the State. Natleaha liked the sound of that, ending a person's life and getting away with it.

At sixteen, she was already a sultry brown beauty, naturally seductive like her father and she's had had three lovers since she was thirteen. The first, a young African boy of sixteen and two white girls she met while she was visiting her grandparents in Moscow. Right now, Natleaha is not sure what sex she like more sexually, but she does like the pursuit.

Strangely enough, given her evil abnormal ways, Natleaha does have great affection and love for her mother. For some reason, she believes her mother is not afraid of her like the rest of the family.

"Why did you marry father?" Natleaha frankly asked Clearessa one day.

"Because it was required of me and now I am trapped, but it won't be that way for you my Nata. You have a choice and you only have to kill for them to keep that choice. Remember never bare children of your own Nata or you too will be trapped like me and your father," her mother grimly informed her.

She would always take these words to heart. Natleaha enjoyed fornicating from Africa, Russia and abroad, but she always protected herself with condoms she most of the time steal from drug stores.

While walking the streets of Berlin, Natleaha wondered how her life would be ten years from now. Would she have a finer killer edge? Would she have her fill of the most beautiful men and women in the world? And would she ever be free of her annoying father and grandfather? Their talk of belonging to the State without choice was tiresome to her, but her uncle Marvin was less annoying and more practical.

"Eventually the State will have their fill of you as long as you kill enough and fuck enough for them," he told her shortly after they first met.

As she is walking with her two friends by some old buildings, Natleaha is looking at one of the girls she's with. The girl is wearing a faded jean jacket and white pants, she has freckles, curly reddish blond hair and her body is thin. The girl may not be too attractive to most people, but Natleaha doesn't mind that, she likes the girl and her other friend who's kind of fat well enough anyway.

Natleaha doesn't look for that despite her own beauty. Sure, the guard she's sleeping with is sort of handsome in an older type of way, but they have to have other qualities.

"If I only fucked physically pretty people with empty heads, I'd never hardly fuck at all," Natleaha said to a friend one time. Sometimes, she would fuck her thin ugly friend if she was in the mood. Though Natleaha had a dark sense of humor, the thin girl managed to make her laugh.

"Nata, Nata what are you going to do now? You're almost of age to join the service, aren't you?" the fat girl asks, coming closer to Natleaha's side.

"Well, I don't know yet," she answered, which was a lie. She knew exactly what she was going to do as soon as she was given the chance. But she opted to lie. Natleaha was also taught at a very young age that you never know who may be listening.

The Soviet Union was strong and their eyes and eyes were everywhere. Later that night after saying goodbye to her friends, Natleaha went back to the border station where her older lover was. Luckily, the few other guards on duty don't pay too much attention to what this man does, also Natleaha is already a master at sneaking in places she's not supposed to be in. The guard is standing near a tool shed, so he hears Natleaha whistle for him from the entrance of the tool shed. He turns around and a broad smile appears across his face.

"Natleaha," he says in a hush whisper as he walks toward her, lifting her up in his thick arms.

Going inside the lighted toolshed, the guard quickly locks the door and blocks the view of the two large windows with a wide dirty sheet. Before any words are said, the guard has his pants and underwear down around his ankle and he's shoving his thick fingers down inside the front of Natleaha's jeans before she begins to unbutton them.

"I've missed you, Natleaha. Why have you kept me waiting all these weeks?"

"You could always do your wife," she teases.

He only grunts in response, biting her earlobe, forcing her jeans off her shapely legs. His middle finger massages her inner with a surprising gentle motion. The guard wasn't a Casanova or Adonis, but he knew what he was doing. An adequate lover for his age, in Natleaha's opinion. She did realize the guard was only interested in her because of her age, not even her beauty.

She was well aware the guard was trying to seduce her fat friend, who was a year and half younger than her. This fact is probably the main reason Natleaha liked the man. He couldn't be controlled by her beauty like most people could and would be. It wasn't even power, it was youth and that fades faster than beauty, real beauty that is. Once he's inside of her, Natleaha teases then guard some more.

"Do you like my friend Brahteena? Do you want her instead of me? Do you imagine how her moist plump body feels wrapped around your pretty cock?" Natleaha asks about her fat friend in seductive tone.

His pace quickens, her theory is right, he does like girls younger than her.

Enjoying her words and body, the guard tries to deny it, "No, no, I, I, uh only want you ooh," he stutters and moans. But she can tell he's becoming more aroused by the thought of Brahteena. She steadily continues with her verbal taunts.

"Would you like to know how her still hairless lower body felt when I touched it, felt the wet moistness of it, the taste? Would you, would you?" she subtly berates him.

To further humiliate and arouse his passion at the same time, Natleaha assaults the guard's buttocks with her sharp nails. This causes him to bite her earlobe even harder. This pleasant torture goes on for the guard and Natleaha for about an hour. When they were done, Natleaha was on borrowed time as she soon discovered. The guard's wife had to be aware of her husband's inclinations. Women were always privy to a man's tastes, especially their husbands' or boyfriends'.

Natleaha believe this also, just like her mother was aware of what her father was and her grandmother knew about her grandfather. Men always have weaknesses you can exploit, so do women, they're just better at hiding them. Natleaha already believed this in her mind. But this experience did put Natleaha in the mind of what her friend would be like in bed.

Hmm I wonder, she thought as she left the toolshed with a still exasperated and exhausted guard leaning on the table against the wall.

There were more moments with the guard like this, but eventually Natleaha grew tired of making him long for her friend to satisfy her. The death of Korcoff Vamitri came at a good time four months later, Natleaha didn't want to attend the funeral, but her mother talked her into it.

"It would be good for appearances if you were there. You'd show your future Russian superiors that you had loyalty toward the benefactor of your family," her mother explained to her over the phone. So Natleaha flew from Germany back to Russia. The funeral was held in chapel inside the building Korcoff use to work at.

As funerals go, it wasn't a depressing as Natleaha had thought it would be. Her uncle Marvin was there with his wife and children. Her uncle Eric was there with his wife as well. All the Fisk men were managing to keep their good looks, even her aged grandfather whom showed gray in his hair, wore it well. And her mother was still beautiful as well, of course.

This reinforced Natleaha's belief that beauty outlasts youth. Following the funeral, the wake was given at Korcoff's home by his wife of twelve years. Another woman who knew the truth of her husband's character.

"You were like the son he never had," Mrs. Vamitri says to Jonah with a straight face, knowing that was an out and out lie given Korcoff's racism. Everyone practically in the government knew why Korcoff was so interested in Jonah and his family and by now even Natleaha and her cousins. But Mrs.

Vamitri said this to Jonah while holding his hand nonetheless. But she couldn't help it, sometimes men like to hear women lie about certain things.

However, for some reason Mrs. Vamitri was interested in talking to Natleaha.

"So, you must be Peter and Clearessa's daughter Natleaha. My, you are beautiful!" the woman says in perfect English. Clearessa nudges her daughter in the side for her to respond.

"Uh yes, thank you ma'am."

"I bet you'll break the hearts of many people during your lifetime, if you already haven't," the woman says with a kind smile.

But Natleaha was alarmed that the woman said people instead of men. And what did she mean by the way she said if you already haven't? Natleaha's young guard was up.

"How much does she really know?" Natleaha wondered. Her parents were right, Russia does have eyes and ears everywhere. Mrs. Vamitri has cleverly shown that she's a sharp lady.

"Korcoff saw something special in you and your family Jonah and he knew if he didn't calm, hon and temper it, that you and your wife would have died on the streets or in a gulag somewhere and nobody would've cared. Your grandmother wouldn't have been aware of it before she died, but you men think you have so many secrets from us, that we don't know, but we do. The reason Korcoff finally married me, he said I was to care for him in his old age, that he could not work for the State for much longer. That was bullshit," Mrs. Vamitri said to everyone's surprise with the American slang term, but she continued.

"You may believe that the world doesn't understand you, but you're wrong. The truth of the matter is the world doesn't know you. That's how you've all survived these decades in this country and that's how you will survive Natleaha, you and your children."

"I won't have any children!" Natleaha blurts out in response to Mrs. Vamitri's calm assessment of her.

"So, you say," the woman says with a slight smile. Natleaha thought the woman didn't know what she was talking about.

"Don't let it bother you Nata, the woman was speaking out of grief, she probably wasn't really aware of half of what she was really saying," Clearessa was saying to her daughter in an attempt to calm her down during the drive back to the hotel.

"She doesn't know what she's talking about, I'm not having children or getting married ever," Natleaha adamantly stated. Her body was her own and she wasn't going to ruin it with children. After that experience, she couldn't wait to go back to Germany.

Another year went by and Natleaha began her training by the Soviets. All of the instructors were very tough on her and the other cadets in her class, grilling into them the importance of completing whatever mission that was assigned to them, using whatever tools they happened to have at their disposal to accomplish this and above all not to get caught. If they happen to be, they didn't want to be privy to what would be the end result.

All the cadets, including Natleaha were told that the Soviet Union was still in a power struggle with America, half of Europe and more recently parts of the far and Middle East. This did not bother Natleaha about what she would be doing for the State. Her parents has already told her how she would sometimes have to use her looks and body to get close to a target. Her one problem was Natleaha had difficulty blending in with other black people from other countries.

When she was in Cuba during part of her training, she walked past a group of women talking.

"Hello, how are you?" one of the women greeted Natleaha.

She didn't know if this was part of a test or if the woman was just being friendly. Natleaha didn't answer, instead she was put on guard. She looked un-comfortable to the group of women. For a moment, she contemplated on using a broken bottle to slit their throats. Luckily, she chose to walk away without speaking. One of the instructors had words with her when they heard about the incident.

"You can't be on obvious guard all the time. You have to learn to appear more friendly to a point. If you act aloft and guarded all the time, people won't let you get close to them. Not all of your targets will be at a distance," the instructor explained. But it wasn't people in general, it was other black people of the world.

Even though she grew up in Africa, she preferred hanging with men and women of other nationalities. She didn't feel comfortable around the other native African children, which is one of the reasons she left Africa where her parents lived.

"If you want to be successful at what you do, you'll have to quickly grow out of that singular exotic trait, especially if you have long term assignments in some places like America," Peter sternly told his daughter. She reluctantly agreed with him because she knew what he was talking about. So, she tried hard to overcome this character flaw.

She wasn't very good at multiple languages, but she did manage to learn three and some Asian dialects, but she wasn't on par with her father though in this field. She did excel at marksmanship, close quarter combat and target seduction of course. Natleaha's superiors were aware that it did not matter to her if her target was a man or woman, she'd get the job done.

"You're progressing in certain areas well Natleaha, but we must work on your language skills. Soon you will be required to eliminate targets that are difficult to get to," another instructor commented.

"I will always complete my missions sir, no matter what," Natleaha answered with confidence.

"We will hold you to that Natleaha, you and your family," the instructor shot back.

Near the end of her training, she was allowed to go visit her parents, instead of talking to them on the phone. She wanted to see her uncle Marvin at his new post in Sweden, but her superiors strongly suggested that she see her parents. Natleaha hated Africa, she hardly understood what the people living there were saying. Unlike her mother and father, she barely spoke the language of the village she spent time in as a child.

"Have they given you your first assignment yet?" her mother asks.

"No, but I would like to go to Spain. I've heard rumors that a double agent is selling Russian secrets there to the highest bidder," Natleaha answers confidently.

"So, the mission won't be a problem for you, whatever they demand?" Peter asks, fully aware of what his daughter was.

"No, that's not problem for me, it never will be," Natleaha casually says as if she were taking an unimportant written test.

To her delight, Natleaha was assigned to Spain posing as a French model on location for a photo shoot. Her first handler was stationed at the Russian Embassy in the country as a technician. Natleaha relished her cover as a model. The photographer and the camera loved her and she posed in beautiful pictures with nice backgrounds. Natleaha was complete professional, able to stay on her true task. With a few well-placed words and flirtations, she was able to find out where the double agent was staying and his scheduled routine too.

To add more ways to get closer to her target, she befriended the double agent's girlfriend. In a matter of weeks, Natleaha had the woman eating out of the palm of her hand. The woman was drawn to Natleaha's wild zest for life.

"You're so free and brazen with how you approach everything in life," the woman told her. "I believe it is the only way to be if you want to cope with life," Natleaha tenderly explained to her with a thick French accent.

It was easy for Natleaha to get the woman talking about her boyfriend. She was in love with him, but she was also lonely.

"What does your boyfriend do when he's not with you?" Natleaha asked her a week after they met. Naturally, the woman was hesitant, having only met Natleaha a short while ago but she eventually opened up.

"Vladen works for an international building design company. He's always bringing home plans and documents for buildings and special rooms for clients. He travels a lot though, sometimes he brings me along on his trips, but not often," the woman said with slight sadness.

"I'm sure Vladen will want to spend more time with you when he becomes more settled in his job. Who would not, you're gorgeous?" Natleaha reassured her. In that, Natleaha was being partially truthful, she did think the woman was very attractive.

"Vladen is a fool to leave this gorgeous woman unattended. Numerous other foreign agents have probably tried to get to him through her, especially Interpol," Natleaha surmised to herself.

Having such an attachment is a mistake, one I can use, Natleaha further thought.

Natleaha did however indulge herself with the woman. The woman was hesitant again, this time about being intimate with another woman, but also once again, Natleaha with her charms, won the woman over. Despite what happened, Natleaha found the time magical.

One night, during one of the rare periods when she was sure Vladen would be home, Natleaha used a grappling hook and line to climb up the couple's building and pick the lock on their apartment window near the kitchen.

Natleaha was dressed in all black with a ski mask and leather gloves. She didn't have a gun, not wanting to chance leaving behind any residue. So, she waited in the dark living room. Her patience paid off when Vladen came into the kitchen, probably to get something to drink. He didn't even see or hear Natleaha as she crept up behind him.

"Mother Russia sends her regards," she quietly says in his ear. And before he can react or turn around, Natleaha reaches up and snaps his neck. Natleaha didn't think it would be necessary, but her instructions were not to leave any live bodies. So just in case the woman might've been secretly watching, Natleaha kill her boyfriend, she crept into the bedroom where the woman was sleeping, knocks the woman on the head with a night lamp to keep her unconscious and smothers her to death with a pillow.

Though she has a small bit of regret about killing the woman, she felt exhilarated by her first kill of human beings. After leaving the building, the same way she came, Natleaha walks all the way to her hotel using the alley ways to avoid street lights and cameras. In the morning Natleaha makes a phone call on a secured line.

When the party on the other end answers she speaks, "The architect won't be able to come to work today."

"I'm sorry to hear that, thank you for telling us," the person on the other end says to Natleaha in code. Afterwards, Natleaha goes back to her cover job as a model. The Madrid authorities are baffled about the double murder at a pose high rise in one of the city's nicer neighborhoods.

The police don't know what the mysterious assailant looked like or how they got into the apartment. Their only deduction was that the killer must have gotten in somehow when the couple was asleep. This is what Natleaha and her handler heard on the T.V news. She continued to enjoy herself in Spain until it was time for her to leave on another assignment.

Her second kill assignment was in Sweden, a renegade diplomat who was trying to gain allies to help them undermine Russia's government. This target was a lot tougher to get to. He had well-trained guards around him every second, even when he went to bed or the bathroom. Natleaha thought about killing him with a sniper shot from a distance, but he kept his men at all the windows in his suite.

And he was always surrounded by many people whenever he went anywhere, so it would be impossible to get a decent shot. His personal car was also out because it was bullet proof and to top it all off, the man was impotent, so seducing him was not an option. Her only recourse was to bribe or turn one of the guards.

But how? she constantly thought.

Natleaha thought about going to her uncle for help, but she couldn't risk being outed as a spy, so she went to her handler for ideas. They met near an iced over lake on the outskirts of winter Halmstad, six miles away from where her target was.

"He's untouchable, I cannot get close to him or take a distance shot at him because of the guards around him every second," Natleaha complains.

"There is always a way, Natleaha."

"How? He doesn't even have sex."

"Patience Natleaha, we did our homework, we have a way in. Go back to your hotel room and wait for a delivery you will receive tomorrow afternoon," the handler says before he gets up from the bench him and Natleaha are sitting on and walks away.

She follows his instructions and returns to her hotel. As predicted, the next day, Natleaha receives a package by special delivery. She quickly opens it up, inside is a thick file with a name stamped on the corner of it. Inside the file are papers with typed information on them and a picture of an average-looking sand-haired white man attached to the papers with a paperclip. Natleaha quickly guesses that the man in the picture is one of the guards of her target. She then reads through the information.

"Specialist in the marines, trained in hand-to-hand combat, skilled in several forms of martial arts, a typical soldier and guard. So what?" Natleaha reads and says out loud.

She continues to read his file with boredom until she comes across information about his marital status, which was single.

"Frequent visits to a club called the Hambone. What the hell is that?" Natleaha asks herself.

The club wasn't listed anywhere in the white or yellow pages and nobody at the hotel knew of it either. Fortunately, the address was listed on the man's file. It happened to be located on the outskirts of town, an hour away from where she met her handler. Putting on a sweater, a warm coat, a hat and thick pants, Natleaha rides a motorcycle to the club.

Catching sight of the place, she decides to park a block away from the club. Walking up to the club she notices a line of people starting from around the block to the entrance waiting to get in. Natleaha sees a tall large man blocking the front. She figures he must be the bouncer and the doorman who collects the money to get in.

Upon further observation, Natleaha notices there are no women in line, only men. She could easily take down the doorman with some strategic kicks to the knees and balls, but she was in no hurry, so she waits in line.

"Women don't find this club popular?" she shouts in English, but nobody responds, they just stare at her with curious looks on their faces.

When it's her turn to pay the doorman, he gives her the same look the other men in line gave her. She pays him with wad of money and walks inside before he can respond. She finds a hook to hang up her coat. Disco music is blaring out of the speakers loudly.

All around, different types of men are dancing on the large dance floor or sitting at various tables and booths drinking. She goes to the bar to ask the bartender questions. Swedish is terrible, so she asks in English while holding up the picture of the man from the file.

"Have you seen this man? How often does he come here? It's very important that I speak to him," Natleaha says and asks over and over to the point where she's starting to lose her temper. The last man she asks gives no words, just a blank look on his face. She nearly yanks off the man's shirt when he doesn't say anything.

Natleaha is frustrated, she's never been ignored like this before. She has a gun tucked in the back of her pants and she's ready to use it to help her get answers. Thankfully for the men's sake, someone answers her.

"I've seen your man yeah," a man says in broken English. Natleaha turns around and sees a medium weight average height man with blond hair, wearing tight pants and a white shirt opened at the front showing off his well-trimmed chest.

"You've seen him?"

"Yah, yah. You his wife?"

"Uh yes I am. It's very important that I find him, our son is sick." The man laughs at Natleaha making her more angry.

"You're not his wife, he have no wife. You play joke yah. Why you want, he a guard? Only like us boys all the time yah," the man says while laughing at Natleaha.

She then realized that this man knew something. If she had the time, she could get him someplace hidden and interrogate him aggressively to find out how much he knew about this guard. But there wasn't time, so she would have to resort to bribery.

"How much would it cost for you to find this man for me?"

"Find him?"

"Yes, find him and keep him in a private place until I got there."

A crooked smug smirk formed across the man's face.

"You freak huh, you like to watch huh yah?" he assumed wickedly. Natleaha decided to play along.

"Yes, very much so. I like to when he doesn't know I'm watching, it makes it more exciting for us after I watch. Will you make this happen?"

"Yah, yah I'll do it, I'll do it. For $800, I'll take him to a place I know."

$800 dollars? So that's what it cost to sell yourself nowadays, Natleaha thinks.

"Fine can you do it tomorrow?"

"Yah, yah I can do it."

"Good, take him to this hotel and keep him there for an hour. I'll give you 400 now and 400 after tomorrow when I see you."

"Yah ok."

Natleaha then gives him 400 dollars and tells him when and where to take the bodyguard.

Early evening, the next day Natleaha gets ready with her photo equipment. She caught on fast on how to operate the professional cameras during her time as a model. She finds it regrettable, she kinds of hopes she doesn't have to kill the prostitute too. Fun was fun, but Natleaha didn't want to be greedy, she felt that would make her clumsy.

She again slipped on her black outfit with the mask and gloves. She then takes the stairs three floors down to the appointed room. As instructed, the prostitute left the door unlocked to the room. Natleaha slips in and sneaks upon the two men having sex. The room has enough lighting to where they don't notice the low flash from the camera. The scene is more than she bargained for.

Their naked bodies were entwined pleasuring each other. The man she paid subtly glances in her direction and smiles, knowing it's her under the mask. The guard who's with him didn't even notice her, he was too caught up in savagely kissing the other man. She didn't believe two men could be so into each other like this. Taking several more pictures, Natleaha then creeps out of the room.

Hours later, she meets the prostitute to pay him. He still has the same smug look on his face that he had at the Hambone and the hotel room. Standing blocks away from the Hambone Natleaha starts to hand the man 400 dollars.

"Keep it, this was worth it. Yah, yah it was turn on to be watched, for you too yah. You enjoyed it didn't you?" Natleaha only looks at him with a quizzed expression on her face.

"I like it when men want me and it's a bigger high when women want me too, especially women like you. The high is better than any amount of money."

"So, you don't want the money?" Natleaha asks.

"Don't worry, your new-found kink is safe. We always take care of our own agent Fisk," the man suddenly says in Russian. Natleaha is stunned.

"H—how did," she mumbles in shock.

"Your handler knew you would need help after you read the file on the guard, so he sent me knowing I would be perfect bait for him. I met the man the day before you came to the club. It is true, I do like it when people want me. So, the State stations me in places where I'm really wanted. It was good to work with you agent Fisk. I hope those pictures you took will help you in your task."

The man then turns to walk away.

"Wait, what is your name?" Natleaha asks finally getting her voice back from shock.

"Flavawn. Flavawn Gorbachin and I hope to work with you again," he says as he disappears around the corner.

How is this possible? The State couldn't allow a man like that to serve openly. He's lying, he's a fool, they wouldn't let him live if they were aware of him back in Russia, Natleaha frantically thinks. But here he was, plying his trade for all to see.

"What the fuck is this?" the guard shouts when he's confronted with pictures at a restaurant he likes to eat at when he's off duty. The other customers look in his and Natleaha's direction when he yells.

"Keep your voice down, we wouldn't want other people to see what you like to do, now would we?" Natleaha urges and teases.

"What do you want?" the guard demands.

"Only a small favor, no one will ever really know."

So, a week later, Natleaha is on a rooftop several buildings away from her target. The guard in question is standing in front of a window. Several feet away, the diplomat he's watching is sitting in a chair right behind him. The diplomat is reading a newspaper, so he doesn't notice the bodyguard moving slightly to his side.

A minute later, a bullet smashes through the glass window past the guard and hits the diplomat square in the forehead. All the other bodyguards didn't even see this particular bodyguard move. This is Natleaha's second successful mission, with a little help of course.

"I was wrong, I didn't have to kill him like my instincts told me I might have to." She was intrigued by Flavawn and she was certain she might see him again.

Natleaha's next few missions involve rebel insurgents from Iran and Afghanistan. The Muslim members are taken aback when they witness a black woman fighting and killing for Russia. Soon, the rebels give her the nickname the Black Spider.

"How can you kill for these infidels? They would kill you as readily as they kill us!" a rebel she overpowers shouts right before she shoots him in the head with own gun. But Natleaha wasn't totally ignorant, she knew enough about Muslim culture and what they thought about women in positions of power. So, she had no qualms about killing as many of these men as was needed.

The eighties were flying by for Natleaha and the rest of the Fisks, namely Peter and Clearessa whom still stayed in Africa, hardly venturing out, except for the occasional mission for the KGB. They both kept their bodies well for their ages. Jonah still cleans at the old office building he first went to decades ago. New people work in the building he cleans now though and his wife Martha rests at their home unable to work due to the bad arthritis in her legs.

Her son Marvin calls her every day from where ever the military has him stationed. Eric lives in America with his wife and children. Even though he's a respected medical examiner for the city police department he lives in, he had to spend years applying for citizenship for him and his family. They finally get it when the United States is convinced they're not Russian spies. In 1987, things are becoming strained all around the world, a deadly disease is ravaging entire populations. Homosexuals are blamed for it even though children, women and drug addicts are contracting the A.I.D.S virus too.

Witch hunts are breaking out all over for gay men. For the first time, Natleaha fears for her father and grandfather.

"I don't want him to die like this," she confides to her mother. Though she doesn't like her father and is annoyed by him, she doesn't want him dead. Africa is one of the places that's hit the hardest by the disease. Not since the famine of Ethiopia has all of Africa known such pain.

With the apartheid rule and the spread of A.I.D.S, Africa was becoming way too volatile for Russia to gain a foot hold, but they still wanted spies there. So, to split the deference, Peter's handler remained in Cape Town to relay any to the Fisks any missions they need to go, which was rare and Peter and Clearessa went to Great Britain.

Once there, Peter got tested, his results were negative, which was a surprise given what he got up to in Africa. Jonah refused to get tested, even after the urging of his children. Natleaha flew back where she was to talk to her grandfather.

"I'm old Nata, it won't make any difference how I die at this point."

"Aw come on, Grandpa, you're not that old," she attempts to cheer him up with kind words, but he's unmoved.

"I'm pushing eighty Nata, if I'm lucky, I'll go into my nineties safely. I've done what I could, not what I wanted or who I wanted for that matter. The greatest love of my life, not your grandmother, died dangling at the end of a rope."

He must mean Willie, Natleaha thinks.

Natleaha recalls when she was a child visiting her grandfather that he would sometimes get too drunk by accident and began talking about Willie, how he looked, how he smelled and walked. By the way Jonah looked whenever he talked about the man, even in his drunken stupor, Natleaha was sure he loved Willie then, to her grandmother's ire.

Although they tried to keep secrets from her when she was growing up, Natleaha learned a great deal about her family through other sources. Her uncle Marvin's wife told her why him and her grandpa Jonah never got along and her handler happen to know why Korcoff Vamitri was so interested in the Fisk family, more than what his wife happened to share years later. It was then she decided to get tested herself. She then thought about Flavawn and what he was doing and if he was still alive.

"It's not over for our family Grandpa, Uncle Eric is in America with my cousins and father and mother are safe in Britain." She knew better than to bring up her uncle Marvin at a time like this.

"At what price Nata? At what price? We're scattered all over the world, only speaking to each other by phone, or seeing each other when somebody dies. The latest world crisis has brought you here, not love for me, but fear of seeing your future when you get old."

He was partially right and Natleaha didn't want to admit it. Believing there was nothing to do to change Jonah's mind, Natleaha left on the next flight to wait in Cuba for her next assignment.

So far, Natleaha's test results were negative, so that was one less thing she had to worry about. But her parents knew her too well, so they constantly called her on the phone urging her to be careful.

"Take care of yourself Nata," is what her mother always seemed to be saying to her nowadays.

"Yes, yes I will, I will," would be her reply to her mother.

Natleaha thought her warnings were Redundant given what she does for a living. Though the disease didn't stop her from indulging herself, Natleaha was more cautious. Picking men and women that to her were safe in their daily life practices, maybe once in a while, seducing a target if it was absolutely necessary.

"What's going on? Things are becoming slow," Natleaha said one day to her long-time handler.

"It's nothing to worry about, Russia will always have enemies to eliminate and you have to remember you're not the only assassin that works for the State," her handler reminded her.

Yeah, that was true, Natleaha thought.

Although her demands appear to wane, she still received missions that required her special touch as the Black Spider, as the KGB even called her now, just like Russia's enemies do. But still she and her handler could not ignore that things were showing signs of collapse in their government.

To take her mind off what was going on with her home country, Natleaha decided to take her first trip to America. She'd heard stories for years about the United States and was curious.

They can't be more bigoted toward people like me than they are in Russia, Natleaha thinks.

"Be careful," her mother again warned.

"Don't worry. You do realize I can take care of myself by now." Her mother shook her head at her daughter the day before she left for America.

"The people who rule the government there maybe gluttonous and foolish, but they are dangerous fools. They will do whatever they must to hold on to their money and power, including kill anyone that gets in their way."

"You talk as if I haven't had to blend in before, that I don't comprehend being in a dangerous situation. I do. Besides, while I'm there, I'll be staying with cousin Ida in Chicago, Illinois. She lives by herself in what she considers a dangerous neighborhood. She'll welcome the company."

Clearessa saw that her daughter wasn't completely naïve about America, but she still had her reservations about her going there. If they found out she is a spy and assassin, the Americans wouldn't bother with questioning her, they would just kill out right.

"Tell your cousin Ida that your father and I send our love."

"I will."

Life in Great Britain seems to be agreeing with Clearessa and Peter. The most they had to do so far since being there is surveillance of key cabinet members, their routines, their habits and any family they might be. Peter wasn't home the day Natleaha came by and told her mother her plans of going to America, so he had to hear it second hand from his wife.

"Does she have the forethought of what she's getting into?" Peter asks his wife with a worried look on his face. Clearessa folds her arms and shrugs her shoulders.

"Partially yes, but I don't think she grasps the full gravity of the coming situation she'll be in. They brag about otherwise being a liberal nation, but they have spies and devices watching every move their people make just like every other country."

"Did she say where she'll be staying while she's there? At the Russian Embassy?"

"No, she says she'll be staying with your niece Ida."

"Ida? I heard she was on drugs from what Eric told me. How can Nata keep a low profile with an addict? The police will be onto her in days and then the secret service. This is a disaster! Our whole family could be in danger."

"Calm yourself, your brother and his family have been there for years and they've never even been caught for so much as a parking ticket. And

Natleaha's handler can also watch out for her. Let's not worry about something until we've cause to."

Peter concedes to his wife's reasoning.

Natleaha could take care of herself.

"Alright I won't over react. Natleaha can handle whatever the Americans can throw at her. By the way, I was thinking we should go see my parents and maybe on the way back from Russia, we could stop in Cuba to see your father."

"When could we do this? Our government won't give us leave to travel from our posts. They didn't when we lived in Africa. It was only in extreme circumstances that we were able to leave. And the only other time was to go to your father's benefactor's funeral, who was well-placed in the government."

"But my mother is ill and my father's not much better off. I'm sure they'd give us permission if we explained to them about why."

"And my father? There's nothing to warrant a need to visit him. The old bastard is as mean and evil as he ever was," Clearessa says with resentment.

Her and her father have never really cared for each other, even when she was a child. He always saw her as something he was stuck with and given the type of man his daughter is married to things have only gotten worse between them.

"Fine, we won't go see your father, but I will ask for permission to see mine and my mother."

Four days later, Peter is granted a pass to see his parents, but the KGB order Clearessa to stay in Britain to monitor the surveillance they have on the cabinet members.

Father and son talk very little when Peter arrives back in Russia after such a long absence. They have little in common, aside from what normal society calls an abnormal flaw. They find the words to eventually speak to each other.

"Your mother has her good days and her bad days. The doctors here don't know how much longer she will last," Jonah relays to his son.

"If mama dies before you, you'll be free to be happy, to find someone to give yourself to fully."

Jonah totally gets what Peter is saying, but he is still shocked by the statement.

"Are you fucking serious! You would bring that up now? I'm over eighty years old, Peter, much too old for any of that. I still love your mother despite everything else."

"Oh, please pop, the love died between you two a long time ago, I could see it in mama's eyes."

"And what about your marriage and the promises you made?" Now it was Peter's turn to be shocked.

"I never made promises to Clearessa. We only married to help fulfill your agreement to Korcoff. There was there, but no real love and we both were aware of it."

"So that's why she was content to let you play around for your amusement in the deepest parts of Africa. Yes, I know all about that, me and your mother. I controlled that part of me for your mother's sake."

"What about Korcoff?"

"That was business and one-sided. There were no others, I didn't make a fool of myself like you have and still are. I couldn't afford to, not here. Think of your daughter."

"What about Natleaha?" Peter asks in offense.

"You were so busy being afraid of her that you didn't teach her how to moderate her own similar behavior."

"She's a woman, it's different for her and it's not like when I was her age and it's especially not like when you were a young black man."

"True, but it's still dangerous for her in other ways. Times don't change for people like us, they just evolve into newer dangers that are harder to see and accept. We can never regain the ground we have lost. We can only struggle not to be destroyed in the process of life."

"You're half right pop, we do have to struggle not to be destroyed, but we can regain the ground we have lost. It's just taking a long time to do so."

Jonah hears his son's words, but he believes Peter is just as worried for their family's future as Jonah is. Rolling into the summer of 1990, Natleaha is twenty-four now, but she's seen much in her young life. The winters are rough in Chicago, but no more so than they are in Russia she's noticed. The summer days are humid and hot as she has also witnessed.

Natleaha has found her twenty-year old cousin Ida is fighting a losing battle with drugs. Ida can barely function, Natleaha has to practically force her cousin to go to her job to help pay for their two-bedroom apartment. Since she moved in months ago, Natleaha has watched Ida sell herself, body and soul, to numerous drug dealers to pay for her habit.

Also, since Natleaha has arrived, she's stopped her cousin from spending all her money on drugs, by grabbing her check from her job and taking most of the money for rent and electricity. Natleaha doesn't really care if her cousin eats, but she wants the bills paid so the heat and air condition works. To pay for food, mainly for herself, Natleaha does odd jobs and if things get really desperate she does secret hits on her neighborhood's drug dealer rivals.

No one has ever seen her face and they don't know her name. To make matters worse for her, she's sexually frustrated. None of the men Ida sleeps with are appealing. It's not their looks, some of them were kind of cute, just that they seemed of very low character and morally disgusting, sub-human. And the women seemed too preoccupied with making babies or chasing after the most successful drug dealer.

"What chu a dyke or sumthin?" Ida asked Natleaha one day after not seeing her with no men after months of being in their place. Natleaha punched her dead in her mouth, causing Ida to stumble almost to the floor.

"Never mind why I don't go out with men, you just make sure you have money for the god damn rent," Natleaha warned Ida. The truth was Ida did wonder why she never seen her cousin go out on any dates with anybody, she was gorgeous.

Things continued to drag along with Natleaha and Ida until some Jamaican gangsters called the Shower Posse moved into the neighborhood. Natleaha could tell by the professional way they carried themselves and of course hearing their accents. Natleaha had heard stories about the Shower Posse from other agents who've had dealings with them.

They were very dangerous and the low rent drug dealers of Chicago were no match for them. They flooded the streets with acid laced cocaine to make it seem like the local dealers were purposely trying to kill their customers. This would cause the addicts to come to the Jamaicans who would charge even higher prices for the crack cocaine.

Ida the fool that she was, almost over-dosed on the laced drugs. The paramedics barely got to the apartment in time to save her life given the paramedics reluctance to come to an all-black low-income neighborhoods. And when they got there they wasted time asking Natleaha stupid questions.

"How long has it been since she took the drugs? What did she take? How long has your cousin been a drug user?" the paramedics asked.

"How the fuck should I know? She's dying you assholes!" Natleaha screamed at them.

Despite what she thought about Ida, she was still family and Natleaha felt that this was an attack on herself. She had to do something, but first she had to wait on a call that she was sure was coming. As suspected, her personal phone she kept for own business rang.

Using a voice muffler, she answered, "Sivosin Extermination Company."

Natleaha says through the muffler, "Uh, yeah I got some roaches in my building dat's outta control. Can you come by and spray?"

"Yes, give me your address and we'll be by in a couple of days to fumigate your place."

"Thanks, dat's cool. My address is 835 Inglewood North Ave."

The neighborhood drug dealer followed her protocol to the letter. The main drug kingpin had one of his corner boys call her from the ad she put in the paper and give her the address of the people they want eliminated. Months back, she pretended to be a hitman's girlfriend and Natleaha carefully approached the drug kingpin about how to get rid of pesky bugs, namely people.

And the address the corner boy gave her was to the headquarters of the Shower Posse. Natleaha has never taken out this many men that's going to be there at once. She had to be cautious and make sure the main leader of this faction was going to be there.

Having a day to put together a plan, Natleaha contacted a shapely black trans-sexual who had her ear to the ground on the street knowledge of everything that was going on.

"Caramel, what would get the main Rusta to their headquarters?" Natleaha asks after meeting Caramel in an alley behind a convenient store.

"Easy honey, the disruption of the cash flow or product. Men in power hate having to deal with silly shit they pay their foot soldiers tom take care of."

"Alright, sounds easy enough," Natleaha replies while noting Caramel's beauty and body filling out a form-fitting green sleeveless dress.

How could this pretty creature have been a man? She's stunning, Natleaha thinks in astonishment.

"Don't get any ideas you're on business," Natleaha chastises herself.

"So, I take it you're gonna give those Jamaicans a special evening they won't forget?" Caramel asks slyly. Caramel always suspected Natleaha was a pro of a high level when it came to this type of thing.

"You'll just have to find out after it happens as always. Your fee will be in your account tomorrow," Natleaha answers her freely, not worrying if Caramel is wired or if they're being watched. She trusted her as well as she trusted anybody she works with.

After that night, Natleaha got to work. Early in the day, Natleaha found the two main stash houses and snuck in without being seen and placed a few fire grenades in each house.

"What da fuck!" the men guarding the houses screamed as they watched the houses go up in flames.

Sadly, some of them got caught in the blazes. This caught the attention of the main Shower Posse man in charge in the city. He played right into Natleaha's hands by going straight to the headquarters in Inglewood to question his men about what happened. He calls his lieutenants to the basement of the headquarters.

"What da fuck is goin on? Who be tryin' to play round wit' me business hmm!" he demands more than asks by his tone, heaving his broad chest, arching his shoulders. His eyes are menacing, sweat beading off his shaved head. His lieutenants are frightened and reluctant to answer because the man is known to kill for the slightest infraction. However, one of them muscles up the courage to answer.

"We don't know what happened boss, da flames jus came outta nowhere, wires and product jus meltin'. Da sprinklers didn't do shit. Same wit da other place. Fire people said dey found shells of grenades," the lieutenant recounts.

"Grenades, what da fuck? Dos low rent drug mutha fuckas ain't got da juice to hit my stashes. We gonna find dis mutha fucka dat's movin on us, startin tonight," the leader says with a thick Jamaican drawl.

Meanwhile, Natleaha has entered the building through the roof, wearing her signature outfit. She has two Smith and Wesson guns strapped to her sides with attached silencers, a metal garret hidden in her necklace around her neck, a Swiss army knife in her boot and cache of bullets and grenades in a small back pack. The guards she encountered on the roof and upper floor are easy pickings, dead before they hit the ground.

"Where is your boss?" she demands of a young guard who looked Barely eighteen who tried to resist harder when she shot him in the leg.

"I ain't tellin' you nuthin' bitch! ON my honor, I die!" the boy proudly says through gritted teeth. So, she shoots him in the other leg. The boy screams, cursing at Natleaha in his native tongue.

Growing bored with the exchange, Natleaha puts a bullet in between the eyes of the boy. She continues to creep from room to room, some of the soldiers are alone, some are with women ravishing them on squeaky beds. The soldiers are so into what they're doing that they don't hear Natleaha inch up behind them and slit their throats. She savagely stabs the women too, believing them as guilty as the men they were with.

One man is in one of the bathrooms showering, she opts to walk past him, figuring to take care of him later. Eventually one of the young soldiers comes to level where the bedrooms are with a rifle. He heard strange muffled noises from downstairs. He is terrified when he witnesses the cut and shot bodies, his hands won't stop shaking. Natleaha eyes him fiercely with her guns drawn on him. She can tell he's very young and not fast enough to use his rifle on her.

"Where is your boss?" she demands once more. "He's in da basement, bout to leave." The boy didn't realize it, but his inexperience and fear saves him.

"Leave! Everyone in this building is about to be dead, including your boss."

Not giving her a chance to change her mind, the boy drops the rifle, turns and runs to the nearest exit. Encountering more guards as she goes down the steps, Natleaha makes short works of them. When a group of them comes at her, she throws some grenades over their heads. The exploding causes the ceiling above them to collapse on top of them, making it easy to shoot each man under rumble in the head.

She traps the boss downstairs by barricading the door with an iron crowbar she found. For added measure, she throws more grenades in the basement. She's so busy with her task that she doesn't notice a man sneaking up behind her until he wraps a thick white towel around her face.

"What cha gonna do now huh, hm, hm!" the man says in gruff voice while he's smothering her with the towel. His grip is strong, she can't breathe, so she stomps on his left foot as hard as she can breaking the skin of the top of his foot. It's enough for him to slightly loosen his grip and her to clip him with a swing of her leg.

Getting the towel off her face, Natleaha gets a good look at the man attacking her. She's shocked to see that he's completely naked. Water dripping from his long dreadlocks all down his tall, bulky body and Natleaha can see he's not ungifted with his middle manhood. Right then she wants to kick herself, it's the man from the shower she saw earlier. She thought he would be too busy with the noise of the running water to hear anything.

"Ya tink ya can come in our house and do dis to us, hm, hm? Ya gonna bleed dis day bitch, ya gonna bleed yeah!" the man sneers.

Natleaha attempts to shoot him, but he dives out of the way, proving he's a lot faster than he looks. Dodging her bullets, he ducks behind fallen debris.

If only I can get behind him and slit his throat with my garret or knife, she thinks in desperation.

Running at her, he uses a loose wooden beam to swing at her and knocks her in the head. It momentarily stuns her, giving him the chance to tackle her to the floor. He bears his entire weight and strength on top of her. He's got her arms pinned and she still too groggy from the blow to the head-to-head butt him off her. He then manages to pull off her mask.

"Ya gonna remember me, remember me always, even after ya kill me ya remember!" he roars in her face, spit and water dribbling out of his mouth and onto her.

"No, no, no!" she screams, she knows what is happening and she can't stop it. He holds her by the throat as he tears open her pants with his free hand. It is a nightmare, he's deep inside, putting his weight on her to keep her from escaping. He grunts loudly when he is done with her. Another momentary distraction gives Natleaha the strength to bite her assailant on the nose. She digs her teeth in, trying to rip his nose off with her mouth.

"Ya bitch!" he spits and screams as he tries to pull away, but he makes the mistake of removing his arms from hers.

Quickly reaching up, Natleaha grabs him by the head, turns and snaps his neck. He falls dead on top of her. It takes her a while for her to crawl from under him. She then brutally stabs the dead body over and over again with her knife. Taking a moment to pick up a machine gun from one of the dead soldiers, Natleaha unlocks the basement door and walks down the steps to finish off whoever is not dead from the grenade explosions.

She pulls off what's left of her pants, slips on one of the soldier's pants and leaves out of the front door, stopping outside to vomit heavily.

"Oh God, oh God!" Natleaha screams. She can't think, she can hardly breath, her vision is blurry, it's horrible.

"Oh God no!" she wails again. She barely makes it home, locking herself in her room, laying on the floor, muffling her screams with a pillow. Weeks go by and the pain she feels doesn't stop, it only gets worse. Word of what happened to the Shower Posse spreads fast, the neighborhood dodges a bullet, if you want to call it that.

"Did ya hear what happened to the Shower Posse? Dey got fucked up, dey and dey houses," people were saying to each other on the streets.

It's a steamy hot day in late July and the vomiting won't stop for Natleaha. She muddles through to the beginning of next month, but the sickness won't stop, so she goes to the nearest hospital where her cousin Ida is still recovering from her overdose. Natleaha goes to the emergency section of the hospital. Her hair is uncombed and she's wearing nothing but a tank top and shorts.

"May I help you?" the nurse at the check in desk asks Natleaha. "I'm sick, I can't stop throwing up."

"Ok, do you have any insurance?" the nurse asks before handing Natleaha a clip board with a form and a pin on it.

Natleaha doesn't even answer the nurse's last question because she figured the nurse can figure it out by the looks of her and her silence. Natleaha uses Sivosin as her last name on the medical form, it's her mother's maiden name and the name she uses in her ad. She answers the rest of the questions on the form the best she can. The doctor finally sees her after a several hour long wait.

"What seems to be the problem Mrs. Sivosin?" the doctor asks half-heartedly. He looks like a thin bearded geek with glasses instead of a doctor to Natleaha.

"I'm sick, I can't stop vomiting. What is it?"

"Well let's have a nurse check your blood and run some tests to see what's the matter," the doctor says as he gets up from his chair and walks out of the room.

As he said, a nurse comes into the room wearing latex gloves, holding a tray with small tiny tubes and a needle on it.

"This may hurt a little bit," the nurse warns Natleaha before she pokes the needle in her arm. She's so numb she can barely feel the needle.

Once enough blood is filled into the vile, the nurse pulls the needle out, plants a cotton swab and a band aid on her arm.

"Wait here, the doctor will be right back," the nurse kindly orders Natleaha as she leaves. An hour goes by and the doctor returns with the nurse who took Natleaha's blood. He has a smile on his face to signal that he supposedly has good news.

"Well, Mrs. Sivosin, we've checked your blood work and the other tests on your fluids and it appears you're expecting," the doctor tells her.

"What?" Natleaha muddles.

"Your pregnant, Mrs. Sivosin, three weeks along to be precise," he further confirms.

Natleaha feels like she's going to be sick right there in the doctor's office. The doctor sees her distress and attempts to calm her down.

"There are several options you have in ways you wish to proceed if you want. I can recommend a good OBGYN that you could talk to."

"No thank you, I'd like to go home now please," Natleaha says with strain in her voice. She leaves the hospital in a self-induced haze.

She sees the man who brutally raped her every time she closes her eyes. Natleaha has other problems as well, with the Chicago police investigating the murders at Inglewood.

"Police is sayin dat der were witnesses who seen somebody goin der fore da place got lit up," her contact Caramel relays to Natleaha, but she's not too worried.

"It's all rumor, they can't prove nothing. They would've came to me weeks ago if they had witnesses," Natleaha states confidently.

But for added insurance she decides to flee the country, but she scrounges up enough money to pay four months of rent on Ida's apartment in case she ever returns. She wanted to go to her grandparents in Russia, but she felt the situation was too serious for them to handle, so she went to her parents who were still in Great Britain.

Sitting in their living room, Natleaha painfully recounts the horrible attack to her parents.

When she's done telling her story, her mother hold her firmly while her father gazes out a window sorrowfully.

"Are you going to have an abortion then?" Clearessa asks frankly.

"I think so, I feel sick all the time just thinking about this baby."

"No!" Peter blares out. Both his daughter and wife are stunned by reaction.

"You can't kill this child, we all live with violence and death our whole lives, putting our fates into our hands every time we go on a mission. This child is just another consequence of the danger you continue to put yourself in."

"But I don't want it Papa!"

"You have to and you have to let it live, if for no other reason than to prove you can live with any consequence of your actions."

"So, what then? She sentences it to the horrors of foster care?" Clearessa asks with an edge.

"No, we can take care of the child until you're ready to be a mother to it, if ever."

"That's not going to happen Papa," Natleaha adamantly says.

"We can tell your handler you were brutally injured during a personal matter, which is not far from the truth. The way things are now, you won't be needed, so he'll be able to convince our superiors for a period of rest time. You can go to a place where there are other young women in your situation until you have the baby and give it to us."

Natleaha thinks hard on her father's words and notes that her mother has become silent and difficult to read.

"Alright fine," Natleaha softly says.

The months are very difficult for Natleaha as she languishes in the center her father sent her to. There are large grounds around the place, so Natleaha doesn't feel too trapped inside. Eventually, in March of 1991, Natleaha went into labor. Following two days of labor pains and contractions, she gives birth to a healthy baby boy, but she and the doctors were shocked to discover the baby was pale white like ivory with bright blond nappy hair. Natleaha could barely stand to look at the boy.

"What would you like to name the boy?" a pediatric nurse asked Natleaha.

"Ivan. Ivan because he's terrible like his namesake was."

Natleaha refuses to hold Ivan, demanding instead to call her parents. Naturally her parents were put off when they first saw Ivan. His grandfather was the only one in the family to hold him. His grandmother also refused to hold Ivan like her daughter.

"You will be loved no matter what," Peter tenderly says to his new grandson.

Ivan was born shortly before a bad ending for Russia. Communism collapsed in the country, leaving the Russian people to pick up the pieces and rebuild. The KGB officially no longer exists anymore.

Their agents where ever they were in the world were stuck there for the time being. Ivan's mother took advantage of this tragedy to sever all ties with the defunct KGB and disappear. Ivan only feels love from his grandfather and was faced with growing up in a changed world.

Chapter 4

Ivan is a delightful baby to have around for Peter. He doesn't give off the dark eerie vibe his mother did when she was his age. Clearessa holds him occasionally, but not nearly as much as Peter.

"His life is gonna be interesting and hard," Jonah states when he sees his great-grandson.

"Why did Natleaha name him Ivan?"

"Something about him being terrible," Clearessa answers Jonah when he asked.

Peter is sort of weary of people coming to see Ivan, especially by members of his own family. He gets the impression that they see his grandson as more of a circus side show attraction than a baby. This grows to irritate Peter, so he restricts visits to Ivan and rarely takes him outside in stroller. This turns out to be a good decision due to the fact that Ivan's skin is sensitive to too much sun.

Months pass by and before Peter realizes it, Ivan is learning how to walk. Potty training Ivan is not as difficult as it is for some babies. Peter manages to watch him closely and coaches Ivan to the training pot.

"Yaya, yaya, yaya," Ivan eventually starts saying to Peter, his word for Papa. He calls Clearessa granmie. He still had problems with calling Peter Grandpa instead of yaya. Nobody from the old Russian regime has come to see the Fisks about Ivan. The Fisks figure that the Russians don't really care about debts to the State at the moment.

"In time, if they want him they will come for him, especially if he shows promise," Clearessa reminds Peter.

"They would only want him to bust his back in a gulag carrying boulders and dead bodies in Siberia. Look at him, he could not be a spy anywhere. No, no that's not how his life will go," Peter says in defiance.

As Ivan grows, it's still no word from his mother. She never went back to Chicago and her uncle Marvin has searched all over the world for her and he cannot find her.

"A child needs their mother no matter the circumstances."

"Peter, you know that's not possible and the reasons why."

"It's been four years and the rapist is long dead."

"You've never been raped, you don't understand the pain, the violation, the nightmares. How could you? You're a man."

Peter looks straight at Clearessa.

"Men can be violated too, in other ways even you can't imagine, especially black men."

Peter is reminded of what he had seen when he lived in Africa during the Apartheid, the beatings, mass forced relocations, the mass murders and the imprisonment of the men and women who attempted to fight back against the injustice.

On the upside, the Peter heard is that apartheid was starting to go out of favor. Both Peter and Clearessa have witnessed things that would terrify the average person. And Peter hopes for once that the newest member of his family won't have to experience total horror growing up.

Soon, Ivan begins school. His grandparents would rather have him attend school in Britain or America, but the investigation of what happened in Chicago involving their daughter is still on going. The new F.S.B that's taken over from the KGB wants Peter and Clearessa to return to Russia.

It's clear there are some whom still find value in the Fisk family. As suspected, it is difficult for Ivan in school because of his appearance. Sometimes, he gets into fights or other kids throw things at him. But some of the teachers have discovered he is special when it comes to how he learns. The principal contacts Ivan's grandparents to arrange a meeting face to face, he's is in the second grade by then. The Fisks don't have to wait long when they arrive at the school.

"Mr. Bolivich will see you now," the secretary says to the Fisks. The principal looks more like a military officer than an educator when they meet him, a stern look and perfect erect posture. He doesn't even sit when the Fisks do, he stands at attention by his desk with his arms behind his back.

"Mr. and Mrs. Fisk thank you for coming today. It has come to our attention that your grandson exhibits advanced skills in reading and math, working at fourth grade level. With your permission, we would like to put him in a special program to better hone his talents."

A special program? How could Russia have the means for a special program? They barely have enough to feed the people, Peter thinks.

"That sounds interesting. Would Ivan still be with children his own age?"

"Of course, Mr. Fisk. We even think that he would better thrive in this environment. Even though our government is shifting, Russia still believes in excellence for its people."

"I guess this special program might be good to try for Ivan, maybe for a little while until he gets older," Peter says half-heartedly.

Clearessa remains silent throughout the entire exchange, choosing to nod at the principal if he acknowledges her.

"Is this something that would interest you?" the principal asks as if they really have a choice.

"Yes we think this might be good for Ivan," answers for both him and his wife.

The more things change, the more they stay the same, Clearessa solemnly thinks to herself. Peter doesn't really regret his decision to go along with the principal's recommendation to put Ivan in special school. Right now, it seems being special means you won't go hungry.

"What are you?" a little white girl asks Ivan one day when they are in class.

"I'm special like you," Ivan answers with child-like pride.

"No, why do you look so pale? Your hair is blond, but it's bushy. Can you comb it?" the girl elaborates.

"I don't know, my grandpa always combs it with a big comb."

"Children stop talking, pay attention," the teacher teaching the class sternly says to Ivan and the girl. Days later, Ivan sees the same girl again at lunch time wearing iron pressed overalls, her hair tied in a pony tail. She's sitting with two other children at a cafeteria table. Ivan muscles up the courage to talk to her again.

"Hi," Ivan casually says to all the children at the table. The other two ignore him, but the brown-haired girl doesn't.

"My mother says you're an albino and my sister says she read a book that people like you are magic," the girl tells him.

Ivan didn't know what to make of that.

"No one's ever said that to me before. My grandpa just says I'm special," Ivan repeats.

"No, you have to be magic, all my family says so. There's no one like you in the whole school."

Could I be magic like the girl says? Grandpa has told me no one else looks like me, Ivan wonders.

This revelation fascinated little Ivan.

Could this be why he felt so detached from everyone else? His deep thoughts are suddenly interrupted when one of the other children speaks.

"He's not magic, he's a freak. Everybody knows it, freak!" the boy yells throwing a carton of milk at Ivan. Ivan lunges at the boy, banging his head on the connected bench to the table.

"I'm not a freak, I'm magic!" Ivan cries as he continues to slam the boy's head against the bench. All the children in the lunchroom are shouting and cheering, including the girl Ivan was talking to. Eventually, one of the teachers present in the lunchroom breaks it up. The back of the boy's head is busted, so he has to be taken to the nurse to have it bandaged.

Ivan is kept in the principal's office for the rest of the school day. Peter has to come get Ivan because the school refuses to let Ivan on the school bus with the other children. Peter spanks Ivan with a belt and gives him a hard lecture.

"You can't beat on children when they say something you don't like! You could have killed that poor boy! Is that what you want? To have people think you're a mad dog, Ivan?"

"But I'm magic, the pretty girl says so!" Ivan cried.

Peter is dumbfounded.

"The principal said that the boy called Ivan a freak. Where did this girl come from saying he was magic?" Peter recounts. Because of the fight and the injuries the other boy suffered, Ivan is suspended for two weeks and Peter was ordered to take Ivan into counseling for his anger issues.

Because of the incident at school, some of the children were afraid of Ivan, but the pretty girl who said he was magic still talked to him, saying the fire magic in his blood made him attack that boy. Him and the girl named Eleanea became friends. Eleanea showed Ivan a book about fairytales with bright colored pictures.

She mainly showed Ivan the story about the magic elf who liked to practice magic and grow things in the forest. Eleanea showed Ivan a picture of the elf in the book. He was colored white with long flowing blond hair. The mild differences between the character in the book and Ivan was the elf's hair was straight and he had pointy ears.

"See, I told you, you were magic."

Eleanea bragged. On the spare of the moment when they were alone in the hall one day, Ivan kissed her quickly on the lips, she didn't seem to mind it. Ivan had just turned ten then.

The long months of counseling helped Ivan maintain his anger issues and concentrate on his school work, but he still believed he was magic for some reason. At ten years old, Ivan was beginning to show what type of personality he would have later in life. There were two other moments that would also help shape Ivan into the person he would be. One of the events he told no one about, not even his best friend Eleanea. Another had to do with a man he'd seen every day after school sleeping outside his grandparents' apartment building.

"Do you have any change?" he'd ask Ivan and other people every day.

Ivan noticed the man's speech was kind of funny and his face was weird shaped. He wore raggedy clothes and had thinning grayish hair. Ivan would always feed the man one of the sandwiches Peter would make Ivan for lunch.

"Thanks Ivan," the bum would always say in slurred speech. Ivan grew to like the man because he believed he might be magic like him because of his strange appearance.

"Could Mr. Survick be magic like me Grandpa?" Ivan asked filled with childish curiosity. Peter smiled tenderly at Ivan.

"No Ivan, Mr. Survick is not magic, he has down syndrome." Ivan was confused.

"Down Syndrome, what's that?"

"It's something that makes a person look different and they can't learn as fast as you or me. It basically means Mr. Survick will have a very hard time in life, harder than you or me."

"Oh that's sad," Ivan says with sympathy. Ivan felt deep compassion for Mr. Survick after learning that. Though he learned the truth about Mr. Survick, he still remained friends with the man.

The second moment was quite a different situation involving a male Greek immigrant who was a teacher for the older high school age children at the special school Ivan went to. His name was Armond Greako and he was very nice to Ivan when he first met Ivan after he wandered to the section where the older kids had classes.

Whenever Ivan would finish school he'd come to Mr. Greako's classroom and he would give Ivan candy and juice, telling him he was beautiful ivory boy. Ivan thought Mr. Greako looked like those exotic male Indian dancers he watched on T.V with a trimmed beard and sparkling brown eyes. Armond seemed glad to shower attention on Ivan whenever he got the chance.

Ivan believed that Mr. Greako thought of him as magic too because of the attention he received. Ivan couldn't quite remember when the moment the attention began to feel strange and now he wasn't sure if it was right. All he knew was Mr. Greako liked to touch and hug him a lot.

"You're a beautiful boy, you'll be strong and handsome when you grow up," Mr. Greako expressed with a wide smile.

One afternoon, Ivan went to Mr. Greako's classroom as always. He had delicious sweet muffins for Ivan to eat. He sat Ivan upon his lap as he ate the muffins. Without warning, he started to tickle Ivan causing him to laugh.

"Stop, stop, heh, heh," Ivan weakly protested. This went on for minutes until Mr. Greako stopped tickling him and began rubbing Ivan's thigh. This felt strange to Ivan, he didn't know what to make of it.

No one had ever touched Ivan this way before, not even his grandfather. The weird sensation was causing great fear in Ivan. He was terrified someone might walk by and see what Mr. Greako was doing, but the door was closed, although Ivan didn't remember it being closed after he came through the doorway. Mr. Greako senses Ivan's fear and attempts to calm him.

"Relax, relax, there's nothing to be afraid of, no one's gonna hurt you," Mr. Greako says softly.

His hand continues to rub Ivan's thigh. Slowly, his hand moves to the middle of Ivan's pants zipper. Mr. Greako squeezes the middle of his zipper until Ivan gasps in shock.

"Don't worry. I'm not going to hurt you, just relax this won't hurt," Mr. Greako gently says as he slowly unzips Ivan's pants.

"What, wha, wha," is all Ivan can utter when Mr. Greako reaches inside Ivan's pants. Ivan can feel a lump from Mr. Greako against the lower part of his back. Before he realizes it, Mr. Greako has pulled out Ivan's small penis and feels on it. He pulls on Ivan until he's filled with a strange sensation. Mr.

Greako reaches into his desk drawer and takes out some paper towels, he tears off some from the roll and hands it to Ivan.

"Clean yourself up, you have to get home soon," Mr. Greako kindly demands. He was right, Ivan's grandparents would be looking for him in front of the school. When he got off his lap, Ivan saw what was poking in the back. There was a bulge in Mr. Greako's pants and he cupped it in a vain attempt to cover it up. Seeing this, Ivan quickly wipes himself off and walks out of the classroom.

This encounter leaves Ivan feeling strange and confused. He's afraid to see or look at Mr. Greako after that. Whenever he sees Ivan in the hallway or lunchroom, he tries to entice Ivan to come to his classroom with offers of exotic candies, juices and rich cakes. Ivan still doesn't tell anyone what happened. He believes more people would think him a freak and not magic.

When he becomes twelve, Ivan goes to Mr. Greako's classroom again after school. By then, he's gotten taller and he has let another older boy touch him. The feeling is different from when Mr. Greako touched him before. The older boy who touched Ivan has blond hair, was muscular and is rumored to be a homosexual some of the other kids say.

"I'm not going to sit on your lap," Ivan flat out tells Mr. Greako in a stern late pre-pubescent voice.

"Would you like some beer, ivory boy? I got some in my drawer," Mr. Greako offers but Ivan isn't moved, he's old enough and smart enough to know what Mr. Greako wants now. His older boyfriend told Ivan all about Mr. Greako and what he does to the other boys.

"No, I'm not going sit on your lap for beer, but you can touch my thing if you want," Ivan offers.

Mr. Greako nods, stands up from his desk and kneels down in front of Ivan. He unzips his pants, pulls out Ivan's penis and puts it in his mouth. This feels good to Ivan.

"You're so beautiful my ivory boy, so beautiful," Mr. Greako praises when he takes Ivan's penis out of his mouth.

Eleanea can sense something is different with Ivan. They're still friends, but they don't laugh and play as much when they were younger.

"Do you want to go see the new Sylvester Stallone movie this weekend? It's supposed to be great," Eleanea offers as they're walking to the bus stop from school.

But Ivan is too distracted with watching the other boys, so he doesn't notice when Eleanea speaks to him.

"Ivan, Ivan?" she repeats.

"Huh, what?" he says finally paying attention to her.

"Do you want to go to the movies with me this weekend?"

"I don't know, my grandpa may need my help with work he has to do in the building we live in. We could probably go next Friday to the movies."

"Oh ok," Eleanea answers feeling disappointed. For a little while now, Eleanea has had a crush on Ivan. She's not sure when it happened, but she gradually discovered she liked spending time with Ivan when they weren't at school.

Unknown to Eleanea is that Ivan likes spending time with his older boyfriend, passing the seventeen-year-old Gregor Feldman as his best friend to his grandparents. Gregor knows something of oppression, being Jewish and all in Russia. Ivan can remember when they first met, it was during a conversation about the American September 11, 2001 attack on the World Trade Center. It was all over the news worldwide.

"Those Arab Muslims won't stand a chance now that the Americans are fighting them as well as my people in Israel," Gregor boasted to Ivan when they were eating lunch outside the school near the race track. Ivan was drawn to Gregor with his dark and wavy thick hair. He had the beginnings of a mustache and goatee, which made him look mature to Ivan. He'd often brag to Ivan about being with girls.

"You're going to love it Ivan, the feeling of full tits, rubbing the thick creases in the middle of their thighs. I love piercing them with my cock, it makes me hard just thinking about it."

Ivan love watching Gregor get all worked up whenever he talked like this.

"Girls are ok, but they're too complicated for me," Ivan freely admits, even at this young age.

"What are you talking about man? Girls are great, they do things to you, you couldn't even imagine."

"Then why does he let me touch him? Why does he let me rub my cock against his?" Ivan silently wonders.

Gregor knew right away Ivan liked him, ever since he caught Ivan staring at him when they were in the boy's locker room getting ready to change for gym class one day. Sometimes, the special assembles they attended would mix the junior students with the older high school students to see how they fare. The truth of the matter was Gregor didn't mind if Ivan touched him or not. It was a personal experiment to Gregor to see if he'd be uncomfortable with it.

"How was school today?" Peter asks Ivan as he walks through the door. "It was ok, our math teacher gave us weird algebra problems having to do with train departure and arrival times."

"How did you do?"

"I got eight out of ten of the problems on the board right. The last two had three sections in them. I was only able to finish two parts of the problems, the last parts of them I wasn't able to figure out," Ivan said feeling disappointed over not getting all ten of the problems right.

"I did good on my English though. Also, I'm doing great on Russian and American history. I can recite all then presidents by name."

"That's good, it will be a useful skill if you ever travel to America. Go do your homework, so you can be ready for dinner," Peter orders.

"After dinner, can I hang out with Gregor? He has a new hand-held video game he wants to show me."

"He can tell you about it over the phone, it's in the middle of the week, you have school for the rest of the week. You can spend more time with him when the weekend comes."

Ivan is disappointed once again, but he knows his grandfather is strictly adamant when it comes to his studies. So, for the time being, he gives into Peter.

"Ok," Ivan says sadly.

Clearessa didn't speak to Ivan when he came home from school, she only nodded to him in greeting. She doesn't speak that much to him at all, only occasionally when she has to. Ivan wonders if she cares for him at all.

"Your grandmother has always been a quiet woman, Ivan. It doesn't mean she doesn't love you," Peter explains to Ivan when he asked why she was so distant with him.

"What are your intentions toward my grandson?" Peter asked Gregor when he came over dinner to their home for the sixth time. Gregor was not afraid of the question.

"We're friends Mr. Fisk. Ivan and I like hanging out together, it's no big deal."

"He's five years younger than you. He's a child and you're practically a man."

"You have nothing to worry about, Ivan is like a brother to me. We have fun together, like he does with other friends like Eleanea."

"Eleanea is his own age and he doesn't ask to go spend evenings with her in the middle of the week."

Peter did not like Gregor. He suspected what was going on, he saw it in Ivan's eyes in the way he looked at Gregor. Clearessa noticed it too, although she didn't mention it. The boy was roughly handsome, he would grow to be more so when he was a man. This was unacceptable to Peter, he had to figure out a way to limit his grandson's time with Gregor before the boy gained too much control over Ivan.

Peter knew what could happen if you let another man gain too much control over you. It happened to Peter years ago when he was still living in Africa, before he married Clearessa and wasn't aware of Natleaha. The man in question was a member of a guerrilla warfare brigade. His group had come to Peter's village for food and supplies.

The reputation of these brigades was well known, they hardly ever asked for what they needed or wanted, they'd just take. Usually, burning villages to the ground. Peter was aware he had to find a way to get rid of them before they had the chance to destroy the village.

"Who's in charge here?" one of the guerrilla fighters demanded after they drove their trucks into the village. Peter volunteered to act as leader because the leaders of the village didn't have the necessary stomach to deal with men such as this.

"I lead here. What do you want?" Peter announced boldly.

"We wish to have food for us, our provisions are low" the fighter explained.

Since this man was the one addressing the people, Peter took him for the one to be the leader of this group. Peter had a large branch cutting machete hidden behind his back and a hand gun in his left pants pocket. With one quick swing, Peter could take off the head of the man he was talking to and kill about three more of them who were closest to their leader before they had time to react. He noticed most of these men were darker than him.

For some reason, Peter didn't think that was possible given his own brown skin like his parents. One of the men caught his attention, sitting in the passenger seat of the carrier truck. He was dark like the rest of them and appeared to be taller by the way he was sitting.

"We can give you what we can, but it's not much. I can give you directions to a village miles up the road that have much more."

"You would give us this knowledge?" the fighter asked with surprise. Clearly, the man was not use to the friendly greeting he was getting from Peter. But he also took note of how Peter had his hand behind his back.

"Show us where you keep your food, give us directions to the next village and we will leave you," the fighter sternly states. Peter nods to one of the female villagers to come to his side.

"Show these men where we keep our food and give them our extra supply," Peter instructs. A few of the men climb out of the back of the truck to go with the woman Peter spoke to.

"Emmubahta come!" the leader of the brigade shouts. The man Peter had seen in the passenger seat of the truck steps out and walks to his leader's side.

"This is Emmubahta, my field commander, he will watch to make sure you are as good as your word."

Peter was right, the man was tall, very tall. With his lengthy frame. he looked like he could play successfully for any basketball team. But it was his eyes that drew in Peter. They were cold, calculating, full of animal ferocity, a look Peter was familiar with all too well. A look Korcoff displayed to him and his father before him.

Surprisingly, the guerrilla fighters left without incident, but months later they returned, this time Emmubahta was at the head of the group.

"We wish to take your women as ours," Emmubahta announced. However, this time Peter was prepared with the help of his handler in Cape Town, he armed the villagers.

"That will not happen today!" Peter said to Emmubahta. Peter had positioned the villagers in the nearby hills and huts.

"Take them," he ordered. Thus began a fire fight that quickly turned bad for Emmubahta and his men. He lost nearly over half of them before they retreated.

"This is not over!" Emmubahta shouted as he drove away.

Peter thought he had seen the last of him after that humiliating defeat, but his gut told him otherwise. Weeks pass and there was no word from the guerrilla fighters.

Word was they were pillaging and burning on another part of the continent.

Thinking things would eventually go back to normal in spite of his gut feeling, Peter went out on another walk in the open Savanah. It had recently rained, so there were puddles of water and mud everywhere. As Peter walks, he sees wild buffalo and gazelles drinking out of the rain made puddles and eating the barren grass. His thoughts drift off to less difficult times before he joined the academy and became an agent. Peter is so distracted by his own day dreams that he doesn't even notice a form rising out of the pool of mud behind a large stone Peter is leaning against. The form attacks swiftly without warning, jumping on top of Peter.

"What tha?" he barely manages to utter as he's assaulted with a series of hard powerful punches to the face. Peter is able to head butt the person and knee them in the stomach. Getting a closer look after forcing the person off him, Peter is staring at a tall lean naked man covered in mud.

"Who the fuck are you?" Peter asks in anger. The man utters a dialect he's not familiar with.

"You've picked the wrong man to mess with. You're going to die for this," Peter promises.

"We shall see sellout Russian scum!" the man shouts, this time in Swahili, which Peter understands. The man charges at him, but Peter is ready for his attack this time and flips him over his shoulder. As he does, he catches his assailant in armlock. Getting an even better look at his attacker's face Peter recognizes him, it's Emmubahta.

"I will break you for this," Peter taunts as he continues to try and break Emmubahta's captured arm, but he uses one of his long muscular legs to hit Peter in the nose, causing Peter to release his grip.

"You humiliated me, caused my men and leader to doubt me. You must die for this!" Emmubahta spews in fury.

The two men square off against each other in the open wilderness, landing a series of punches and judo kicks upon each other as they wrestle to gain dominance over the other. Peter appears to be stronger than his taller foe until Emmubahta manages to lock Peter in between his powerful thighs. Peter struggles to get free, but his hands can't reach Emmubahta's face or arms, so he reaches for the only thing he can get to.

Peter bites down on Emmubahta's balls, but his grip grows tighter, so Peter bites down harder. He feels his neck breaking and he can't resist much longer before it does. Finally, he finds the strength to pry Emmubahta's thighs open, but the effort exhausts Peter and Emmubahta knees him hard in his own midsection. Kneeing him hard again, this time Emmubahta cracks Peter's ribs. Peter lays on the ground reeling in pain. Emmubahta stands over him clutching his bleeding balls.

"This is not over Russian sellout! I will kill you, count on it," Emmubahta promises as he staggers off half beaten. Peter lays on the ground for what seems like hours to him. He eventually forces himself on his feet and slowly makes his way back to the village. One of the villagers uses his jeep to drive him to a distant hospital to tend his broken ribs and fractured neck.

"He beat me and he knew who I was, how!" Peter demands to himself in frustration. Peter's handler could offer no real answers, only that the divided apartheid and guerrilla fighter factions had spies everywhere like Russia. This was unacceptable to Peter. He withdrew himself even further from Ugandans he had to see every day.

Peter was ever vigil, waiting for the guerrilla fighters and Emmubahta to return. The defeat by his hands haunted Peter. They never returned to the village Peter lived in, but their presence was always known. Even after Peter married Clearessa, he was very cautious, especially during his trips to outer underdeveloped tribes for male fertility rituals. Emmubahta's memory held Peter in its hand along with what he did to him.

"Ivan is not as immature as you think. He knows what he wants and what makes him happy as a child," Gregor says snapping Peter back to the conversation.

"How do you know what my grandson wants? You barely know what you want. Ivan is a passing fancy to you, a thing to make you feel worshipped," Peter says effectively ending the conversation. He then calls Ivan to dinner while Clearessa sets the table.

Chapter 5

"Grandpa, I'm gay," Ivan suddenly says to Peter out of the blue.

"What?" Peter asks in response.

It's Sunday, they're watching T.V and Ivan is preparing to start his training with the F.S.B. Ivan is a striking figure at only seventeen. Even though he's an albino, women find him exotically attractive, but he doesn't want them, he only likes them as friends. He's heard the words homosexual and gay before when he was a small child from adults when they thought he wasn't listening.

Since he was thirteen, he knew he was this way as they call it. And now he wants to tell his family, hence his announcement to his grandfather.

"What did you say, Ivan?" Peter asks again.

"I said I'm gay, I like other boys, sometimes I like older men."

"It's nothing new, we all are, just like your great-grandfather before he died."

Ivan is shocked, he doesn't know what to make of this. "But you and Grandma…"

"There was passion in the marriage in the beginning, but we were both aware of what I really desired. It's a funny thing to be different, especially for a black man in this day and age. Imagine what it was like for me, even further back for your great-grandfather? We did our duty and hid our true feelings of what we really wanted. But still Russia hasn't caught up with the rest of the world on how to handle men like us yet. So, you still have to guard who you are even now. I've known for a long time about you and your friend Gregor and what he's involved in."

"But I love him," Ivan adds.

"You may think you do, but you will find others to sate your so-called abnormal desires as well all have in this family."

"Does Grandma have lovers?"

"We don't like to talk about it, but I'm sure she does, she's a beautiful and passionate woman."

"Was my mother passionate too?" Ivan asks wanting to know more about her.

"She was many things besides that. She had a strong will, could rise to any challenge and was a fierce fighter."

"But why didn't she want me?"

"You came to her at a very difficult time in her life. Caring for you was a challenge she couldn't rise to. Having you, giving you to us to raise was the hardest thing she ever had to do."

Peter didn't have the heart to tell Ivan the real reason Natleaha gave him up or the circumstances of his mother's pregnancy.

"What you should concentrate on now is your training for the F.S.B. When you are done at the academy, you will be able to serve any place in the world, other places where you can be free to be yourself." Ivan liked the sound of that.

Maybe Gregor will want to come with me Ivan thought.

Ivan was fortunate to live in a city that had modern conveniences, unlike the more distant towns that were less developed and poor. When he thought his grandparents were asleep, Ivan slipped off later that night to meet with Gregor. Ivan walked to an alley behind a hardware store. It was cold like it always was in the city. Ivan rubs his hands together in his thick leather gloves to gain more warmth.

After waiting for half an hour, Gregor rides up on a motorcycle wearing wool pants, overlapping combat boots and a heavy leather jacket with a wool black hat.

"Did you have any problem getting away?" Gregor asks with concern.

"No, no problem," Ivan answers. On instinct, Ivan reaches over and puts his hands on Gregor's face and deeply kisses him.

"I can tell you missed me," Gregor slyly notes showing off his full-grown mustache and goatee with a grin. At twenty-two, Gregor was a handsome lady killer, able to talk his way into any woman's bed he wanted, but he still enjoyed what Ivan could give him.

"When do you leave?"

"Tomorrow, but I wish you could come with me," Ivan sadly moans.

"You know that's not possible, 'sides I got other plans, other than working for the F.S.B."

"Yeah, yeah I know, you want to be an adventurer, free and in the wild, having your fill of different kinds of women."

"That's right, but I bet you'll make a cute soldier making any drill sergeant want to dominate you and get in your pants. You're white as snow, they'll go crazy for you."

"Maybe the girls will, but I don't want them," Ivan says flatly.

"Speaking of girls, how's your girlfriend Eleanea?" Gregor knew Ivan didn't like Eleanea to be referred to as that.

"She's not my girlfriend. She's staying in school to become a computer analyst," Ivan answers irritably.

"She's cute, you should throw caution to the wind and give her something to remember you by," Gregor teases. But Ivan is not amused.

"I don't think of her that way, we're just friends, that's all we'll ever be."

"Shame, I bet she's a wild fuck. You know she wants you. You're just a big tease for her, admit it, you like it when people want you."

"I like it when you want me," Ivan says seductively.

"You always talk about wanting someone or them wanting you," Ivan further says as he rubs on Gregor's thigh.

"I like to fuck, I won't apologize for that, it feels great when I do it. I like when we do it, you do too," Ivan practically straddles Gregor on his bike when he speaks to him that way.

They passionately hug and kiss for minutes.

"Let's go back to my place," Gregor suggests. "Aw I want to, but I can't, I have to get back home to finish packing up to be ready tomorrow."

"Then why did you bother meeting me here?"

"I just wanted to see you before I left. We'll talk on the phone and I'll write you."

"Aw, whatever."

"Please, don't act like you'll be lonely. You probably have some pussy waiting on you right now." Gregor doesn't answer, he just smiles. He holds Ivan by the waist and pats him on the butt.

"Let me know what soldiers or officers want you," Gregor demands softly. Ivan doesn't know when he would see Gregor again, all he knew is that he would miss him terribly.

The next day, Peter drives Ivan to the nearest F.S.B training facility miles away from the city they lived in.

"Be good and make us proud," Peter says as they part ways.

"Don't worry, I will," Ivan reassures his grandfather.

"You are here to become new extensions of the state. You have been chosen because you are the best of the best in everything you do," the drill instructor states after having several staff members rouse all of the recruits out of bed at 5:00am. The female instructor speaking has a stern, serious look and a face to match it. She holds a long pointer in her gloved hands as she speaks.

"Some of you may be the best at what you do, but some of you won't make it through this program, that is a fact. A fact that has been proven time and time again since the early days of the KGB. The first lesson is paramount when completing a mission. When performing a mission for the state, you use the weapons you have and the ones you don't think you have."

"What does that mean?" a cadet asks after being called on when he raised his hand.

"It means you use your looks, your sexuality, your exotic mystery."

Ivan swears he can feel the instructor's gaze on him when she made that last statement.

"These tools some of you have are nothing new, you've used them every day in your life. We will help you perfect them better, to help you serve the state."

Many tasks await Ivan and the other recruits, training marksmanship, knife fighting, martial arts and computer skills. All of the tasks lessons with tough instructors, male and female. Ivan does well with all these tasks, except the ones dealing with seduction, naturally with young women. Several times during class, the recruits were taken to back rooms to learn how to disarm a target with their charms.

Using various made-up scenarios with agents acting as unsuspecting targets, Ivan watches with the other recruits as some of their fellow cadets engage in different acts of sexual manipulation. Ivan is understandably nervous, even more so when an instructor, another female calls on him.

"Ivan come here," the instructor orders. So, he slowly walks from the viewing room to where the instructor is.

She then explains the scenario.

"Your mission is to retrieve a valuable computer chip that can be used to advance our weapons program by a decade. But the only copy of this chip is hidden in the home of the technician who invented it. You have reliable intel that it's there but the technician's wife is always home. How do you neutralize her without lethal force? Because sometimes, lethal force is not necessary. What do you do?"

Ivan hasn't a clue and he's watched different scenarios of recruits and agents for months now. What could he do? He is an albino, no one would talk to him in their right mind. He could see the instructor is growing impatient with waiting for him to get started.

Ivan has a plan. He thinks about his martial arts teacher whom Ivan is a honey as he heard some good-looking people be referred to on T.V. The teacher reminds him of Gregor, only the teacher has blond hair instead of dark black wavy hair Gregor has and both men has the same handsome shaped face. Ivan imagines that the teacher wants to have him and that he has lewd pictures of him in his desk in a den, but he has to get his wife out of the way.

He also imagines that she like to watch her husband who is the martial arts teacher to be ravished savagely by another man, especially a strange looking one like Ivan. He was now ready. Ivan went up to the makeshift door and knocked, he had removed his undershirt and left his uniform shirt open at the front, showing his still developing barreled chest with kinks of blond nappy hair on it. His nipples were erect and his belly button slightly poked out. He was a sight.

"Is your husband home? I'm a friend of his he likes to jog with sometimes," he says to the woman who answered the door.

"My husband doesn't like to jog," the woman says in perfect English in keeping in character.

"I've been training with him at the Y, so he can get toned up. We do it during his lunch break on the running track above the basketball court," Ivan says while remembering hearing about how the Y.M.C.A are built from his cousins in America.

"He asked me to come by and wait for him to run for the first time together outside in the heat," Ivan could tell by the woman's body language he is starting to get to her.

By the way he moves, the way he bites his bottom lip, sweat starting to form on his exposed chest, looking at the woman like he wanted to devour her as if she was delicious meat. All he could think about is getting the martial arts teacher naked and getting him aroused.

"We could wait for an hour or so until your husband gets home," Ivan suggests in a sensual base voice.

"Yes, yes I could fix us something."

After Ivan comes through then doorway, the woman's hands remove Ivan's uniform shirt and pants. He pictured himself being watched by the martial arts teacher as he slowly plowed this makeshift wife. It was his first time with a woman. He bit and licked the woman's earlobe before the instructor ordered Ivan to stop during mid-thrust. The woman appeared hesitate to release Ivan from her embrace.

"That is good Ivan, you did well. What have we learned? How to mix fact with fiction to gain our objectives. Mr. Fisk learned something that was true about the woman's husband and used it with an elaborate lie to convince her to let Ivan into her house. Furthermore, he used his body language to entice his way in. This is useful in case the objective is not that attractive. Thank you Ivan, you may go back to your seat in the viewing room," the instructor tells Ivan as he's getting dressed.

Oh shit! he thinks in frustration with a raging hard on. He still can't get the vision of the hot teacher out of his mind. It was times like this that he wished Gregor was here.

"Know your target, learn their routine, their habits, to better engage them and eliminate them," the marksman instructor always tells the recruits. The computer instructor mainly demonstrated the skills, as did the combat specialist with knives. The martial arts teacher liked to talk and show recruits.

"Keep your opponent guessing, never attack the same way twice, use your skills to throw them off balance," the teacher would say. Ivan is afraid to be called on to demonstrate his various techniques for fear of visually becoming excited. So, he lags back, watches and learns from a distance.

One day, the recruits are introduced to a new instructor.

"Hello recruits my name is Flavawn Gorbachin and I'll be teaching you on the better points of espionage."

Espionage huh, Ivan thinks. He is intrigued, now the F.S.B was getting down to the bare bones of the matter. Flavawn specialized in intelligence gathering without computers, using your wits if your body fails. But after observing Flavawn for several weeks, Ivan gets the feeling the man was kind of flamboyant and liked to be seen by everyone.

"That's impossible, the government wouldn't let anybody like him in the academy to teach, let alone be an agent," young Ivan reasons.

But upon further examination, Ivan and the other recruits realized Flavawn knew what he was talking about. He often described with relish about a mission he was on that helped eliminate a rogue diplomat in Sweden. He openly spoke of a stunning beauty that helped him take pictures of a guard to help with the take down of the target.

"The woman was a consummate professional, I would love to work with her again," Flavawn recounts joyfully.

"What was the woman's name?" a recruit standing near Ivan asks.

"Natleaha, ahh a lovely creature," Flavawn expresses. The hairs on the back of Ivan's neck stand up.

This man knew my mother, Ivan thinks with hope. *Maybe he can tell me more about her or where she might be*, Ivan further wonders. What Ivan did know was that he had to speak to Flavawn more closely.

"Do you still keep in touch with Natleaha?" Ivan anxiously asks Flavawn when he manages to get him alone.

"Alas not really, the last I heard she was in Spain or was it Italy, I'm not really sure. It was one of those hot-blooded Latin countries, but that was twelve years ago, a little after the fall of the Soviet Union." Ivan saw this was getting nowhere talking to Flavawn.

"Why do you want to locate Natleaha?" Flavawn asks suspiciously.

"She might have information about someone close to me," Ivan quickly answers Flavawn to change the subject. He couldn't run the risk of Flavawn warning his mother he was looking for her, so, he made up a lie to throw him off.

"Things are getting difficult here, but I'm keeping up. There's an instructor here who met my mother, but he doesn't know where she is now, but I won't give up, I'll find her one day and have her tell me the real reason why she gave me up," Ivan says to Gregor over the phone. They've spoken three times since Ivan came to the academy.

"Don't sweat it, she couldn't be that much to care about if she dumped you on your grandparents' doorstep. So, are you finding any hot-blooded boys or older men to play with?" Gregor asks in an attempt to change the subject.

Ivan takes the bait.

"There is this one instructor that reminds me of you, but he has blond hair."

"Blond hair, what the fuck, you think I'd look good with blond hair now?"

"Well, he looks like you in a certain way, but he's not interested in me that way, they did make me have sex with a woman weeks ago." Gregor's interest is peaked when he hears this.

"So, how'd you like it? Have you thought about doing a woman again?"

"Not really, all I did through the whole thing was think about you and that teacher with the blond hair."

"That sucks."

"It is what it is. I still wish you could come up here to visit me to ease the tension."

"Don't worry you'll find somebody to warm your bed eventually."

"Maybe you're right."

"I am, you're magic remember, an ivory elf," Gregor teases Ivan with what he used to say about himself. "I'll talk to you again soon Ivan."

"I hope so Gregor, I miss you."

"I miss you too," Gregor admits before he says goodbye and hangs up.

Ivan hasn't really gotten to know the other recruits to form bonds. He mainly sticks to his Studies and training, day dreaming about the martial arts instructor or Gregor. It's been awhile since Ivan has been with anyone, save that woman he play acted with, but nobody else has caught his eye that returns the interest.

He's positive some of his female classmates are attracted to him, but he's definitely uninterested in that regard. After being at the academy for little over a year, a visiting lieutenant comes to lecture there. The man is from the Cuban counter part of the F.S.B of the training academies. He's kind of fat, but he's tall with a pretty round face and tan colored skin.

"I'm here to teach you what to expect when your target is also being pursued by the military of your home country as well as the secret service. First you should always compare info with the led officers stationed in the area and see if they can be of any assistance to you in the field."

"What if the officers stationed in the area can't help you with your objective?" Ivan eagerly asks Lieutenant Ingramisck.

"Then you have to improvise to where the military can help you," he responds to Ivan's question with a slight smile. Ingramisck looked like a big cuddly cute teddy bear in his uniform to Ivan. He waited for Ingramisck to finish answering questions from the other recruits before he approached him.

"How long are you stationed here?" Ivan asks while staring deep into the Lieutenant's eyes.

"About a few weeks. I will give other lectures in the nearby area before I return to Cuba, but I'll mainly be resting here with you recruits." Ivan likes the sound of that and the way the Lieutenant was looking at him.

"You're a negro albino, that's exceedingly rare, especially here," Ingramisck comments with a friendly smile.

"Is anyone else in your family like you?"

"No just me. I'm unique," Ivan had to catch himself, he was about to say magic.

"Maybe we could further discuss more about what to do when you're behind enemy lines with your home country's military," Ingramisck suggests.

"I'd like that. Maybe we could someplace where you could give me notes on your next lecture," Ingramisck and Ivan are definitely feeling each other.

Strangely enough, the staff offer no questions when the lieutenant suggest that Ivan accompany him back to his room to answer more questions he has about the lecture today. Ingramisck embraces Ivan in a big bear hug, he feels like a firm cushion in the lieutenant's chest.

"You're beautiful. How did your family come here?"

"My great grandfather migrated here from the United States South back in the 1930s," Ivan answers as he practically rips open Ingramisck's buttoned shirt. He's wearing a tank top underneath holding up his bulky plump chest. Ivan reaches under the tank top and rubs his round hairy belly.

"You like that?" Ingramisck urges as he returns the favor of rubbing Ivan's own flat belly and chest.

Ivan sucks on the full flesh of Ingramisck's nipples, they're like a woman's breasts and just as sensitive, which Ivan quickly discovers from Ingramisck's moans. He literally devours the larger man, undressing him. Once they are both undressed, they fall to the bed with Ivan on top clutching Ingramisck's engorged chest.

"How did you know I wanted to?" Ivan asks while griped in passion.

"I recognize the look of all boys who want me to hold them, but nobody has ever been as hungry as you, you're not even fully grown yet and you're so firm and strong."

They take turns entering each other. Ingramisck is tight and his ass muscles clutch more tightly around Ivan's dick when he invades him. Ivan on the other hand is looser, but he still enjoys it when Ingramisck ravages him.

"You're so beautiful, I can't believe it, oh Ivan, oh Ivan," he pants as he rides Ivan like a white stallion. The man is heavier than Ivan, so it's a bit uncomfortable with him on top of Ivan, but he bares through it.

Ingramisck grunts softly and keeps himself from crying out. Both men are soon spent from mounting each other and collapse onto the bed.

"I hope to see you again after complete your training to be an F.S.B agent."

"Maybe, I'm not really sure if I want to finish now."

"But why, you would be a good asset to the agency. Is it because you like men? No one really cares anymore about that, as long as you do your job and succeed."

Ivan lets Ingramisck's words sink in as he rests on his chest. Since coming to the academy, nothing makes sense to Ivan. He thought he wanted to be an agent for the State, but now he realizes that's more about wanting to find his mother and just learning the skills to better locate her.

So, a week from completing his training with the F.S.B Ivan quits the academy and returns home to a disappointed grandfather. Soon, he's back with Gregor who makes a tempting proposition.

"The Bratva are the new power in Russia, dating their roots back to imperial Russia."

"I've heard of these men. They don't want anybody like me."

"It doesn't matter, as long as me and some other friends of mine sponsor and vouch for you. They would be willing to overlook what they call a character flaw. With your skills and smarts, you'd be the perfect enforcer. You could travel the world and they could help you in your search for your mother. And you wouldn't have to hide your tastes in the shadows like you do here, you could have your fill of any man in the world."

It sounds like real freedom to Ivan, all he had to do was play enforcer for an organization that was worldwide.

Chapter 6

It's 2015 and Ivan has spent six years with the Russian Bratva, among the most dangerous of mafioso organizations. Gregor had kept his promise, the Bratva had resources at their disposal that rival any government and to the extent the F.S.B, but it seemed every time Ivan came close to finding his mother, she would manage to elude him somehow. Natleaha has never been part of the Bratva, but she was somehow aware of their tricks.

In spite of the circumstances of his making, Natleaha probably couldn't help but be proud of how her son has effectively risen through the ranks as an efficient enforcer and good sniper with the help of his best friend and still sometimes secret lover Gregor.

Ivan still had connections to the Russian government through another acquaintance, Lieutenant Ingramisck, now of the special forces.

"How can you be so brutal and tender at the same time?" Ingramisck often asks Ivan whenever they were together after hearing or if he witnesses his physical brutality against an enemy of his organization.

"I just am," would be Ivan's only response.

The days of the Fisks owing a debt to the Russian government were coming to a close. The pact Jonah Fisk made to Korcoff Vamitri was going out of fashion. Ivan's uncles were on different paths. His uncle Marvin was a colonel in the military, but privy to the intelligence of the world, but his children were not and didn't live in Russia, yet other parts of the world. Eric Fisk has made a home in America and is busy with problems of being a medical examiner and an aging black man in the country. Also, none of his children show no interest in working for any of the Russian or United States intelligence agencies.

As for Ivan's grandparents, they are not as well-known in the intelligence community as they once were, but still agents of note in some areas. Natleaha served the Russian State well for a time, but after the fall of the Soviet Union and her unwanted pregnancy, she disappeared from sight. Her son had the potential to serve the Russians faithfully, but quit the academy near the end of his training. Also, others in the State believed he might've had additional difficulty working for the Russians due to the fact that he was an albino.

Another promise Gregor kept to Ivan was that although the Bratva did not approve of Ivan being gay and were put off by his appearance, they ignored these things as long as he followed their orders. So, they let Ivan do as he wished, using Gregor as a go between for giving orders, where to meet other members for large manned operations.

The only times Ivan has to see the chief members of the Bratva are at ritual initiations, weddings and birthdays for a chief member's family events, attendance at these events were mandatory. Ivan always feels like a freak at these things, but he does enjoy the freedom the Bratva gave him whenever he isn't working on a job for them.

Ivan has other lovers besides Gregor and Ingramisck, lovers who were as unusual as him.

One is named Calhoun Williams who suffered second degree burns on his face and half his body from a grease fire in his mother's kitchen in her house as a small child. Even though his body is disfigured, Calhoun plays college football for Oklahoma state.

Ivan meets Calhoun when him and other members of his organization along with a lieutenant in the Bratva is setting up a drug operation in the state, as they've been doing in other parts of America for decades. It is the second time Ivan is in America, the first time is in New York city to see a ballet a Bratva chief's girlfriend was in. The next time would be in Stillwater city two years ago. It would be the first time Gregor isn't with Ivan when he goes to work for the organization.

"Don't worry, you'll be fine. You don't need me there with you. It's just like any other job. Only I won't be sitting at a strip club where you're breaking somebody's bones or putting a bullet in someone's head. 'Sides, they want me back in London to help stand guard at a location of a major meeting."

Gregor still look handsome to Ivan, even after him shaving off his hair and beard.

"Ok I guess, I can do whatever they want until I can meet up with you in London," Ivan replies lazily.

He wants to hug and kiss Gregor, but Gregor stopped him by patting Ivan on the shoulders. There were other men around and he didn't want them to give Ivan a hard time during his trip to America. Ivan flew on a private plane with six other members guarding the lieutenant in charge of setting up the Bratva's operation in Oklahoma. The rest of the men working under this lieutenant sailed on a freighter where their weapons were hidden from the prying eyes of the coast guard.

Days after arriving, Ivan was sent along with two other members to scout out locations to make the drug product they would be selling. They settled on Stillwater city with the lieutenant's ok.

There are already several Bratva posing as college students at Oklahoma State University handing out samples of cocaine and heroin. As they were setting up production in a warehouse on the outskirts of Stillwater, one of the student/dealers came rushing in unannounced almost getting his head blown off.

"You've got to see this football game tonight! The running back is something you can't believe!" he announces with excitement.

"This is what you bother us for? Some cheap American version of football?" one of the workers asks irritation. It was widely believed in Europe that America didn't play real football.

"No, no, not the game, the player. I've seen him without his helmet, he looks like a scarred-up monkey with thick lips, it's true."

"Are you sure of this?" another worker asks the student.

"Yes, yes, you have to see him, it's weird."

Ivan had just walked back into the room where the men were talking, when the student points to him.

"He looks even more weird than him,"

Ivan was intrigued. Who could look more stranger than him? He had to see this for himself. So, a few of the men along with Ivan and the college student went to the football game. It was an easy task to gain some tickets to the game. They all wore plain clothes, so they wouldn't standout. But no matter what Ivan wore, he would always standout.

It was cold out, so Ivan was able to wear a hat to cover his nappy hair. He was a sight to see with a blond afro. The game started out as suspected with a quarterback running with the ball, the offense trying to help the quarterback score, the defense fighting against the offense of the other team. The Oklahoma Cowboys were playing against the Cincinnati Xavier Musketeers. Ivan saw a few people staring at him, but not as many as he had thought would.

"That's him, Calhoun Williams the running back!" the college student shouted pointing to a man running up and down the field near the quarterback.

They weren't seated on the frontline, but Ivan and the other Mafioso were still seated close enough to see the players. The Mafioso still couldn't see what all the fuss was about, that is until halftime. Some of the players sat on the long benches and remove their helmets, including the running back for Oklahoma State.

"Aw shit he is ugly," one of the men Ivan is with said.

"I told you. Didn't I tell you?" the college student boasts.

The man's face was scarred and his lips were indeed thick. His hair was shaped in dreadlocks. Ivan had seen this type of hairstyle before when his superiors did business with some Jamaicans.

He's not ugly, his face is just burned, Ivan thinks. He also notices the player's butt did appear round when he got up to go play again.

"I could not look upon my child if they were burned like that. How could a mother let her child live like that?" one of the men insults as he looks at the player. Ivan feels that he wasted his time coming to the game, but something in him wants to see the football player again.

Several weeks goes by and Ivan watches Calhoun Williams play in three more home games. As luck would have it Calhoun has a girlfriend who was a customer of the Russian college student. The girl is a chunky Latina with a pretty face. The Bratva college student has a crush on her, he would always offer her discounts in an attempt to get her to notice him.

"She's pretty, I could do her better than that messed up monkey," the student would say in frustration every time Calhoun's girlfriend would turn him down. Ivan thought the Bratva student was a skinny pencil nosed geek who was drunk on power. This same geek would try to rape Calhoun's girlfriend in the men's locker room when he lured her there with a written note pretending to be Calhoun.

"Just stay here and make sure nobody disturbs us until I'm done," the college student ordered Ivan when he brought him to the hallway near where the locker room was.

"Don't they have practice every afternoon?" Ivan asks.

"These American idiots are never on time, we got them strung out on our product."

"But what if their coach comes by?"

"Kill 'em and get rid of the body. No one knows you're here. We entered through the blind spots of the area where there are no video cameras. Now stay here and do as you're told or I'll tell my uncle and he will cut your head off."

This was a threat Ivan could believe because the college student's uncle was high up in the organization. He could have Ivan chopped into pieces, along with his family that lived in the United States. To add insult to injury, they knew about Ivan and Gregor, so they'd probably kill Gregor too to keep him from acting out any thought he might have of revenge.

"Fine," Ivan dully utters to the student.

Ivan stayed hidden and watched people come and go, including Calhoun's girlfriend who was walking to the locker room with a smirk on her face while holding a letter. The locker room was far enough away from where Ivan was standing that you couldn't hear anything. But then the unexpected happened. Minutes later, Calhoun came walking down the hallway. He didn't want to do it, but he had to distract Calhoun or he was dead.

"Uh hey you're Calhoun Williams right, the running back?"

"Yeah, who are you?"

"I'm Ivan, I went to a couple of your games, you really can play."

"Thanks dawg, 'preciated it."

"Dog, what does that mean?" Ivan asks himself. Knowing that Calhoun was about to walk away, Ivan uses more flattery on him.

"It must take great skill to play as good as you. How long have you played?"

"Since I was ten, back in the pee wee league."

"I bet it takes heart to play."

"Yeah it does, a lot of heart. You been a fan long?"

"Oh, about a couple of years, just something I got fascinated by." Ivan didn't realize he let something slip by the way he said his last statement. He was trying to ask about the accident that burned his skin, but didn't know how.

"How long have you been going to Oklahoma State? You're pretty big, you could probably play a good tackle."

Ivan didn't know what that meant, but Calhoun accepted the complement anyway.

"Thanks, I'll keep that in mind." Ivan was hoping that Calhoun wasn't getting suspicious by the way Ivan was speaking English to him.

I wish that geek would hurry up already, Ivan thought in a haste. He was running out of things to talk about with Calhoun. But now Calhoun appeared to be taking an interest in Ivan. His albino skin wasn't even an issue.

"So, are you on your way to practice now?"

"Aw damn, dat's right! Thanks fo' remindin me dawg, I gotta go."

"Can I walk with you to get a feel of the place in case I want to try out? I just transferred here, I want to keep all my options open."

"Sure, dat's cool," Calhoun answers back as he was beginning to take a liking to Ivan.

As they walk toward the locker room, Ivan purposely speak loudly so that his voice would carry and maybe the Russian college student would heed the warning and get out of the locker room before Ivan and Calhoun arrived. The sight that greeted them shocked both men. Ivan's boss's nephew was laying on the floor in a pool of blood, while Calhoun's girlfriend was huddled into a corner shaking, holding a butcher knife with her shirt torn.

"Help me, h—help?" the Bratva college student weakly pleaded.

"Baby what the fuck happened?" Calhoun yelled out.

"He, he, he tried to rape me," she says through clenched teeth while crying. While Calhoun is distracted with his girlfriend, Ivan lifts the wounded Russian college student over his shoulder and carries him out of the locker room running.

It is a disaster, come to find out Calhoun's girlfriend isn't the first woman the geek Bratva attacked. He has raped three other women, but scares them into silence by having his uncle threaten their families. Because of this, the man responsible for the rapes has to leave the country in a hurry. Fortunately, Ivan explains away his part in it by telling Calhoun he saw the man on the floor dying and his instinct was to help, but he didn't know what he had done.

For his sake, Calhoun has bought the lie. No telling what would have happened to Calhoun had he found out the truth. But sadly, the Bratva knows Ivan well, better than he thinks. They have him get closer to some of the athletes to reel them in as customers. Ivan's growing affection for Calhoun is an unfortunate circumstance of his grim mission.

"Is your girlfriend doing any better?" Ivan asks Calhoun eight months after the attack. It is after Homecoming and they were sitting on the bleachers drinking beer. Calhoun had already drank six cans and Ivan had four.

"It's a slow process dawg, a slow process," Calhoun repeated.

Ivan could see the sadness and depression in Calhoun's face. He wanted to help, but Ivan really realized Calhoun knowing the truth would only make matters worse.

As predicted, Calhoun and Ivan got closer, spending much time together. Ivan isn't even looking for physical intimacy with Calhoun, it just happened. Ivan went to take a piss at the bottom of the bleachers behind the fence. Without warning, Calhoun was relieving himself besides Ivan. Calhoun looked glazed over as he stared at Ivan.

"Whoo, dawg dat shit's good!" he hollered almost pissing on Ivan's shoes when he looked in his direction.

"Careful man, you almost wet my shoes," Ivan playfully says.

"Man, fuck you. I can piss anywhere I want whitey," Calhoun teases.

Ivan could see after about nine cans of beer Calhoun is drunk and horny by the way he was holding himself. He didn't even bother to put himself back into his pants, he just continued to stare at Ivan with that glazed-over look in his eyes.

"What are you doing man? Pull yourself together Cal," Ivan orders in an attempt not to stare at what Calhoun is showing off, free of burned flesh. Calhoun isn't a small man, so he almost knocks Ivan over when he leans in to hug him.

"Come on man you're drunk, come on," Ivan keeps saying in a half-hearted attempt to dissuade Calhoun.

"I know you want me, you want it," Calhoun utters in slurred speech.

"Come on man you don't know what you're saying. You'll feel better after you've slept it off Cal."

But part of Ivan doesn't want his words to be true, he does want Calhoun, scars and all. But before Ivan could catch his breath, Calhoun was kissing him roughly on his neck.

"Mm, mm," is all Calhoun utters as he sucks on Ivan's neck. Ivan figures that Calhoun misses having sex with a girl and that he only turns to Ivan, desperate for affection.

Feeling himself giving into it, he pulls Calhoun off him after letting him suck on his neck for a while.

Ivan then practically carries Calhoun to his dorm room bed.

The next morning, Ivan is talking to Gregor by skype.

"Whoa, what happened to your neck?" Gregor asks pointing from the computer screen.

"What?"

"The mark on your neck, it's right there."

Gregor says pointing to his own neck to show Ivan what he's talking about. Gregor then bursts out laughing.

"You got a hickey! You've must've had a wild one last night, I'm jealous," Gregor comments while continuing to laugh loudly.

It wasn't the fact that they were monogamous, they weren't. It was that Ivan never received a hickey before. Taking a moment to look in a hand-held mirror, Ivan could see it was noticeable on his ivory white skin. He was so embarrassed, no wonder the other men were laughing at him.

"So, tell me how'd it feel? They feel great, don't they? I've had a couple myself over the years, you'll get used to them. So, who was it, that you let them blemish that pretty white skin of yours?"

"Nobody you'll ever meet."

"Uh huh, don't be so sure, that's an animal I gotta meet. Is he another older daddy for you?" Gregor steadily quizzes knowing Ivan's main type.

"No, he's a few years younger actually."

"That's unusual for you. How young is a few years? You're not turning into Mr. Greako are you?"

"No, he's nineteen," Ivan answers sharply, remembering how Mr. Greako molested him and other boys.

"Well, have fun, you've never had to teach them before. I'll bet he's young and hot, hardly any hair on his body."

"He's cute in his own way."

"What does that mean?" Not wanting to describe Calhoun's condition, Ivan rushes Gregor off the video phone.

"Look, I got a lot of work to do to get the product out here in this state. I'll call you back next week when I can." And he clicks off without saying goodbye to Gregor.

Ivan had practically hoped Calhoun wouldn't remember what he did to his neck, but it didn't seem so when he met Ivan later that afternoon at study hall.

"When can I see you again?" Calhoun whispers to Ivan, admiring his braided hair that Calhoun's girlfriend's sister did when she visited for days after the attack.

"I'd thought you'd have a hangover from last night," Ivan comments while feeling sort of uneasy about how everyone is looking at the two of them.

"I remember everything, everything. Maybe we can talk later?"

"Sure, but no hickeys," Ivan demands while feeling Calhoun's eyes zeroing in on his neck.

Gregor is right about one thing. Calhoun is animalistic in bed. He enjoys being rough, he tries biting on Ivan's neck again, but Ivan resists that, so he left marks on other parts of his body.

Calhoun has no roommates, he is lucky enough to get a single, probably because he play football for the university. His girlfriend almost catches the two of them together when she comes by his room unexpectedly one day. Calhoun has just returned from then shower room and he wants to get up in Ivan when she knocks on the door.

"I was on my way to the weight room and I wanted to see if Calhoun would spot me."

Ivan's lie was convincing because she knew him as Calhoun's friend. Afterwards, Ivan decided it would be best if they met off campus. To this day, Gregor hasn't seen Calhoun, so he doesn't know what he looks like and the other members stationed with Ivan haven't told Gregor whenever he was there in the state either.

One of Ivan's newest lovers he met only six months ago and he's a Puerto Rican who is only three and a half feet tall, who's trim and fit. Ivan was shocked to see the length of his penis reach halfway down part of his short muscular thigh. Emmanuel has a regular sized head, but it appears huge on his compact body with a full beard topped off with a buzz cut. Emmanuel was a runner for one of the drug cartels the Bratva traded product with. Ivan was becoming somewhat of a popular hushed rumor and Emmanuel admitted he liked to dabble, so he wanted to meet Ivan.

"Si, si, you all legs hommes!" Emmanuel exclaims in lust. He couldn't take his eyes off the ivory giant when he first laid eyes on him. Emmanuel did have the habit of being crass at times, which Ivan discovered when he slept with the man.

"Man esi you fucked a Jew, a cancer patient and a fat Cuban?"

"He's not a cancer patient, he's a burned victim and the Cuban is not that fat."

"What about your Jew?"

"He could kill you with one of his bare hands," Ivan remarked. The one thing he liked about Emmanuel was that he's from a culture that is superstitious about albinos.

"Is it true you payos got magic in your blood?"

"That's only white men albinos, I'm black," Ivan jokes.

"Si, you don't have to tell me hommes," Emmanuel would always say, being and standing at eye length at Ivan's crotch.

These are then men Ivan sleeps with, some he likes more than the others. When he lays on Ingramisck's chest, he has an understanding father, with Calhoun he likes his wildness, Emmanuel is silly and Gregor will always have his heart. That will never change, depending on the ever-changing events in Ivan's life that is.

"I've some bad news for you Ivan," Gregor says to Ivan over the skype screen with a serious expression. He has Ivan worried.

"What is it, what's wrong?" Ivan asks anxiously.

"Your grandfather is dead."

"Grandpa Peter?"

"No, your other one, Ocscarious."

Ivan had to think for a moment to place the name, but then it came to him.

"Oh, Grandma Clearessa's father, I didn't even know he was still alive at this point. He was over hundred years old."

"Do you want to get permission from the head chiefs to go to the funeral?"

"Hmm, no we weren't that close, I barely ever saw the man," Ivan answers casually without any show of grief.

He didn't know the man and his grandmother hardly ever talked about him. The funeral was a somber affair, other than Peter and Clearessa, the only other people to attend were a much younger baby sister of Ocscarious and the nurse who cared for him in his old age.

The only thing that is depressing his daughter is the heat of Cuba, where the funeral is held.

Gregor is called into a station of the organization in London on a rainy day. It is a tailor shop that's a front business to launder money for them. A worker uses a device to scan for any listening devices. Satisfied that they're not being bugged, the chiefs present begin the meeting, speaking only in their native Russian.

"Your boy is doing well for us. We see a bright future for him with us so far. We've learned we are making much money from our endeavors in the American state of Oklahoma."

"Thank you sir," Gregor says to the Bratva chief addressing him.

"You made a good decision to sponsor him when he wanted to join us. His success has benefited you as well. You are to attend a ceremony in two weeks to have your proper bands and be made a lieutenant of our operations in London and a couple of other major cities in Britain."

"Thank you, I live to serve and advance our interests sir."

"Glad to hear it and may you someday rise even higher in our organization," the Bratva praised.

The meeting is concluded shortly after some other business. In a little while, the ceremony comes to pass for Gregor. His family feels it is a great honor the Bratva has placed on him, given that he's not part of their orthodox religion. Gregor's wife and children wait inside the church in Moscow.

In a room dimly lit in another part of the church, a group of men stand around Gregor who's stripped at the waist. Ivan is invited to celebrate Gregor's promotion, but he's not allowed to attend the ceremony. He waits at the banquet hall where the reception will be held afterwards. The tattoo artist present at the ceremony uses an ink filled flesh piercing pen to draw the honored tattoos of the Bratva on Gregor's chest and back.

"You are truly part of us now," a chieftain announces after Gregor kneels before them when he's finished receiving the tattoos.

The Bratva bring their cooks, not bothering to hire a caterer just in case an enemy of the organization might attempt to poison them through the food and drink.

"You've finally made it my friend," Ivan congratulates Gregor at the reception.

"We've made it, you're gonna rise with me too, they promised," Gregor informs Ivan.

Throwing caution to wind, Ivan hugs Gregor in front of everyone present at the hall. They know about them and Ivan doesn't care if they see him expressing his feelings for his oldest lover. But from a far distance on the rooftop of a building several blocks away, someone is watching them through an advanced long distance camera scope.

The person has a long-range sniper rifle perched on the edge of the roof they're standing near, but they seem more interested in taking pictures than blowing someone's head off.

"Enjoy your happiness while it lasts, you white devil. It'll be fleeting, I'll personally see to that," they say to themselves as they snap pictures.

Chapter 7

"I love you, I always have," are the words that freely spill out of Eleanea's mouth. Ivan is speechless at the revelation. Their day started out good enough, Eleanea came to London on business through the computer company she worked for after she left the technical.com division of the F.S.B.

She heard he was in town and opted to call him to have lunch.

"Sure, that's fine. I'll take you to Deliah's Rov ways, an Italian restaurant an hour away from your hotel," Ivan suggested and at the same time feeling uneasy about how too many people outside of the organization know of his movements.

When Ivan met her at the restaurant, he couldn't get over how radiant Eleanea looked. It had been five years since he had seen her. It was right after he left the academy and he told her he'd be leaving the country for a while. Ivan didn't realize it at the time, but Eleanea was heart-broken.

"Are you sure this is what you want to do? You're so close with completing your training, you could be a great agent, the first of your kind," Eleanea said, meaning being the first albino. He couldn't tell her the whole truth then, so he tells her a part of it.

"I have to do this, the people my friend know can help me find my mother, so she can answer the questions I have of her."

"Well, I'm going to miss you, you're my best friend," she says fighting back tears.

Time has not changed the feelings Eleanea had for Ivan, they only smoldered. She decides to make him see what she thinks he is missing by wearing a form-fitting yellow dress suit.

The jacket buttoning up front in a way that caused her bosom to appear fuller.

"You look nice," Ivan admits to Eleanea when he sees her in her dress suit.

"Thank you. I'd thought you'd like it. I've had this outfit for a year. I bought it in a dress shop in Paris when I was on vacation there."

"Well, it fits you good, your husband is one lucky man."

"Oh, I'm not married," Ivan is stunned, he thought a beautiful woman like Eleanea would be with a good man by now and her intelligence would be an added bonus.

"So, are you seeing someone?"

"Oh no, I'm single at moment, curse of the modern woman. Concentrating on my career," Eleanea jokes feeling good about seeing Ivan again.

"So how about you? Are you seeing anyone special?" Ivan laughs not wanting to reveal what he's been up to, so he plays it off.

"Well, no one special, but I am dating here and there," he said feeling bashful. Eleanea always had that effect on him, even when they were children.

They spend the next hour eating and talking about what else they've both been up to since they last saw each other. Ivan leaves out key details, but Eleanea is an open book. She tells him after she graduated from school they both went to, she worked with the F.S.B for a few years honing her computer skills, through them she got a job with a computer conglomerate company that does International data transferring for various people and businesses. She's in charge of overseeing sectors that do business with half of Europe and part of the United States.

"It sounds like you're a modern success story. It's true, you can have it all."

"Well, I don't have everything."

"Oh, what don't you have?"

"Someone special to share it with."

"Please, that'll be rectified in no time. It's not like it was in our grandparents', men aren't afraid of strong women anymore, they prefer it. I still have a little time before I have to get back to work. Would you like me to drive you back to your hotel? My car is parked only a few blocks away."

Eleanea sees this as her chance with Ivan.

"Sure, I'd like that."

They both decide to split the check to be fair and walk to Ivan's rented car. Eleanea thinks Ivan looks so handsome in his dark brown business suit with matching tie and blue office shirt. His hair is freshly braided back, two small gold loop earrings in his pierced ears. It's an hour away, but Ivan drives him and Eleanea back to her fancy hotel within forty-five minutes.

"Would you like to come up to my room for a drink?" Eleanea asks pressing her advantage.

"Sure, I still got a few minutes to spare," Her heart jumps inside her chest as she walks beside Ivan past the front desk. She doesn't mind the stares. She believes she's snagged the most beautiful man in the world.

Ivan can't get over how nice Eleanea's suite is. Spacious, luxurious, with an open bar, a king-sized bed with fancy linen in the next room and sliding doors that led to a balcony.

"What would you like?" Eleanea asks graciously as she walks to the bar.

"I'll have a screw driver, if you can make it."

"I think I can manage," she answers while recalling what went in it from one of her managers. She makes his drink and makes a vodka tonic for herself. She leaves her suit coat on the barstool before walking over to Ivan with their drinks. They clink their glasses together.

"This is nice, us being together again," Eleanea comments.

"Uh yeah it is," Ivan answers, not sure where Eleanea is going with this.

"There's something I've been meaning to tell you and I've been wanting to tell you for a long time."

"What?" Ivan asks with curiosity.

"I love you. I always have."

"What do you mean you love me?"

"It means what I've said."

"But how, you're so beautiful and I'm—"

"A black man who's an albino, yes I know all of that Ivan. Is it so hard to believe?"

Ivan hesitates to answer at first. He knew Eleanea always liked him, but he always figured it was out of curiosity, fascination, not love.

"Yes it is, I didn't think anybody could love me, my own mother doesn't. I don't see how any woman could love me."

"That's not true, I do love you and I worked up the courage to tell you how I feel before we separated again." Ivan feels his heart sink, he had no idea Eleanea felt this way about him.

"Eleanea, I can't love you like you want."

"Why, because you think you're different? Because of what your family or mine might think? Who gives a shit, it's nobody's damn business about how we feel!"

"No, no it's not that at all. There's something I have to tell you. The main reason I can't return your feelings you have for me is because I'm attracted to other men only. You've probably heard the rumors about me and my family." But he was wrong, she didn't know about the hushed rumors concerning his family, so he has to spell it out for her.

"I'm gay Eleanea."

"Gay, you mean?"

"Yes Eleanea, third generation, like my grandfather and my great grandfather before him."

"But didn't they both have wives?"

"Back then they had to keep people from finding out their secret."

"And you've always been like this?"

"Yes."

"But your grandfather still has a wife, you can be attracted to women too," Eleanea urges with hope.

"That was youthful confused passion with my grandparents, it wasn't real love, I don't feel or want that for you. I'm the first in my family to be completely free to live as he wants."

"And your mother, you think that's why she gave you up as a baby?"

"I don't know, it's one of the reasons I have to find her to ask her, her reasons."

It was a lot to take in, here she was hoping to reunite with the lost love of her life, but come to find out he couldn't love her like she loved him.

But Eleanea felt no regret about telling Ivan how she felt, she could move on now. But she would always love him, even if he didn't feel the same way.

"It was still good to see you again Ivan. I hope we can still be friends after this?"

"I don't see why not. And I'm right, you will find someone who loves you soon enough," Ivan reassures her as he hugs and kisses her on the forehead.

"Why do we stay together? It makes little difference what society think of us at our age," Peter says to Clearessa as he looks at her from across the dinner table.

"It must matter what people think of you still, especially here in this country or else you would've left and divorced me years ago. It's not like you have no place to go. You could stay with your brother and his family in America."

"He has his own problems dealing with a daughter hooked on drugs and another child in prison. No, we stick to the illusion out of an outdated sense of honor and uncomfortable promise. You are over seventy-one and I'm not far behind, both our parents are long dead, we don't know where our daughter is, whether if she's alive or dead and our only grandchild is a member of a dangerous organization that would gladly kill him for what he is."

"He's been with them for six years. They think he has value and is loyal to them."

"Only as a novelty act. The Bratva don't care about people like us, they barely tolerate us when they want to use us. You'll see I'm right, when they have no further use for Ivan, they will kill him."

"We are not completely helpless without resources. We still have contacts in the government that can watch over him from a distance. Isn't there that lieutenant from the Communist Cuban sect that Ivan is close to?"

"This lieutenant can only caution and warn Ivan of certain events and things, he can't keep him from being disposed of if the Bratva wanted to."

"You forget that Ivan is not a helpless victim. He has his own set of skills for survival. He could live and survive anywhere in the world, like we've had to."

Peter weighs his wife's words. If his daughter can last this long without being discovered, then his grandson could do the same if forced to. Finishing up his food, Peter gets up from the table, puts his plate in the kitchen sink and rinses it off.

"I'm going out for a while," Peter announces as he grabs his hat and coat.

"You should be careful if you're going to play in the park at night."

"You give me too little credit, I would at least go home with them instead of running the risk of being arrested in the woods of a park," Peter responds, fully grasping Clearessa's meaning.

But she knows her husband is too smart to be caught like that. No, she knows the situation with Ivan and Natleaha is weighing heavily on his mind.

The same person who is watching Ivan in London is observing Peter walking out of his building putting his coat on. It's dark out this time of year, so Peter can't see them eyeing him from across the street.

"Everything you care about will be taken from you and you'll be forced to watch."

"Traitorous monkey, you and your family were never really part of Mother Russia," they retort to themselves.

They follow Peter for a while until they see he's only walking around the neighborhood. Given Peter's reputation, they half expected to go to a local park to see him fool around, but that didn't happen. So, they break off the surveillance of Peter and go back to their van.

"What did you find out?" another mysterious figure in the van asks when then person watching Peter returns.

"Not much, only that he likes to walk outside sometimes when he's worried."

"What makes you think he does this when he's worried?"

"Because he always has this stressed out look on his face whenever I see him walking anywhere at night."

"Good, we will give him something to worry about as well as his daughter Natleaha when we find her. What is the status on the search?"

"She's managed to elude our people, but our sources know for sure she's somewhere in Canada. It's only a matter of time before they find her and eliminate her."

"We don't want her killed, not yet. We want her and the rest of the Fisk family to suffer, starting with her errant son and we indeed have the means to make Ivan Fisk suffer."

"How do you want to proceed?"

"Keep surveillance on the Fisk family, especially the ones who are in prison or on drugs, they're the easiest targets. And let our friends in Africa in on our status of watching the Fisks."

"Yes I understand."

They then get out of the van and head to another nearby vehicle.

"How can it get any worse?" a detective Sam Givens asks out loud as he surveys a brutal triple homicide scene at a parking lot to a high-end grocery store.

One of the victims has his neck snapped and the other two are shot in the head at close range by the looks of it. Chicago is a rough town, but people in this suburban area are still not use to this sort of thing close up.

"What can we get off the cameras that watch this place?" the detective demands. A uniform officer answers him.

"They disabled, whoever did this wanted no one to see who they were."

"Well, that's obvious," Sam responds sarcastically.

"There are no finger prints on any of the bodies or signs of the.32 caliber that fired the bullets that killed two of them. Lividity of the bodies puts the time of death about nine hours ago," the coroner on the scene adds. Sam leans in to get a closer look at the victim who had his neck snapped.

"This guy looks like somebody tried to turn his head in the other direction. Whomever did this was pretty strong, but bold. They left the bodies out in the open for us to find in an upper middle-class neighborhood. Do we have I.D's on these guys?"

"All we know is they're Caucasian males that looked to be from the ages of thirties to mid-forties. I'll probably find out more when I get 'em on the slab in the office," the coroner answers.

"Givens, the owner of the store wants to talk to you," another uniform officer informs him.

"Tell 'em he'll have to wait, I'm busy, this is a crime scene." But before anyone can stop the heavyset man, he pushes his way through the officers. Ignoring the yellow tape around the three bodies and surrounding area he gets close to Givens.

"How long is this going to take? I have special orders of expensive meats, not to mention my bakers have to begin baking our different styles of fresh pastries," the owner tells Sam. Because Sam Givens was short the larger man must have thought he could intimidate him, but he was wrong.

"This is an active crime scene sir and you can't reopen your store until our people are done with canvassing and examining the area to find clues of who did this. And it's always in such a place where the crime takes place. Now I'm sorry you're losing daylight over this, but you have to wait, that's the law. Officer Simms, take this man back to his car so he can wait until we're done," Givens demands sternly.

"But you can't do this, I own—" But the man is dragged away before he can further protest.

"Fuckin rich people are a god damn pain in the ass!" Givens mumbles under his breath.

At the 21th precinct, Sam Givens is sitting at his desk glancing through the photos of the crime scene. Somebody was trying to make a statement, the bodies were popping up everywhere, not just in the poor areas, but the well to do neighborhoods too. Chicago was more of a carnal house than usual.

"Do you have any leads?" Givens' Lieutenant asks him when he walks up to his desk.

"No sir, it all still appears to be random, but I'm waiting on the M.E to give me further clues."

"Well keep me posted, I've got the chief of detectives and the assistant police commissioner on my ass about this. They're asking can anybody go anywhere without getting their head blown off," the lieutenant states as he goes back to his office.

Just then Givens' land line rings.

"Yeah ok, I'm on my way down," he says, then hangs up the phone. Minutes later, he's down in the M.E's examining room where the three bodies from the grocery store parking lot are displayed on long wide tables.

"What have you got for me, Paula?"

"For starters, an ID on two of the bodies. I ran all their finger prints through the data base. This is Marko Fantone and over here is Eddy Luckcos, known associates of the O'Connor crime family."

"What about the third one?"

"He's not in the system, but he's probably mobbed up like these guys."

"Just like the others we've found in various parts of the city, belonging to different crime families."

"It looks that way Sam, I'll give ya a ring if I find anything else that can help you."

"That sounds good Paula, thanks."

Sam then goes to wait for his partner Repen Stello who was pulled for uniform guard duty at a function with the police commissioner.

"What's the word on the case?" Givens' partner asks when he's back from guard duty.

"Same as the others it seems, more mob gittin' killed. I'm glad you're back we gotta hit the pavement and start askin' people who live near the store where it happened if they saw anything."

"But didn't it happen late at night? Nobody would be out that time of night in front of their houses like they maybe would be in the lower income neighborhoods."

"There's always somebody who's nosier than most in every type of neighborhood Repen, we just have to find 'em. Now let's go, we gotta long search ahead of us. Sam and Repen speak to people from seven different houses that are close to the high-end grocery store before they spoke to someone who points them in the direction of Ameila Saunders, the neighborhood watch dog."

"Nothing goes down without her knowing about it," a man from the seventh house tells Sam and Repen when they are questioning him.

"Where does she live?" Sam asks the man.

"Three houses down," the man answers pointing them in the right direction.

Mrs. Saunders is a window in her sixties that always likes to walk her dog day and night, using that as an excuse to spy on people. Sam leads the questioning when she lets him and Repen into her home.

"Mrs. Saunders did you happen to see anything late last night?"

"Well, as a matter of fact, I did. I walked my dog Betsy to stretch her legs, so she can have a good bowel movement in the morning after I feed her breakfast. The parking lot of the grocery store is just over the wide hill of grass by my house. I was out on my walk with Betsy coming back to my house when I saw six men carrying three long sacks that appeared to be large enough to carry human bodies."

"Did you see what any of them looked like ma'am?" Sam inquires.

"I'm sorry no, they were all wearing dark masks, but I could tell they were large and tall men by the way they were handling the sacks. I did get a good look at the men who were in the sacks though, white men. The masked men dumped them on the ground. One of three men tries to beg, but one of the masked men stepped forward, reaches down and snaps his neck. The remaining two scream in horror, that's when they got shot by another of the masked men."

"Did you happen to notice anything else, maybe about their hands, the type of gloves they were wearing?"

"Oh, why yes one of them took his glove off to scratch his hand. I could see through my binoculars under the parking lot lights that the man's hand was white."

"So, he was Caucasian?" Repen guessed dryly.

"No, I mean it was white like snow, like you find on those people who are albinos."

An albino, that's interesting, Sam thinks to himself.

"How did you manage not to be seen by these men ma'am?" Sam asks with concern. "I was too far away for them to see me and it was dark where I was standing at."

"Well thank you, Mrs. Saunders, you've been a big help," Sam says getting up to shake her hand.

"I'm glad I could help."

When Sam and Repen step outside they head back to their parked car.

"So, one of the killers is an albino, that's not much help at all, there are a number of men in the city that are albinos."

"Yeah, but I don't think any of them are mobbed up, except for this one. Somebody has to have seen this guy without his mask, we just have to figure out where to look," Sam tells his partner.

What Sam was saying was partially bravo, true there weren't that many men who were albinos who were mobbed up, but this guy was a professional, it was only a small fluke that the woman saw his hand. And this only occurred because he thought nobody else was looking. At the end of his shift, Sam heads home to his apartment. When he enters he feels something is amiss, everything is where he left it as he feels around in the dark.

"Who's in here!" he demands while holding his gun.

"I'm impressed, I was careful not to touch anything," a female voice says.

Sam still holding his gun clicks on a nearby light switch. He's stunned to see a beautiful brown colored woman sitting in his sofa chair. She appears to be in her forties, wearing an all-black leather outfit. She has a Smith and Wesson hand gun trained on Sam.

"Who the fuck are ya? How'd ya get in my place?" Sam firmly asks in a stern tone.

"It was an easy task to scale up the back of your building without being seen and to slip into a window with a proper lock pick. I hear you're looking for someone I know," she informs him.

"Looking for whom?" Sam asks in an attempt to play dumb.

"An albino who you think works for the mob. I assure you the people he works for are far deadlier than you could ever imagine."

Sam's mind is racing.

So, this is an out of country, I can tell by her foreign accent, Sam thinks knowingly.

"So, you're here to give me a warning? Lady, I don't scare that easy."

"Oh, I'm sure, but think about the people close to you. What would happen to them if you pursue this? This organization has a long reach. The man you are looking for already knows you are searching for him and he's probably out of country by now. Save yourself some grief, do not pursue this any further, it will end badly for you."

Then before Sam can react, the woman pulls out a hidden weapon and shoots him in the stomach and the leg causing him to drop his own gun and slumps to the floor. The woman holds her guns to him as she inches closer.

"Think on my words, you won't get another warning, I assure you," the woman tells him before she steps over him and walks out the door. The woman's guns had silencers on them, so nobody heard the shots. Sam weakly reaches into his pocket and pulls out his cell phone to dial 911.

"I've been shot, send help, you can trace my phone for my location," Sam says in a struggled voice.

While he's recovering in the hospital, Sam is grilled by other investigating officers including his partner.

"Did you ever see her before that night? What did she look like? Did she say what other ties she had to the man we're looking for?" Repen rapidly interrogates Sam as if he's a victim.

"I already gave her description to the other detectives, an attractive foreign black woman in her mid-forties with wavy black hair. I've never seen her before. She had information on one of our suspects. You gotta get out there and find her."

"That might be harder than it seems. An airport surveillance camera caught the woman you described boarding a plane for Italy. After that, we lost track of her, but our precinct got a package and inside it had a message saying the Bratva are in town," Repen explains to Sam.

"So, I was right, it is a foreign mob that's been killing the local outfit. We gotta do something fore they start killin' cops to get their point across."

"How? These guys are keepin' a low profile, no clubs, warehouses or anything."

"They're near, we just have to find 'em and fast," Sam states through bodily pain.

Chapter 8

Ivan is sitting in a park in Havana Cuba waiting to hear what his superiors are going to do about him being identified at the job in Chicago. Though the woman didn't see Ivan's face, some of the Bratva are still concerned he showed carelessness, little as it is.

"If you hadn't left in such a hurry, the Americans police would have eventually found you. It's a question if you can show proper judgement doing jobs in the field. If it's believed you can't, then it would be unfortunate for you and all who are close to you."

The head of Ivan's sect firmly warns shortly after finding out that an albino was identified among the group of gloved and masked men Ivan was with. A lucky guess by a woman whom saw Ivan scratch his bare hand.

"Just go to Cuba, our superiors will decide what to do with you about your lapse in judgement," the head of his sect had ordered after warning him about the incident.

So, since he's there for an extended period, he calls Ingramisck to see if he wanted to spend some time together. Gregor is keeping his safe distance, so Ivan knew he couldn't count on him in situations like this. And Calhoun and Emmanuel had their own lives in America, he couldn't ask to uproot them from their homes for casual sex. So Ingramisck was the logical choice and he was the easiest since he lived in Cuba.

As Ivan sat on a bench in the park, his thoughts drift to his family and if they understand the reasons for the choices he's made for his life. As the questions go through his mind, Ivan's cell phone rings.

He lets it ring at first because only Gregor and the sect leader has his number and Gregor said he wouldn't be contacting him by phone until a decision is made and the sect leader wouldn't bother with phones. If he wanted to see Ivan, he would send people to get Ivan for him. But ignoring the ringing is difficult, so eventually Ivan answers it.

"Hello!" Ivan yells in annoyed tone.

"Somebody is in a bad mood," the person on the other end of the line says.

"Who's this?" Ivan asks not placing the voice at first.

"You asked me for information about your mother years ago, well not that long ago, but it's still been some years," the voice reminds Ivan. He had to think for a moment, but then he remembered.

"Flavawn?"

"Ah you do remember, your memory is good, but I hear you're being disciplined for bad judgement."

"How did you get this number?"

"You're not the first to enjoy the company of other men, especially those with a pretty face. Some are part of the powers that be. Using them, it wasn't hard to acquire your so-called unlisted number. A strange woman was seen by an American policeman whom was shot by this woman. They were unable to find the woman because she fled the country."

Ivan feels hope swell in him.

"You think the woman might be my mother?"

"We're not sure, but it was strange that she appeared right after they started looking for you. We believe there has to be a connection." Ivan knows none of this, all he knew was that the Chicago police was looking for him.

"Oh, your friend Ingramisck won't be coming to meet you," Flavawn suddenly says.

"What?"

"The lieutenant in special forces, he's not coming."

"Why do you say that?"

"This is an internal Bratva matter and despite what people may say, our military gives them great leeway in certain matters. You do realize they could just kill you and be done with it. You're just a soldier in a vast army that will exist long after you're gone."

"I'm not that expendable," Ivan says with pride, recalling the special tattoos he received to show his status in the organization. He knew they wouldn't get rid of him right away.

"Perhaps you're right, but your mistake will cost you," Flavawn reminds Ivan.

"I'll deal with that when it comes."

"I hope you can, good luck. But don't worry, so your present lovers are unavailable, you are an interesting boy, somebody in Cuba will be drawn to you and not all who want you are afraid to be seen with you." Ivan knows he was probably talking about Eleanea.

"I don't like women," Ivan states flatly.

"That isn't what I'd seen in the academy. Besides, it's not about what you like, it's about easing the tension and anybody can do that for you if you're lonely enough, man or woman."

"Well, that doesn't happen for me," Ivan says before he ends the call.

After waiting for another hour for Ingramisck, he decides he's not coming, so he walks back to his car, which is parked four blocks away. While walking to his car Ivan gets stares, some are looks of attraction.

Dressed in a white tank top and black slacks, the shirt shows off his broad muscular shoulders and arms, clean shaven and hair braided back like he comes to like it. Despite his own protests along with other because of albinism, Ivan is a handsome man. He does notice there are a lot of strikingly handsome men in Havana.

If they weren't so homophobic here, Ivan thinks. *That's all I would need, to be caught chasing after some pretty boys by the police. They'd kill me for sure*, Ivan further muses.

Right as he reaches his classic rental car, a beautiful honey brown woman in a summer flower covered dress approaches Ivan. Although he knows she is near before she comes behind him, he wonders what she wants.

"Excuse me, Mr. Fisk?" she asks in English with a thick Spanish accent.

"Yeah that's me," Ivan responds, unsurprised that she knows his name.

"I have a letter for you here," she tells him as she hands him an envelope. Ivan opens and reads the note.

"This is your punishment, meet your new shadow for the time being until we can trust you can follow the rules. Her name is Rosa. If you break the rules again, she has orders to kill you and whomever you're with," the typed letter says, signed with an ancient Russian symbol that means authority.

Ivan took the note seriously, mainly because he's seen what the organization does to people who break their rules.

"Does this mean you hold my dick while I take a piss too?" Ivan asks his new unofficial keeper sarcastically.

"Maybe, but it does mean you will have to be far more careful."

"On my downtime, I'm not that careful with certain things."

"Yes, I'm fully aware of your sexual lifestyle and I'm not put off by it or you for that matter," Rosa says in a matter-of-fact tone. Ivan doesn't like the way she looks at him, like a predator eyeing moving meat.

"How did you get here?"

"I have my ways, but now I guess I'll ride in your car with you back to your hotel," Rosa answers right before getting into the passenger side of Ivan's car. He's sort of uneasy because he remembers that side of the car being locked. Ivan then gets into the car and starts the engine.

"My day is fucked up," Ivan says to himself in frustration. During the whole drive to the hotel, Rosa has a smug smirk on her face as she stares at Ivan.

"There will be further retribution for your mistake that you didn't read about," Rosa casually says to Ivan days later when they're back in Moscow.

Ivan is worried at first, but days and weeks go by and nothing has happen to him. So, he figures he will probably be severely beaten or something until he's back in the states and get a call from Gregor.

"You'd better call your grandfather," he urgently demands.

"Wha, what's the matter? What's happen?" Ivan anxiously asks.

"It's better he tells you Ivan," Gregor explains before he hangs up. Ivan calls Peter on a satellite phone hours after speaking with Gregor. Peter answers after two rings.

"Grandpa what's going on?" Ivan demands without saying hello.

"Your grandmother is dead, Ivan," Peter answers in a cold tone. Ivan didn't know how to take the news, him and Clearessa were never close. He felt sad, but not filled with grief as he would have if it were his grandfather or his uncle Marvin, who he was much closer to. Obviously, Ivan had questions.

"How'd it happen?"

"The police are not sure, they think it might've been poison or asphyxiation, but they can't tell because her body was so decomposed from the icy water of the river where they found her."

"Do they have any suspects?"

"This is Russia, Ivan, not America, people disappear all the time every day. You know what me and your grandmother did for the government, there could've been a number of people who had a grievance against us." Ivan senses his grandfather is holding back something, but he doesn't know what.

"When is the funeral?"

"Maybe, it's best you don't come, you can pay your respects later."

"But why? I want to be there," Ivan protests.

"You're under restrictions now. It's best you don't aggravate your superiors with requests of going to funerals, even if it is for family. A request like that might be all the excuse they need to kill you."

How does he know about my punishment? Did the Bratva kill Grandma Clearessa? Ivan wonders. But his grandfather did have a point, he was on thin ice with the men he worked for.

"Are you going to bury her in Cuba with Great Grandpa?"

"I'm not sure, I haven't decided yet. I'll call and let you know. Take care of yourself Ivan, try not to get killed."

"I won't Grandpa, goodbye."

Ivan is right, Peter is holding something back. He does suspect who might've killed his wife and the fact he is certain she was dead when she went missing a week ago.

"I'm going out to the store to get some groceries," were the last words Clearessa said to her husband before she left their apartment.

Peter didn't bother to respond because it was nothing out of the ordinary for her to go to the store for things they needed. But when three hours passed without her return, Peter was aware something was wrong.

"She's dead," Peter quietly says to himself when another passes with no sign of his wife. When she disappears, Peter thinks that something Ivan did, that the Bratva might kill Clearessa as punishment for the mistake Ivan made in Chicago, but the way they do things they would've killed Peter too, especially since Ivan loves and cares more for him than Clearessa.

Somebody else is behind her death and his suspicions are confirmed when Peter gets a strange phone call a day after the police found Clearessa's body. When the phone rang, Peter let it ring. Given that his wife of forty odd years is found murdered, he doesn't feel like talking to anyone, but the phone keeps ringing nonstop for two hours. So, Peter finally picks it up out of frustration more than curiosity.

"Who is it!" Peter yells.

"Ah, I see we've worn you down," a male voice answers.

"What the fuck is this? Who are you?"

"Tsk, tsk, temper, temper, Mr. Fisk, all in good time. Did you like our little present we left for you?" Peter doesn't even have to ask what he meant.

"What do you want?"

"What we want Mr. Fisk is to erase Korcoff Vamitri's mistake, which is your family. A family that's bred three generations of amoral character, depravity that was nursed by an amoral unnatural man. Korcoff should have been eliminated when the state first found out about his unnatural tastes. But no, the government let him live to corrupt other young men, to bring in other unnatural elements like your father who made you, then producing your grandson."

After all this time, Peter still couldn't believe homophobia is still alive in Russia.

"You killed my wife because me and my grandson are both gay?" Peter asks in disbelief.

"No, Mr. Fisk you and your family are going to die slowly because you're an unnatural cancer that's poisoned Russia and its allies long enough."

However, Peter is not frightened by the unknown enemies who is attacking his family, he is enraged.

"You kill my wife and think to threaten me? Me and my family have survived, lived and worked in your racist country probably before you and yours were born. I'm not some helpless animal who lays down and dies when he's wounded. I fight back, I attack as does the rest of my family. You'll make a mistake like people like you always do when they think they're landing the killing blow, that's when you show yourself and that's when my family will end you."

Peter doesn't wait for a response. He just hangs up and cuts off the phone. He is furious beyond belief. This presently unknown is going to be relentless, but they made an error. They mentioned Korcoff and his father, those like them, meaning they were mainly after Peter and Ivan since his father and Korcoff had been dead for years. His daughter is still safely hidden, they would've mentioned her death if she wasn't.

I'd better warn Marvin and Eric just in case, Peter thinks, even though it would be clear to them that their wives and children won't be the primary targets.

So, when Peter speaks to Ivan over a week later, he chose not to tell him of the threat against their family. He figures his grandson had enough to worry about with keeping on the good side of the men he works for. Besides, Peter believes if Ivan behaved himself and continues to rise in the ranks, he would be less of an easy target and they would protect him out of some type of loyalty.

Rosa watches Ivan like a hawk but she does give him some small amounts of privacy, like letting him go to the bathroom. It was during one of these trips that Ivan gets a text message from his grandfather. Sitting on the toilet, Ivan read the message.

"I decided to have your grandmother cremated instead of being buried in the town we lived or Cuba. It made little difference since there was nobody left alive on her side of the family to object. I didn't have a funeral either. Knowing her, she probably wouldn't have wanted one anyway. I did call your uncle Eric and Marvin to let them know what happened and what I did for her. In some ways, it was unnecessary, we aren't that close and we don't know each other's wives to be too concerned."

"What I didn't tell you the last time we spoke was an outside force not connected to the Russian government or Bratva was responsible for your grandmother's death. They called and gloated about it. I'm not sure who they are, but they want to eliminate men like you and me and by extension your mother if they can find her, which I doubt. They may have ties to the Bratva, but this I also doubt. Given if they did, you'd already be dead. I cannot stress enough for you to watch yourself, especially now that we have an enemy that wants to personally destroy men like us."

"Take care and delete this message. Sign; Grandpa Peter."

Ivan does as the text instructs and deletes the whole message. The text has Ivan worried to say the least. He has to call Gregor, Calhoun and Emmanuel to make sure they were still safe.

"Are you done in there yet?" Rosa shouts as she bangs on the door.

"Yeah, I'll be out in a minute!" Ivan shouts back. Just then, Ivan had an idea. He came out of the bathroom in the hotel room.

"I gotta make some calls," Ivan says to Rosa when he comes out of the bathroom.

"To who? One of your boys?" Rosa asks snidely.

"Just one of them and an old friend, who's not a boy."

"Really?" Rosa is intrigued. She is aware he is close to Eleanea, but they an't sexual. Ivan's first call is to Gregor.

"I need you to be extra careful for a little while."

"Why, what's wrong?" Gregor asks with concern.

"I can't get into it over the phone, I might not be able to see you for a while."

"Ivan what's this about?"

"I gotta go Gregor, I'll contact you when I can." Ivan then hangs up on him. His next call stuns the person on the other end.

"Ivan? This is a surprise. What can I do for you?" Eleanea enquires with a slightly subtle tone.

"I need your help with something."

"What do you need?"

"Your computer skills."

"My computer skills, for what?"

"I don't wanna tell you over the phone. Can we meet somewhere?"

"Where?"

"How about Bordeaux in France? It's not on too many people's radar."

"It can't be today. How about in a week? It's the best I can do in such short notice."

"That's fine, Eleanea and thanks, I owe you."

"Anytime, I can't wait to see you, bye."

In the meantime, Rosa watches Ivan's body language as he speaks to Eleanea.

"You really do care for her, don't you?" Ivan doesn't answer, he just looks for his pants to put on.

The lieutenant Ivan was sure could take care of himself, but Calhoun and Emmanuel he wasn't so sure of. These two weren't quite aware of the truth about Ivan, so he opted to tell them half of the truth.

"Yo, what chu into hommes, how can I be down?" Emmanuel asks with excitement when Ivan told him he was involved with something shady that was too dangerous to talk about.

"It's nothing you wanna mess with, it just might be a good idea for you to go back home for a while."

"Wow, dat's crazy hommes, I been meaning to ask when can we fuck around again. But if you wanna chill fo awhile cause of yo business dat's cool, but I hope to hear from you again," Emmanuel cheerfully says at the end of their conversation.

However, Calhoun wasn't so easy. Ivan contacted Calhoun by skype on his computer. As suspected, Rosa was put off by Calhoun's appearance, so she left the room while Ivan spoke to Calhoun.

"What chu mean we gotta cool it fo awhile?" Calhoun asked in a bothered tone.

"I got a situation that's too dangerous for you to be involved in, it's hard to explain."

"Look if you droppin me cause you don't wanna be wit me no more, be a man and jus say dat shit. Don't come wit no bullshit bout bein in a dangerous situation shit."

"Look this is serious, you know how I've told you I can't tell you what I do for a living because it might be bad for you."

"Yeah so, I always thought you was a drug dealer or sumthin, ain't no big thang, you ain't the first. I grew up round dat shit. Is it cause you a fag and I'm tryin to go pro? Dat shit don't matter, everybody fuck around in sports, I still fuck wit females, don't nobody have to know."

Ivan could see Calhoun wasn't making this easy and realized for a long time that Calhoun had feelings for him. So, he saw no other choice but to layout the whole story to him.

"I'm an enforcer for the mob Calhoun, the Russian mob." Calhoun just stares at Ivan through the computer screen before he responds.

"Man, yo pale ass is fulla shit, you ain't in no damn Russian mob. Dey ain't got no niggas in da Russian mob, especially no pale ass niggas."

"Does this look like I'm bullshitting!" Ivan shouts at Calhoun in Russian while lifting up his shirt showing off his tattoos. Though Calhoun has seen them before, he's never known what they meant. Ivan then continues to speak to Calhoun in the thick Russian accent that he's cleverly learned how to hide.

"I kill for the Bratva, I break bones for them and they protect me because of the work I do for them. But some outside force wants me and my family dead for some reason and they're not above hurting those closet to me. You knew you were not the only one I fuck with, but I still care for you enough to warn you about this." Ivan further states while reverting back to proper English.

Calhoun has a stunned look of disbelief on his face, he can't wrap his head around it, but he tries.

"You really do work for 'em? Did you, I mean, were you born in Russia?"

"Yes."

"There are black folks in Russia?"

"Yes, my family has lived there for generations. The man who tried to rape your girlfriend awhile back was a nephew of one of my superiors and I was told to keep people from disturbing him, that's how we met. I'm telling you this so you believe the truth of what I'm saying to you."

"You knew what dis guy was doin all along?"

"Yes, but I was glad your girlfriend fought him off, that's why he was shipped out of the country never to return."

"Do you know what dat did to her, to us? She could hardly function after dat. I couldn't even touch her, she still ain't right today and now you tellin me you worked wit dis guy?"

"I'm sorry Calhoun, I wish that wasn't the truth, but it is."

Calhoun can't even look at Ivan after what he has revealed to him, he only silently clicks off his computer. Ivan's head is heavy after this. Part of him hopes Calhoun can forgive him, but he feels he never will.

"Are you done with your calls?" Rosa asks walking back into the room.

"Yeah, I only have to kill time until my meeting with Eleanea," Ivan solemnly answers.

He doesn't bother trying to call Ingramisck when he decided to do so out of paranoia, but he goes with his earlier assessment because he was with special forces. It seemed the day to meet Eleanea came quickly. The flight to France from where he was coming from appeared to take forever. Once the flight touched down, Ivan called Eleanea at her hotel.

"Yeah, I'm here at the airport, I can meet you anywhere in Bordeaux."

"We can meet at a small park near the middle of the city, I can give you directions," Eleanea suggest.

"That's fine, just text them to me, I'll read them during the train ride there. Oh, somebody will be coming with me to meet you."

"Really, who?"

"It's a long story, I'll explain everything when I see you," Ivan then clicks off the call.

"We've got a train to catch, I'll tell you where we're going after we get off it," he tells Rosa who's close by his side.

The train ride to Bordeaux is two hours and another hour by taxi to the park Eleanea texted Ivan directions to. To say Eleanea is confused when she sees

Ivan with a beautiful woman is putting it lightly. But Ivan quickly gives an explanation. This time he tells her everything, leaving nothing out, including the reason he's with Rosa. Being Russian herself, she takes it far better than Calhoun did. In case someone is listening, they all speak in Spanish, although Ivan is not familiar with most languages like his grandfather, he gets by.

"So, you're Bratva and they're punishing you for being identified by your hand when you were doing a job for them?"

"That's right, it's why Rosa is here, to watch every move I make so I don't mess up again."

"So, who do you think is after you and your family, if not them?"

"I don't know, that's why I need your help."

"To do what?"

"To use your computer skills to hack into the street cameras in the city my grandfather lives."

"What for?"

"The people who are after us killed my grandmother and they had to have somebody watching my grandparents. I need to see if somebody was following them the night my grandmother was killed. If it's true, I need you to check other street cameras in other in other parts of the world I've been to see if somebody was stalking me too."

"I'll do what I can, but it won't be easy, the Russian government have difficult counter measures in place to keep outsiders from prying into their network."

"Yeah I thought about that, but your skills are among the best, besides there's a friend of mine who can help you get past certain fire walls." A curious look forms on Eleanea's face when Ivan says friend.

"What kind of friend and what does he do?"

"We're close, let's leave it at that."

"He's in special forces, isn't he? There were rumors that one of their lieutenants stationed in Cuba that travels to and from Russia giving intelligence instructions liked young men."

Ivan doesn't answer Eleanea's accusations, he only stares at her funny. She then smiles at him making him feel embarrassed.

"I never knew you had an eye for men with power," Eleanea slyly says.

"So, can you help me? My life and my family's depend on it," Ivan subtly pleads.

"I'll see what I can do, but we will have to go to one on my company's main offices in Budapest."

Eleanea was true to her word, she had the proper tools in Budapest.

"They're clients who want to see the inner workings for a task our company is doing for them," Eleanea told the clerks and guards who worked at the building when they asked why Ivan and Rosa was with her.

"How long is this gonna take?" Ivan anxiously asks.

"Just a few minutes. Just give me the name of the city your grandfather lives in and then address," Eleanea casually demands.

"Kazan, 9632 West end zip code 53217," Ivan tells her. Eleanea goes through lots of footage of the building Ivan grandparents lived in, especially at night. Eventually something catches Ivan's eye.

"There, someone is following my grandfather when he goes out on a walk this night. They tail him until he returns home, but they're covered up, I can't tell if it's a man or a woman."

"Let me enhance the image," Eleanea offers. With a few clicks on the section image on the computer, they get a better picture of the person doing the tailing of Peter.

"It's a woman, but where is she going after she left my grandpa?"

"I'll check the other street cameras to track her. There, it looks like she's meeting a man in van. He appears to be older about maybe in his sixties. I'll check more footage of the city to see if this man or woman shows up again."

They don't see the strange man, but they do see who murdered Ivan's grandmother after she left her building. Once she's a few blocks away from her building, a tall dark-skinned black man runs up and attacks her. She manages to fight her attacker off at first, but then he jams something in her neck and she falls over.

Afterward the black man wraps a large rag around her face, stuffing part of it in her mouth and picks her up and carries her body over his shoulder.

"Can you print out a close-up picture of this man and the other two people we saw?" Ivan asks in an uneasy tone after witnessing the death of his grandmother.

"I think so, give me a minute," Eleanea responds before using her computer mouse to click a button. She then walks to another room and quickly comes back with three photographs and hands them to Ivan.

"What are you going to do now?" Rosa suddenly asks. "I'm going to see my grandpa in Kazan to see if he can recognize any of these people, then I'm getting him the fuck out of the country before these people kill him too."

"The Bratva won't like you going on unauthorized trips picking up baggage," Rosa warns.

"Someone is personally trying to destroy me and my family! I can't ignore that," Ivan fires back.

"Look Eleanea, they probably won't hurt you because they don't consider us that close. We should keep it that way until we can find these people."

"I understand," Eleanea says half-heartedly.

Leaving her at her building, Ivan and Rosa take the next flight back to Russia.

Chapter 9

"His name is Emmubahta, a hardcore guerrilla fighter from Africa, I'm not sure which part though. I first met him years ago when I was stationed in Uganda," Peter explains when his grandson shows him the picture of the man.

"What about the other two?" Ivan asks.

"They're not familiar to me, but I would guess that they're ex-intelligence, which would probably explain how they had knowledge of Korcoff and our family. Your friend in special forces could probably help us find out."

"That's a good idea, I'll give him a call, but right now we gotta get you someplace where these people can't get to you."

A look of disbelief forms on Peter's face over Ivan's words.

"Ivan, Ivan you know better than that there's no hiding from these people, you have to find them and kill them before they kill all of us."

"Well, my mother's been good at hiding all these years."

"That's probably because whomever we're facing wasn't ready to make their move until now, but you can be sure where ever she is, she's in danger too. But you are partially right, I have to go with you, if only to help your back. The loyalty of the Bratva only goes so far in certain situations," Peter says while eyeing Rosa with skepticism.

"The Bratva aren't afraid of bitter relics from a dead era and their monkey stooges," Rosa announces proudly.

"Well, they should be. These are very dangerous people, they've nothing left to live for but their ideals and they're willing to do horrible things you can't imagine to protect them. They have no honor, no restrictions on morality, little regard for human life, which is why we have to stop them. They won't be satisfied with just the deaths of the Fisk family. They'll probably eliminate anything and anyone who they think aren't clean Russian in their eyes."

Rosa weighs Peter's words carefully. Communist Russia never really accepted the existence of the Bratva, the government always thought the

Bratva would die out like imperial Russia, but then the fall of communism happened and here the Bratva are stronger than ever.

"How do we explain your presence to our superiors? They will protect your grandson as one of their ranking soldiers, but I don't think that protection extends to you," Rosa firmly states as Peter mentioned in different words earlier.

"Of course, it doesn't. Which is why I'm bringing your superiors something valuable; information. Information on a possible native African organization in criminal enterprise that's attempting to encroach on the Bratva's businesses. After hearing this, your bosses will keep me alive long enough at least to verify what I know, hopefully long enough to deal with Emmubahta and the rest of those trying to destroy us."

"It might work, but I'd be careful if I were you, the high-ranking members of the ruling caste are no fools. They'll kill you and your grandson if they even suspect you're attempting to play them," Rosa replies.

"We won't go straight to them," Ivan then says.

"What?" is his grandfather's and his human shadow's response.

Ivan then further explains, "We go back to the scene of my crime. Whoever is after us won't expect me or any member of my family to go back to Chicago where they're looking for me. We go to Chicago, contact the main police detectives looking for me and make them an offer they can't refuse."

"Which is what?" Rosa asks, not liking where this was going.

"I offer myself as a mole in the organization, I tell them that I had a change of heart, which is why I allowed myself to be identified. They can't help but believe it, meanwhile I maneuver them into helping us distract the people after us."

"Hmm, it might work," Peter comments.

"Are you insane? The Bratva would surely kill you and your whole family before these other people had a chance to."

"I'm not really betraying the Bratva, I'm only pretending to bring a cop under their control. Besides, wasn't this particular cop shot by an unidentified woman in her forties who might've been my mother?"

Rosa is surprised Ivan knows that detail, she thought her bosses left out that part of what happened in Chicago.

"The Bratva already have enough police under their control, we don't need more."

"Please, Rosa we could always use more, especially those who would be grateful enough to do anything to prevent a bloody gang war. We just have to find out the cop's name, which should be easy enough and approach him with our fairytale. Once I'm done with him, our superiors will have Chicago and the rest of the state of Illinois free to quickly branch out to other neighboring states. We just have to explain my plan in the right way, so they approve it."

Rosa doesn't say much after Ivan is finished explaining his plan. She feels it is too dangerous to play these type of games with the Bratva. If the plan backfires, it could mean a fate worse than death for Ivan and his family.

They may go for it or they may not. What will he do then? It's bad enough that he wants to go back to Chicago where he got into trouble in the first place, but he wants to make contact with the police involved. Its' suicide, Rosa thinks rapidly to herself.

She also wonders how Ivan has lasted this long thinking like this in the Bratva. His grandfather appears to have no problem with what his grandson is suggest.

"Do what you must, but time is growing short," Peter advises Ivan.

The next day Ivan is granted an audience with some of the governing members of the organization. He tells them of his family's plight and his plan to help them get out of it.

"We are sadden By your family's misfortune. But what does this have to do with us?" one of the men Ivan addresses asks.

"Because the Bratva is about honor and loyalty without fear, not a person's skin color or what they might personally be. These people who hunt my family don't believe I and my family belong in the world because we're different. By extent, they want to dictate how you run things and if you don't do what they approve of, this gives them permission to attack you anytime they want to."

"And you think they would use African guerrilla fighters against us just to make us stick to their standards?" another senior member asks.

"I do. That's why I want your permission to seek out this policeman who's investigating us and to turn him as an ally to be the first of the soldiers to help my family in the war to rid us of these people."

After Ivan has presented his case, the men take an hour to come to decision and the one who first spoke to Ivan gives him their answer.

"You and your family have our leave to use any means necessary to combat this threat and any member of our organization who wants to help you can do so. But if this threat you speak of hurts us more than you say, then you and yours will die ugly."

"I understand, thank you."

Ivan is grateful for this because it also means unofficially Gregor, Ingramisck and maybe his old instructor Flavawn Gorbachin can now help, that is if Ivan can get a hold of him.

Though it took some heavy convincing, but his grandfather agreed to go with Ivan to Chicago. Though Peter started to regret his decision when Gregor met them all at the airport.

"We don't need him in this, I can understand you having a shadow as punishment, but he's not part of this."

"You heard what they said Grandpa, I can use whatever means at my disposal to help us in this war. Gregor can help us."

"You mean you, not us. This is no time to appease your appetites, that can wait till later," Peter says with an evil side look to Gregor. Ivan wasn't thinking about that at the moment, but it had been awhile since him and Gregor had been together.

"What's this cop's name who's investigating me and my tires to the organization?" Ivan asks quickly snapping to business.

"Sam Givens and his ride along partner is named Repen Stello if that helps. Givens not too long ago just got out of the hospital from gunshot wounds he got from unknown black woman," Gregor tells Ivan as he pats him on the shoulder in greeting.

That has to be my mother, Ivan thinks. Not wanting to draw too many nosey passengers, the small group of them collect what little luggage they have and walk outside.

"We'll have to take a bus to where my car is parked," Gregor informs them when everybody is outside of the airport. So, they take one of the shuttles to the parking garage where Gregor's car is parked. When they're on the road, Ivan continues his questions.

"What else do you know?"

"About what you do, that Givens interviewed a woman who saw your hand when you took your glove off to scratch it and that Givens figured out we were eliminating resistance to us setting up here."

"We need to make contact with Givens now. Does he have any C.I. informants?"

"I don't know, but I could find out."

"Good, find them and pay them to give a message to Givens that somebody has information about the coming gang war he's expecting."

Sam Givens is back at his desk at the 21th precinct when his cell rings.

"Hello?"

"Sam I got intel 'bout them Russians settin' up shop in Chicago," a male voice on the other end says.

"Well, what is it?" Sam anxiously urges.

"Some guy reached out to me saying he wants to defect from the Russians, but he needs help, said he'll only talk to you."

"How did he sound?"

"That's the funny part, he sounded proper, didn't even have a foreign accent." Sam found that strange, but his curiosity won out.

"Set up the meet."

"Where?"

"At Lelha's."

"The dyke bar? Why there?"

"The owner owes me a favor and some of the female cops I know go there, so I'll have extra backup besides my partner. Set it up for tomorrow night at 9:30pm."

"Al'ight bet, it's done." The call then ends.

"What's up?" Repen asks as he sits across from Sam.

"I just gotta a tip that somebody from the Russian mob wants to talk. Said they wanna defect."

"You think it's legit?"

"I'm not sure, but the timing has got me concerned. A little after I started investigating these gang-related murders, I get warning shots that land me into the hospital. That's why I'm goin to Lelha's in case they wanna make this bloody."

"Man, them bitches don't play. Most of them bitches is ex-military and it's even rumored dat some of 'em are mercenaries and terrorists, including the owner."

"Exactly, whomever this man is that wants to talk won't be expecting to walk into a ready-made army there."

"Hey, Lelha!" Sam yells to the owner by the bar over the loud music.

"What's up Sam? How's it hangin baby?" the tall stocky well-dressed woman asks in greeting.

"Same as always baby. Has my guest arrived?"

"Ten minutes early in full view, showing off his ivory skin," Lelha says pointing to Ivan dressed in a long-sleeved green button up shirt and matching pants.

"That's a big fella."

"I'd take care baby he's got back up, a gorgeous sista at the bar and a Greek lookin' boy hidden round here somewhere."

"That's ok, you know I got my own too and I can always count on you and your girls to distract 'em long enough for me to clap back," Sam comments while eyeing an attractive lesbian black couple.

Both of them are thick with big round butts. One of them is wearing brown tights cut to the thigh and the other is earing shredded black jeans shorts with fish net stockings showing off her ass with a black thong. Sam can't help but stare.

"They came out in public like that?" Sam asks himself.

"Do women actually feel sexy in that?"

"I don't know baby, whatever make 'em feel good."

"Would you wear something like dat?"

"Hell naw baby, I don't need to feel dat good wit my body. But I don't think your friend over there is interested in what my girls is showin'."

A bewildered look forms on Sam's face.

"What, he wasn't looking you mean?"

"Yeah, he had more eyes for his Greek friend than the girls."

"No kiddin! Shit, this just got a lot more interesting." Sam then walks to the table where Ivan is sitting at. As Sam is walking to the table, Repen enters the bar.

"I understand there's something you want to discuss with me," Sam addresses Ivan in proper English without slang.

"Yes, Mr. Givens, you are correct. I can tell by your stance you're kind of uncomfortable with men like me," Ivan states while giving Sam Givens the once over.

Sam realizes this man was very observant. Sam always thought he had a pretty good poker face.

"Don't worry Mr. Givens. I'm used to it. Sit down. I didn't come here to waste your time."

"You have information about the people you answer to and you want to break away from them. That sounds like some dangerous moves, especially if they find out what you are."

"They already know, but that's beside the point. The only danger is me giving you the names of the lieutenants who are in charge of setting up shop here in Chicago and all over the state."

Sam Givens' suspicions of Ivan were teetering before he came to this meet, but now that he's face to face with Ivan, it's off the scale.

"No man willingly helps murder several people without blinking and then weeks later, decides he wants to just quit! It doesn't make any sense," Sam reasons in his mind.

Meanwhile, everybody's hand is on the trigger from both sides. Gregor and Rosa have Ivan covered in the bar from different angles and his grandfather is watching through a drilled hole from the roof with a state-of-the-art sniper rifle. But Sam has Ivan out-flanked, half the women in the bar, including the owner are armed. Although the slight advantage Ivan has is that Sam Givens and his people don't know about Peter, whom informs Ivan of the odds.

"There are more armed than we anticipated, you'll have to adjust this scenarios quickly," Peter warns his grandson through an ear piece all four present.

"Yes. I see them, we just have to be more careful of how we talk and move. Sam Givens wants to believe what I'm saying, he just doesn't realize it yet," Ivan announces arrogantly under his breath. But Sam was losing interest, so he had to work fast.

"I have the names of the said lieutenants right here along with where they'll be, so you'll find them with illegal weapons, drugs and young girls they use for prostitution. It's in my pants pocket," Ivan says loudly to everyone trained on him. Ivan then hands the written information to Sam.

"You can verify it if you want before you act on it."

"Thanks. I will, I'll be in touch if this pans out."

"Good, til' next time."

And just like that, the meeting is over. As the two men get up to leave, they don't take their eyes off each other until Ivan walks out the door first.

"What did that ivory-colored muthafucka have to say?" Repen asks as soon as he's in earshot of his partner.

"Gave me some names and whereabouts of these supposed lieutenants who according to him are setting up in Chicago as we speak."

"Do you believe 'em?"

"Not really, something about this doesn't smell right, but I'll check out the info anyway to see."

"Al'ight bet, let's get on it," Repen urges.

"Who were those names I actually gave that cop?" Ivan asks with curiosity.

"Some thieving subordinates who caught with their hands too many times in the cookie jar," Gregor oddly puts it.

"It must have been a lot of times to warrant prison and death," Peter adds.

"Don't worry, they're lowlife sum and the perfect pasties to sell Ivan's plan."

"Let's hope so or this plan will go south in a deadly hurry," Rosa says.

"But in the meantime, this should keep Mr. Givens busy for at least a week or so, which means we have time to kill until he contacts me again," Ivan says to everyone while glancing slyly at Gregor out of the side of his eye.

"We could go to Vegas," Gregor suggests.

"What for? Gambling is a waste, we need to hold on to the money we have," Peter advises.

"It shouldn't be too bad, the Bratva has a presence there," Rosa reminds them.

"Gregor, why would you want to go to Vegas? You don't gamble."

"Gambling is not the only thing to do in Vegas, there's the fights, Ivan."

"I don't wanna watch no boring boxing matches Gregor, we can see bareknuckle boxing right here in the underground fighting pits."

"These are not just boxers my friend, these are U.F.C fighters. They do kickboxing, mixed in with various forms of martial arts. You be seen what I'm talking about on cable TV, fighters built like shit brick houses, wearing spandex shorts that barely fit. I heard the welter and heavy weights fighters are supposed to be fighting in a Las Vegas show this weekend."

Ivan liked the sound of that and so did his grandfather. Ivan loved watching these matches on TV, it would be a treat for him to see a U.F.C fight live. He often had fantasies about which of the fighters were closeted or bi curious at least. Peter still has a healthy appetite at his age and would love the chance to get close enough to touch one of those well chiseled fighters.

"Alright, I'm in," Ivan eagerly agrees.

"That sounds interesting, count me in," the elder Fisk says with the same attitude as his grandson.

Since Ivan was given the go ahead with this venture with Gregor's help, the organization doesn't expect much from him and his allies for the time being, so they wouldn't notice if they took a few days to go to Las Vegas. So, four hours later, the motley crew are riding in four first class seats to Las Vegas, Nevada. They all take a day to rest before they go to see the scheduled matches at Hera Dome Arena.

"They look promising," Rosa says when she sees the welter weight fighters.

The fighters in these matches were European, from Latin America, France, Spain, Sweden and Dominican. But these matches doesn't hold Ivan's attention. The fighters are good, but nothing too special to Ivan or Peter, but Gregor is intrigued by the Swedish fighter who gives Gregor a slight smile near the beginning of his match.

"You always were a sucker for blond bombshells, male or female," Ivan teased.

After three hours and two intermissions, the welter weight matches are over, it was time for the heavy weights to begin. Ivan and Peter couldn't see the fighters when they were walking to the ring because they were covered by their robes and hoods, but you could tell by the color of their flags that one was from Ireland and the other Brazil.

A tall white man with brown hair wearing a black suit grabs the mic hanging over head and announces and introduces the fighters, "Ladies and gentlemen, welcome to the heavy weight main event! In this corner we have from the emerald isle standing at five foot eleven and weighing in at 235 pounds, winner of twelve matches, three of them by knock out, Patrick O'Malley! And in this corner standing at six foot two, weighing in at 240 pounds, winner of ten matches, five by knock out, hailing from Curitiba Brazil, Savante Eurico!"

By then, both men have taken off their robes revealing their bodies. They are both modern forms of Adonis, pure muscle, curved calves, washboard stomachs, tight chests and as suspected both are wearing tight spandex fighter shorts showing off their firm butts and crotch cups. Each Fisk man has a favorite, for Peter it's Patrick O'Malley, fiery red hair, a square jaw covered by a well-trimmed beard. For the past ten years, Peter has had a weakness for hot-blooded white boys. They're like walking talking bags of addictive cocaine to him. All he could think about right now is could he somehow get a private conversation with that fiery white devil. Ivan chooses to admire Savante Eurico, who's taller than O'Malley with his black nappy hair cut into a mohawk, the top dyed blue and blond. When Savante dances around getting ready for the fight Ivan gets a clear view of his brick-crushing thighs.

"Fuck, he's turning me on, I bet he fucks as wild as he fights," Ivan whispers in Gregor's ear while squeezing his right thigh.

The fight is fierce, the opponents go for ten rounds, inflicting as much damage on each other that no one thought was humanly possible. During the fifth round, it looks like O'Malley would win because he is landing devasting blows to Savante's face and torso, he appears to make it to the end of the round barely. But at the beginning of the sixth round, Savante finds his second wind, connecting with powerful kicks to O'Malley's sides and knees.

He even manages to get O'Malley in a scissor hold at one point, clamping one of his arms nearly breaking it. By the tenth round, Savante and O'Malley are battered, bloody and nearly beaten, it shows on their bruised-up faces, but neither fighter is willing to give in. In the end, Savante wins by decision. Even with his face all messed up from the match, Savante still looks sexy to Ivan.

"Damn I'd love to take you to my bed, I'd even share you with a woman if that's what it took," Ivan says out loud softly and he doesn't care if the man might hear what he says. He notices that Gregor is looking good too, in his sagging jeans showing off the rim of his red jockey underwear topped off by a tank top.

"See, I told you you'd enjoy this. It's the best ain't it?" Gregor boasts.

"Yeah it is, this night couldn't get any better, unless we thought of something better to top it all off." Ivan then puts his arm around Gregor before he can protest.

"Come on man, calm down, people are watching us," Gregor says to Ivan in an attempt to dissuade Ivan from doing anything unseemly to him in public.

"I don't care, all this blatant testosterone has got me so horny. It's been months. When are we gonna be together again?"

"You haven't exactly been celibate when you've been away from me."

"Come on, you bothering about Calhoun and Emmanuel, they're jump offs, they ain't serious for me."

"What about your special forces Daddy lieutenant Ingramisck? He's definitely more than a jump off and you were sexing Calhoun so much these past few years that he fell in love with you."

Ivan doesn't know where all this was coming from. Gregor had a wife and still liked fucking her, as well as other people.

"Why is Gregor acting all jealous all of sudden?" Ivan wonders.

"I've told you how I felt about you from the beginning, but you've kept me at arm's length for years. What did you expect me to do? Deprive myself of what I need? You always send mixed signals, like now. You arrange for us to watch well-built men sweating and fighting in front of us, knowing I'll react to it, but you push me away."

At this point, both men don't care who is watching and listening to them.

"There's a time and place for certain things. You've never understood that, Ivan. I can't be touchy feely out in public like you do, I have standards I have to protect."

"I thought I was one of those things you wanted to protect."

"Look, you are. I wouldn't be here helping you and your family fight the people who are trying to kill you. But I have other responsibilities too, besides you."

"Yeah I know, your wife and two sons. Do what you want, I'm going to have a drink."

Painful as it was, Ivan had just walked out of the relationship with Gregor. And though he hated it, Ivan went to bed alone.

"Is everything ready to go?" Sam asks Repen as they suit up with dozens of other officers close to a warehouse located in a factory district in the city.

"It's all ready as it's ever gonna be," Repen answers.

"Alright, listen up. What we got here are bad guys who are heavily armed and ready for anything, so watch your asses! We clear? Good, let's move out!" Sam Givens orders the officers.

Then seconds later, they move in on the warehouse. All the men and women following Sam's lead have listening ear pieces so they can whisper to each other without tipping off the renegade mobsters that they were coming. It's dark and all the officers are wearing black, so it's hard for anybody at the front of the warehouse to see them approach.

"I see five guards at the entrance," one of the officers softly warns into his mic.

"Copy," Sam responds. Signaling with his left hand, several of his people go to the side of the warehouse to sneak up on the guards at the front.

"What the fuck?" one of the guards shouts in Russian a moment too late.

He's cut down by a rapid hail of bullets along with the other four at the front, but not before they hit one of the officers in the chest with some of their own bullets. Quickly, another man grabs the wounded officer and drags him back to the squad vans.

"Rickter's down. I repeat Rickter's down," the officer dragging the wounded man says into his mic. Quietly, they continue to the inside of the warehouse.

"Ok McAuthor, we copy, we'll carry on without you, we got this," Sam responds as him and his team enter the building.

Unfortunately, the mobsters inside heard the noise of bullets from outside, so they are ready with weapons aimed in all directions when Sam and his team enter.

"Chicago P.D, freeze!" Sam yells, but that seems to start the fire fight.

The fight is brutal and the officers manage to take out the Russians, but three more cops are lost in the battle. Afterwards more officers arrive to canvas the scene.

"How many more of these muthafuckas we gotta git at, Sam?" Repen barks in frustration.

"Three, a couple of whore houses and another warehouse. But I'm gonna not only ask our lieutenant for more men from our precinct to use, but I'm gonna recommend all the other precincts that wanna get in on this."

"Sounds like a plan."

It doesn't take too much convincing on Sam's part to get his boss to put in some calls from other houses to lend a hand in taking down these rogue Russians. All the police who get involved share the same desire, to get the drugs and child prostitutes off the streets of Chicago. But they also know that's an uphill battle, but it's a war they're willing to fight.

The two whore underage houses are not that heavily armed and are easy to take down. The drug factory warehouse is another story. Like at the other warehouse, the police take losses when they seize it. The entire amount of manpower and time it takes for the police to raid all of these places spans out in wccks.

"Looks like the albino was right."

"I don't know, Repen. I still get the feeling we're missing something," Sam says to his partner at the scene of the last warehouse they raided.

Chapter 10

The stale humid air in Las Vegas is almost canceling out the air-conditioned hotel room.

Even though it's a luxurious suite, the people in the room can still feel the heat from outside, probably due to the strenuous pleasant punishment they're putting their bodies through.

"Fuck! Dis is better than gittin' drunk and high on Saint Paddy's Day! Fo' fuck sake man where'd ya git da strength to do dis shit at yer age?" Patrick O'Malley screams as the back of his head hits the wall with his legs up in the air.

"I ain't never felt a white boy so tight!" the much older black man exclaims.

O'Malley's wife is laying on the floor unconscious in a drunken stupor after being brought to two orgasms by the same older black man who's now pounding her husband. With the aid of Cialis, poppers and a little ecstasy along with masculine enhancing vitamins, Peter felt like a man less than half his age. His ragged elderly body enjoys the sensations and energy the drugs and vitamins give him.

"Oh, oooh, you my Irish star. Fuck, fuck yeah!" Peter shouts, his body dripping with sweat.

"I knew I'd enjoy you. I knew I would from the first moment I saw you fight, I knew it. You were so god damn beautiful, you Irish muthafucka!" O'Malley can't even respond because Peter is reaching the spot inside of him that makes him want to explode as he touches himself while being fucked.

Months ago, after the Fisks found out the names of the people who are allied with his old enemy Emmubahta, Peter decides to take a cautious break, knowing his grandson and the people he's working with have things well in hand. And he himself is trained enough to still take care of himself.

If I'm followed and killed, Ivan will avenge me, Peter calmly thinks.

So, he goes back to Vegas to watch the kickboxing matches, mainly to see Patrick O'Malley again. Peter is well aware that he is too old to be chasing after young boys, although for some reason unknown to Peter, he doesn't look as old as most men his age. But something about O'Malley has him intrigued. This time, Peter pays for a seat closer to the ring than when he was here the last time.

The man's moves were superb like the last time Peter saw him fight, even though he lost. Whenever the fighters go back to their corners in between rounds Peter would glance at Patrick and then look away whenever his manager look in Peter's direction. Around about the fourth round of the fight Peter could have sworn O'Malley was looking at him when Peter was looking in his direction. Peter is experienced enough to know the look the Irish fighter is giving him, but Peter decided to play it off and continued to watch the fight, which Patrick O'Malley wins.

A night later, Peter is sitting at a bar connected to one of many casinos in town having a drink.

"Sakes alive a man your age shouldn't be havin' a drink alone, it's right dangerous."

Peter suddenly hears from the back of him in a thick Irish drawl. Peter turns his head and eyes the handsome red headed fighter smiling at him, deep cuts and bruises on his face covered by bandages. Patrick is wearing a tight silk purple button up shirt and form-fitting black jeans.

Peter's warning senses were up because this meeting was telling him too much, but he went along with it anyway. It had been years since he had good sex and deep down, Peter felt he was a dirty old faggot like the rest of the horny old men his age.

"Now, why would it be dangerous fo' me to drink by myself white boy?" Peter asks in a fake slang teasing tone.

"It's criminal is what it is. A fella yer age should be at home watchin game shows wit his wife, lookin at pictures of ya grandkids."

"My wife's dead son," Peter answers sharply.

"That's a shame, der's nobody to keep ya outta trouble, is der now?"

"Ya got it half right, I do have grandkids, but I don't spend my nights lookin' at pictures of 'em." Peter says exaggerating a bit.

The truth was he didn't care if this man was sent to kill him, he wanted him badly, but he still decided to be careful. O'Malley then steps closer to Peter and leans in to whisper in his ear.

"I caught the way you were lookin' at me durin me fight. I may not be from dis country, but even we back home can fathom what dat look means. Thankfully, fur ya sake I got Daddy issues ya can help me work out wit, me wife," he whispers seductively in Peter's ear.

Suddenly, without warning, Peter reaches out and grabs O'Malley in the crotch in full view of customers. But to his surprise, the Irishman is not shocked or embarrassed.

"Fer fuck sakes, dat's a fine ass answer! Ya black fuckers in America are a bold lot aren't cha now!" O'Malley shouts with a broad smile on his face.

"My wife is Spanish Catholic, but she'll like yer feisty old ass!" the Irishman continues to shout, drawing attention. Peter continues to grip O'Malley's crotch tightly as he speaks to him.

"I'm probably older than yo Daddy son, but I will give you points fo boldness, but I jus wanna have a drink alone right now, so you can go fuck yo Spanish wife now or whatever groupie pussy you got waitin' on ya. But next if I see ya again, will talk." At that, Peter releases O'Malley, but he still keeps that broad smile on his face.

"Fuck yeah we'll see each other again, yer a feisty old black fucker."

Peter couldn't believe that Patrick O'Malley had the nerve to be sexy and a racist. The man then walked away from Peter rubbing his sore crotch from where Peter gripped it.

Believing in full disclosure Peter told Ivan about the encounter. Ivan just laughed.

"Damn Grandpa, I never pictured you as a daddy. For such an old head, you still got it," Ivan says while snickering under his breath, but he senses what his grandfather is also thinking.

"So, you think it might be a setup by the people who are after us?"

"I'm sure of it, it seems too convenient. Now, I think I still look good Ivan and I could still draw them my way if I wanted, but come on I'm not stupid. I'm old, I know that. Patrick O'Malley is too young, too handsome and he was too aggressive," Peter expresses with partial disappointment.

"So, Patrick O'Malley is a person you and me don't need to be bothered with?" A sly smile forms on Peter's face after Ivan asks that.

"What?"

"Well, that's not what I had in mind."

"Aw come on Grandpa? You said yourself you're too old for this shit. A guy like that will break your back."

"It's a honey trap, but it still might be fun to find out how far this white boy wants to take this. Part of what he said seemed true. He also mentioned he had a wife who likes to play around with him."

"He has a wife?"

"Yeah, don't be so surprised some women like messing with guys like us. Besides half your boyfriends have wives or girlfriends and I was married to your grandmother, remember. He seemed to really want to lure me in, so I'm gonna take the bait and see where it leads."

Ivan plainly sees where he gets his raunchy sexual appetite from, but he also knows it can get him into trouble.

"Just be careful ok?"

"I can't lose you now. You're the only one who really understands me."

"Don't worry, I didn't survive this long by being careless."

So, months later, Peter arranges to see O'Malley fight in New York city. His seat was in the front row this time. O'Malley beat his opponent to pulp and more all through the match. O'Malley couldn't smiling at Peter whenever he looked his way. After the fight, Peter walks to bar in the arena where the fight took place. His plan was to approach O'Malley as he was walking out of the place with his manager and entourage to see if he was serious or full of shit like Peter partially suspects.

"This shit is ridiculous. I must be out of my fucking mind chasing after a boy less than half my age, it makes no sense," Peter chastises himself.

An hour passes and Peter still hasn't seen the man, so he decides to call it a night and head to the airport to catch a flight out of the country.

Fuck this, I should've known this was a bad idea, Peter thinks. But as he's walking to the exit, a young white woman stops him.

"Excuse me, sir, the man whom fought tonight told me to give you this," she says handing Peter a letter.

"Uh thank you," Peter responds to the woman before she walks away. Peter then opens up the envelope and takes out the letter and reads it.

"Meet me at the Carlton Hotel suite room 321, the concierge will have your description. I told my wife about you and she waits to meet you. Sign; Patrick."

"This is gonna be way more interesting than I thought," Peter muses quickly heading out the door. The Carlton is about an hour away by car. Fortunately, Peter has a rental and makes it there practically speeding within forty minutes. On the way there, Peter takes special drugs in case he's slow to perform. Peter parks a block away from the hotel and then walks to the entrance. The doorman nods his head in greeting to Peter as he comes in.

Peter is not dressed in rags, but in clean casual clothes, however he still feels out of place in this fancy hotel on Park Avenue with everybody wearing expensive suits and other tailored made outfits. Yet as the letter said the concierge was expecting Peter.

"Ah, yes sir, the O'Malleys are expecting you. Here is the card key for the elevator to access the floor their suite is on. Please remind the O'Malleys to call the front desk if they need anything."

"I will, thank you," Peter could have sworn he saw the concierge smile slightly as he turned his head away from him, but when he looks closer the man has a straight face.

"Hello," Peter says to an older white woman getting off the elevator.

"Oh, hello young man. How are you this evening?" she asks.

"I'm fine. How are you, ma'am?"

"Oh, just lovely, have a nice night."

She then walks by him to the front doors.

"Young man, I haven't been called that in decades," Peter says out loud in amazement. He wonders if it was blatant racism or if the woman was half blind.

Peter goes to the left of him after stepping off the elevator and looking at the numbers on a square plaque on the wall. Finding the intended room, Peter knocks on the door.

"Yeah!" a voice yells.

"It's Peter," he answers.

"Who?" the male voice asks.

Peter is irritated at first, but then it dawns on him that he never told Patrick O'Malley his name.

"The man from the bar," Peter reminds him.

After a minute of silence, Patrick answers, "Oh yeah, I've been waitin' on ya!"

When the Irish fighter opened the door, Peter's jaw dropped to the floor. Patrick O'Malley was standing there before him wearing nothing but a red thong, which barely contained his equipment in front. Peter knew the fighter had a nice body from seeing him fight in tight spandex shorts, but seeing more of him in the flesh made Peter's old body come alive.

"Come on in and have a drink lad," Patrick says turning around and walking back into the room, giving Peter a clear view of his well fit ass. As he follows Patrick further into the spacious room, Peter is greeted by the sight of a gorgeous naked, shapely brown skinned woman with long raven-colored hair with smoldering dark green eyes. Patrick then boldly, without warning, reaches out and grabs one of the woman's full breasts and bites her ear.

"Mm ay dis me wife Tapella. She's a fine lass, ain't she?" Patrick asks Peter proudly.

"Hola Bella dama," Peter says to her in Spanish.

"Estoy bien distinguido hombre negro," she answers.

"Vamos, vamos, in English we're all gonna be friends in the immediate future now," Patrick urges.

Tapella sorts of reminds Peter of Clearessa, but Tapella appeared more sensually wilder than Clearessa was in her prime. And wild she was, it didn't appear she believed in trimming her bush like her husband did, it was full and nappy looking. Tapella's next words of course are in English.

"I like fucking old men, people don't think they can please a woman anymore, but I know better. Si, I know a good old man has experience at pleasing a woman. I bet you have lots of experience hombre negro."

"I do ok, but what I know, I mainly learned from my late wife."

"She probably was a good teacher by the way your carry yourself. You weren't afraid to come knowing Patrick had a wife. Tell me, do you prefer men or women more?"

"I prefer men, but I don't mind the company of a woman if the situation warrants it," Peter explains as he starts to undress. When he pulls off his underwear, he's semi-erect.

"You're more experienced than you realize, I can tell," Tapella says while slyly eyeing Peter's growing penis.

Peter walks forward and grips Tapella's ass and rubs Patrick's back at the same time.

"Your wife's an interesting woman."

"Iy dat she is. She knew I fancied other lads' cocks 'fore she married me. On our honeymoon, she used ole Charlie to git me in da mood, right fancy fun dat was."

"Old Charlie, who's that?" Peter asks in puzzlement.

"Honey, why don't cha show our guest Charlie, I'm sure tha bonny lad will git a kick outta 'em."

Tapella gently breaks free from the two men's grip and goes to the nearby chest of draws in the next room. She returns to them holding a long thick vibrator, silver-colored attached to a strap on. Peter's bulge out of his head when sees it.

"He's a beauty ain't he? Changed my life after I met 'em, makes our sex downright monstrous," Patrick says licking his lips in anticipation causing his bulge to grow larger.

Despite being gay, Peter has little experience with toys. With the few women he's been with, including his wife, Peter has always managed to perform and as far as with other men, it has never been a problem for him to get aroused. But Tapella looked determined to take charge of the situation.

"It looks like I get to go first," Peter says volunteering.

Peter is so fixated on the object Tapella is holding that he doesn't notice Patrick remove his thong and go into the bedroom where the chest of draws was and lay on the bed with a fully erect dick waiting for Tapella and Peter to join him.

Tapella turns on the vibrator and glides it across Peter's ass causing it to clinch. She then fastens the buzzing object around her waist. Taking Peter by the hand, she leads him into the bedroom.

"I've been lookin' forward to this since I caught ya lookin' at me when I was in the ring."

"I'll admit I was curious bout chu, but I wondered if you were serious or not."

"And what do ya think now?"

"I think you wanna watch me get fucked by yo wife," Peter answers with cat daddy slang as he gets on all fours on the bed.

Patrick is nose to nose with him waiting for his reaction to his wife entering Peter with her toy. Taking her position behind him, Tapella starts off slowly, inching Charlie into Peter's aging rough ass. It has been nearly fifteen years since Peter has been penetrated, so it's naturally painful and tight for him at first.

"Ooh ah, ahh I fuck! S-shit god damn!" Peter yells. He's standing at full attention now through his penis and Patrick grabs and strokes it.

"Yer feelin it now, aren't cha? Ole Charlie knows you're nice and tight, dat's why he's gotta open ya up. Ya can feel 'em goin deeper up inside ya can't ya? It's what Charlie does, makes a lad or lass surrender to 'em," Patrick says as he continues to use his hand to gratify Peter.

Feeling Peter loosen up, Tapella's pace quickens. Grinding his teeth in frustrating pleasure, Peter grips Patrick's wrist and deeply kisses him. Minutes go by until Peter feels two intense build ups in his body, one good, one embarrassing. It had been so long since he's done something like this that he had forgotten how to properly prepare.

"Oh, oh, oooh God, I, I need to stop now. Now!" But Tapella ignores Peter's words and Patrick is busy milking him and wetting his hand in the process.

"Off now!" Peter orders, getting off the bed causing Tapella to slip out of him and fall to the floor.

"Aw shit ya oozing man," Patrick points out noticing the stool dripping out of Peter's ass. He forgot to take an enema before he came here. Feeling humiliated, Peter runs to the bathroom to further relieve himself. As he's sitting on the toilet, Patrick walks into the bathroom.

"Jus leave me alone man."

Peter says shamefully.

"Don't worry laddie tha lass isn't offended, it happened to me the first time she used Charlie on me, ya jus haveta git use to it. He's right fine when ya do. Come back to bed, we both can rub our cocks inside me wife's furry nice walls til she goes to sleep. Then we can really get to know each other better."

Peter is tempted by Patrick's words, but he still feels a little uneasy about what happened. He felt he needed to be better prepared when he would next meet the O'Malleys.

"That sounds nice, but I think I better call it a night."

"Well, if dat's how ya feel lad I hope to see ya again, it was still nice," Patrick says with a bit of disappointment in his tone.

Peter wipes his ass with toilet paper and flushes the toilet. Peter then pauses to use a washcloth to clean himself with soap. When Peter walks back into the bedroom, he sees Tapella laying on her side with the vibrator laying by the nightstand, her smile is seductive and wanting. Peter can only walk away from her to where his clothes are.

"I look forward to seeing you again Mrs. O'Malley, it was still nice getting to know you."

Peter doesn't even stay in the suite to get dressed, instead he opts to walk out naked holding his shoes and clothes getting dressed by the elevator. It was at night, so Peter figured he probably wouldn't run into anybody in the hallway.

More months go by and Peter indeed meets the O'Malleys again, back in Las Vegas when Patrick was there once more fighting another match.

"Peter me boy it's good to see ya again. Me and Tapella have missed ya."

"Thanks, it's nice to see ya too."

"And so has Charlie," Patrick says in a devious whisper Peter's ear.

"What are we standin' round in the lobby for? Let me ditch me crew right quick and we can go up to the room where Tapella is probably watin'."

"Sure, why not?" Peter answers to Patrick's forward invitation. His manager attempts to say something, but Patrick waves him off as he begins to walk away with Peter.

As suspected Tapella is waiting in the hotel suite. She's wearing a light purple matching lace silk panties and bra with a garter connected to the rim of her panties.

"Es Bueno verte otra ves," she says when she sees Peter.

"Ingualmente," Peter answers back.

"Hey, hey I said only in English now."

Patrick reminds them.

"You don't like Spanish?" Peter asks while wondering why Patrick married a Latin woman.

"Oh lo hago, yo solo prefiero English," Patrick readily answers back.

"Enough talk, we've both wondered if you were jus talk," Tapella sternly demands.

In response, Peter walks over and takes hold of her by the shoulders and kisses her passionately on the lips. Slowly, his lips make their way down to her neck and then to the middle of her panties, which Peter uses his teeth to slide them off. He sensuously and savagely uses his mouth and tongue to gobble up her inner walls and clit, causing it to pucker in his gums. He lifts her up with his mouth still on her clit and carries her to the bed while her husband hungerly watches, getting undressed in the process.

Taking a minute from his feminine meal to take off his mown clothes with a little help from Patrick, Peter then throws them off in a heap on the carpeted floor. His body shows time, but it's still in pretty good shape for a man Peter's age. True to his word, Peter came prepared, taking an enema before he came to the fight along with the proper masculine pills and vitamins.

"Ay, papi, measustastc!" Tapella expresses, breaking her husband's rule as Peter resumes his assault on her quivering mound.

"You like mit don't cha lass? Say ya like it," Patrick urges as he's taking out Charlie and running it against the tips of her full breasts.

From the sensation of what Peter was doing along with Patrick's assault on her tits with Charlie, Tapella has a violent first orgasm. Not giving her time to recover, Peter grabs her roughly by the thighs and enters with his engorged penis. Patrick pulls them both back so Tapella's ass lands on his own waiting erection.

Patrick has taken a little help also after his fight right before he met Peter in the lobby. They go at it for what seems like hours causing Tapella to have two more orgasms along with their own. She then falls asleep on the floor while the two men catch their breaths on the bed.

Resting for an hour, Peter and Patrick then go at it again, just the two of them this time. As Patrick is cursing at Peter about how he's fucking him Peter decides to take this moment to question him.

"Who do you work for? What cell, what black ops agency?" Peter continues to demand. When Patrick doesn't answer him, he grabs him by the throat, pumping inside of him faster.

"You know who. I work for the U.F.C. Ack, ahh, what tha fuck?" Patrick says struggling for breath.

But Peter's grip grows tighter and tighter until Patrick puts his waist and back in a vice grip using his legs. Strange as it sounds, Patrick is kind of enjoying himself. Peter slightly relaxes his hold on Patrick's neck when he feels his back beginning to buckle under the press it's in. Patrick uses this moment to flip Peter off the bed onto the floor.

"Who do I work for? I work for, I work for the U.F.C and sometimes da I.R.A who trained me to be a fighter!" Patrick says in a lustful rage as he lifts one of Peter's legs up and roughly enters him.

"Are ya a fuckin fed? MI6? Are ya Interpol? Are they usin' dirty ole fuckers to seduce suspected terrorists now?" Patrick screams in heightened frustration as he savagely fucks Peter, causing himself to come.

"Now, git tha fuck outta my room!" Patrick says angerly as he throws Peter's clothes at him.

Peter realizes now that he's made a terrible mistake and tries to rectify it.

"I'm sorry, some rogue agents from the government I worked for along with some African guerrilla fighters have been trying to kill me and my family," Peter quickly explains.

"What now?"

"I thought you only came onto me cause you worked for them, but I realized you don't."

"The shocked look on Patrick's face was priceless."

"Are ya tellin me yer a fuckin spy?"

"A former Russian sleeper agent for the defunct K.G.B actually."

"Ya shittin me? Der's no niggers workin for Russia."

"How can a white man with blatant racism have the nerve to approach a black man for sex? And why am I still attracted to him?" Peter wonders to himself.

"There are and have been too, for a long time. The people who are after me are very dangerous, they've already killed my wife."

"You had a wife?"

"Yeah, I already told you that weeks ago."

"I thought you were jus sayin that fer Tapella's sake, so ya wouldn't look bad."

"Yeah? You have a wife. Why's that so surprising? I mean it's no more surprising than a man in his twenties making a pass at a man who's over seventy."

"Shit ya don't look it and I thought you were kinda cute and I thought I could trust ya to be discreet. And me bucko the way ya wore me and me wife out was bonny, til ya tried to off me."

"Sorry bout that, not many young men are bothered with me nowadays."

Once the misunderstandings are out of the way, the two men spend the rest of the night talking.

"Oliver Quartz and Janet Rinka, those are the two rogue agents, now xenophobic terrorists we saw on the cameras in Kazan," Ingramisck says to everyone present.

Ivan, Eleanea and Gregor had already suspected that former agents were involved by how well they observed Peter and Clearessa without being spotted. Naturally Peter came to that conclusion. Rosa just thought the people after the Fisks were clever criminals.

"But it has to be more than them wanting just to kill all the gays in Russia." Gregor says in bewilderment.

"There is, these people want a pure Communist Russia, like it was decades ago when they first killed the last Russian royal family, when blacks and gays were not tolerated."

"Ingramisck that doesn't make any sense, men like Korcoff who were gay existed and flourished in Communist Russia."

"I know Eleanea, I told you all what their goals were, I didn't say they were within reason."

"They shouldn't be too hard to flush out in the open, we've already destroyed several of their safe houses."

"Don't be fooled Ivan, these people managed to be undetected and not seen for years, so they've probably been prepared for an eventual attack. We have to assume they still know more about us than we know about them."

"That's a situation that's quickly changing by the day," Ivan says to Ingramisck. After the briefing in Havana, everyone present promptly leaves Cuba by different modes of transportation.

Next Ivan meets his grandfather at a nautilus and weight-lifting gym in Orlando Florida.

"So, how'd it go with the U.F.C fighter?" Ivan asks Peter, anxious to hear what happened.

"He used to be part of the I.R.A, nothing major, not a spy and he doesn't work for the people we're at war with."

"So was he interested?"

"Let's just say he had interesting ways to express himself."

Ivan was disappointed, he wanted to hear all the juicy details, like how the Irishman looked naked and what he liked to do sexually.

Ivan never mind taking about this sort of stuff with his grandfather because they both had similar tastes.

But Peter was going to keep what happened to himself. Now that he knew who Patrick really was and what he was about, Peter wasn't going to involve him in his family's situation. But then again he made that same type of promise about not telling his grandson about what fully happened to his grandmother and he didn't keep it for long.

"Do you think your plan worked with getting those cops to help us from Chicago?" Peter asks Ivan as they begin to ride a pair of exercise bikes close together.

"Rosa says that our superiors got reliable intel that Sam Givens along with his partner Repen Stello led successful raids on all the places I gave him addresses to. It shouldn't be too hard to persuade him to help us further on the American front against our enemies if the fight happens to spill over here."

"Careful son, he may be police, but he's not corrupt and he still sees you as a criminal he wants to put in prison. White America has never been our friend, especially the police part of it."

"All cops are corrupt in a way Grandpa, either they take bribes, look the other way on certain procedures to get a conviction on criminals or over time they get so jaded that they use whatever means they have just to get the job done. Sam Givens is the latter. If we show him that it's in his best interest as a cop to help us in our fight, he'll be on board. We just have to feed him enough of the truth to make sure he's thinking he's doing the right thing for law and order."

"That might not be easy as you think, white policemen, even sometimes black policemen may sometimes do whatever they can for law and order, but if that doesn't work for them, they'll find some kind of way to shoot you down like a dog. And it happens every day. The news in this country shows us that."

"We won't get gunned down by cops Grandpa, if anything we might get killed in this war or make a misstep and be disposed of by the Bratva, but not by the police."

Taking thirty-five minutes on the bikes, the Fisks then move on to other nautilus machines and spend five minutes on them. They then move to the hand weights and finish their workout with twenty minutes on the treadmills.

"Aw shit this sauna feels good, I needed this."

"I just want to sweat out the uneasiness I got built up in my body," Peter says back to Ivan while they're relaxing in the sauna. Thanks in part to both their training, the Fisk men have a high tolerance to extreme cold and heat, so they sit on the benches without towels around their waists, opting to have them around their necks instead. They bare the heat for ten minutes as other men come and go.

"Hi," a man coming in says.

"Hey, what's up?" Ivan responds. Peter however doesn't speak.

"Do you come here often? I've never seen you here before and I've been coming here for two years," the man then says.

Ivan doesn't see the man at first because he has his towel over his head, but he does notice that the man's speech is sort of slurred. So, Ivan take his towel from his head and looks at the man. By the way one of his arms is situated against his chest and by the way his legs causing him to stand funny, Ivan could see the man was physically handicap.

"Oh, I'm not a member, me and my grandpa are just visiting in town for a little while. We thought while we're here we should checkout a gym."

"Well, you came to the right place, this is a good gym. My name's Chris. What's yours?"

"It's Ivan, it's good to meet you Chris."

"Likewise, I hope you come back again Ivan," the man says smiling through the corner of his mouth. After about four minutes, the man leaves the sauna.

"Bye Ivan," he says right before he leaves. Peter was silent, but took notice of the entire encounter.

"Man, they don't care anymore do they?"

"What do you mean?"

"That gimp was tryin to holla at chu as they say."

"Aw no he wasn't, he was just being friendly, trying to show he wasn't a threat to be afraid of cause of how he looks. I know how that shit feels. Not every man who talks to us with a smile is not trying to kill us or get in our draws."

"Yeah well this one was, handicap or no, gimpy Chris wanted to get to know you better in ways that would probably make even you uncomfortable."

"You trippin' Grandpa, you paranoid about everything, even by the way a person talks to you."

"I have to be and so do you or we're not going to survive," Peter reminds Ivan.

Of course, Ivan knew Peter was right, they had to be on guard for the slightest thing.

Following five more minutes in the sauna, Peter and Ivan step out and head for the showers. There are three other men in the shower room when they entered. Ivan takes a spot farthest away from the entrance and Peter takes a nozzle a few feet away from his grandson. Both Fisk men start out their showers with cold water.

"Damn this shit feels good. I feel like my body is gonna go numb. That sauna was hot, I don't know how your old body can stand it."

"It's been through far worse strain than that over the years, let me tell ya. You're still young, you've yet to experience the true rigors of time," Peter warns Ivan.

During their shower, various different men come in and out. The Fisks don't pay attention until four seven foot tall very dark-colored men come in the shower room. They are all sort of well-built for their heights, one of them has long thick dreadlocks, another has a small well-shaped afro and the other two are bald headed. Taking nozzles across from each other, they speak in an African dialect no one understands in the club. But thanks to Peter's time in Africa, he understands bits and pieces of it.

"What the fuck are they saying?" Ivan silently mouths to his grandfather.

"I think they're talking about seducing some white businessmen's wives for coming into their shops and insulting them or they're insulted the white men's wives tried to seduce them. I'm not really sure, the clearest word I heard was seducing."

Meanwhile, an Asian with a grim scowl peeks his head in. He mutters something in his native foreign language and ducks back out.

The dark men are attractive in a foreign way and Ivan can't help but to glance at one of them.

He hopes that the man didn't catch him looking. But when Ivan turns his head in the tall man's direction, he's staring right at Ivan.

I'm not trying to get into a fight for looking, Ivan cautiously thinks to himself.

Though their conversation appears unimportant, something about the men makes the hairs on the back Peter's neck stand up. One of them eventually leaves while the other three stay. A few minutes later, another of them leaves. The one with the dreadlocks eyes are locked on Ivan. He doesn't think Peter notices, but the other remaining man is messing with one of the fixtures in the wall. To the untrained eye you couldn't tell, but the one with the dreadlocks is inching closer to Ivan subtly while fiddling with the back of his locks. Suddenly, one of the four that left the room shouts something in the same African dialect they were speaking earlier.

"Let's take out these faggots!" Peter hears in their tongue.

"Ivan look out!" But Peter's warning almost comes too late as the one with the dreadlocks goes for Ivan with a sharp combat blade that was hidden in his hair. He lunges for Ivan's throat, but Ivan moves slightly, so he catches him in the shoulder. By the man being taller, Ivan gives him swift kicks to his legs and knees.

As his grandson tackles his assailant, Peter turns to face the one by the wall.

"Your old friend Emmubahta says hello faggot," the man says in English with a thick accent.

He then flings the loosened brick from the fixture he was messing with earlier at Peter. He dodges it, but the man catches Peter in a tackle to the wet floor, making it hard for Peter to maneuver. The man is stronger and bigger than Peter, producing a blade between his teeth, he attempts to slit Peter's neck as they struggle. Peter catches the blade in the palm of his hand, taking it out of the man's teeth.

"You fight well for an old man, but it's no use, you and your family are dead," the man says punching Peter savagely in the face. Peter uses the man's blade to slash him across the eye, he screams, but Peter doesn't let up on his assault.

Ivan is faring better against his opponent. Catching one of his long legs in a breaking grip with his knee into the man's groin.

"Where is your boss!" Ivan demands, his grip tightening.

"Fuck you!" the dread headed man says in defiance.

Next, Ivan tries to break the man's leg, but he uses his free leg to knee Ivan in the back and force him off. While they're busy, Ivan and Peter don't see the other two of the four return carrying machetes, but before they can attack one of them is caught from behind with a flexible wire garret around his throat held by Ingramisck who's wearing only a towel. The last of the four is surprised by the Asian man who peeked in earlier. Sporting his own yakuza tattoos on his body he uses the wall as leverage to leap up and catch the much taller man in the face with a drop kick.

The battle is joined with knife fighting, kick boxing and martial arts. Ingramisck makes short work of his prey, burying the garret deep in his throat. However, the remainder of the fight is taken from them when Rosa comes in wearing workmen's coveralls and a military snipper mask.

"Get down!" she yells. In response, Ivan, Ingramisck, Peter and the yakuza hit the floor and watch as bullets from her Uzi fire into the heads of the three remaining African attackers.

"We have to get out of here now!" Peter orders. Sensing someone is approaching from behind, Rosa turns and aims ready to shoot. Seeing it's the crippled man they spoke to earlier in the sauna, Ivan yells out.

"Rosa stop, he's harmless!"

"Wha—what?" the handicapped man mutters startled.

Seeing the gun pointed at him the man pisses down his leg.

"Go!"

Rosa casually tells the man. He moves as quickly as he can on disabled legs.

"I'm sure somebody heard the bullets Rosa shot. If you don't want to kill everybody in this locker room, we better leave like Peter said," Ingramisck further states.

"Rosa should be the one to go first through the exit to the workout room."

Before Peter can say more, she's already gone leaving behind her mask and Uzi.

"Let's do this shit quietly and not run out drawing attention to ourselves. By the way, where did that yakuza come from?" Ivan asks as they are forming a plan to go, but then he also notices the Asian is also already gone.

"The Japanese owe me a favor. Now, can we go please?" Ingramisck sternly says.

Not bothering to turn off the shower water, three men go back to their lockers, but not before Ivan takes the time to wrap Rosa's gun and mask up in his towel. He puts the bundle under his arm, not feeling shy about walking around naked half erect from the thought of wrestling with another man for his life. He enjoys the awkward stares nowadays. Swiftly getting dressed everyone meets outside in the parking lot across from the gym. They happen to leave just in time because a minute or so later another member of the gym walks into the shower room to discover the carnage.

"Oh my God! What the fuck!" he screams.

"Somebody, somebody get help, help!" he further yells.

"Well, I was right, they did make another move on us. It was a good idea to have Rosa and Ingramisck lag back as backup in case something like this happened, Ivan."

"Thanks, Grandpa. They still got us all under close surveillance somehow, we gotta go after more key members of this group now."

"We have to set a trap for them with the type of bait they can't resist, but to come finish us off personally."

"It'll have to be something major for that to happen."

"I know, which is why we'll have to contact all our sources worldwide to make the plan work, including your friends in Chicago. And your former and present lover may be able to play a part too. Ingramisck how many of the yakuza could we count on to help us? Or was it a one-time thing of a closet lover."

"He's placed pretty well in his organization, he could rally about twenty men to help us if I asked."

"Good, we may need them before this is over. Let's go someplace more secure, out in the open like this it's too easy to be watched and listened to."

Following Peter's suggestion, the small group get into different vehicles and drive in various directions to throw off any tails that might follow.

A week afterwards, four people meet in the country of Italy in the city of Venice at an old paper making factory. The four people present are a woman and three men, two of men are black and the third man is a white native Russian like the woman.

"You failed, Emmubahta! You said they were four of your best!" the woman yells at him.

"They were Janet, you and Oliver didn't tell me they had yakuza fighting with them. Your niece didn't mention this to you either, Marvin?"

"We only speak in coded emails every several months. She doesn't want to be discovered by anyone, so she doesn't speak to her father in anyway, so she wouldn't know about the yakuza's involvement," Marvin explains to Emmubahta.

"Our goal is the same, to get rid of your half-brother's kind along with his freakish grandson. This would be only the beginning. Their deaths will make the Russian government get rid of Korcoff's lingering influence on their own," Oliver continues to reiterate.

"I warned you all this would not be as easy as you first thought shortly after you had an agent approach me about joining your little cabal. Just because they're gay doesn't mean my half-brother and nephew are helpless flower arrangers, they're fierce killers. You've fought Peter for years Emmubahta, you should've known better. Sending men in without properly briefing them on what they were up against was foolish."

"I did, but it appears we all underestimated Peter and Ivan along with the ties Ivan has with the Bratva and law enforcement in certain cities in America."

"His ties with the Bratva are a problem, destroyed safe houses, resources and dead operatives prove that. Fortunately, we've studied Ivan more closely than you think and I believe we may have a way of subtly eliminating Ivan. Once he's gone along with his allies in the Bratva, his grandfather will be easier to get rid of."

"How?" Marvin and Emmubahta ask in unison to Janet.

"Patience, it will not happen right away. This war is taking longer than expected, but we will win."

"We also have an ace in the hole as the Americans put it. We have a mole in the Bratva organization, someone well-placed enough to where they can help bring about the kill order on Ivan when the time is right," Oliver adds. Janet and Emmubahta show agreement, but Marvin still remains skeptical.

After the meeting, the small assembly disperses and heads for different flights out of the country. Marvin opts not to go right away. He has some thinking to do and he couldn't do it around the others.

"Jonah made a mistake favoring Peter all those years before he died. Given what I know, he didn't treat Eric hardly any better than me and he was his son like Peter. And what a pathetic nigga Jonah was, runnin round on mama, makin her live in misery while he was Korcoff's toy. His son forced his own daughter to carry her rapist's child instead of letting her get an abortion like she wanted."

Marvin's mind continues to produce thoughts of his hated half-brother. He's known for quite some time that Jonah wasn't his father. Years ago, his real father tracked him down through his other half-brother Eric. Eric called and asked Marvin to come to America to see him to discuss something important.

Marvin thought this was strange because he just visited Eric and his family weeks ago.

"It's really important, I need you to come here if you can," Eric urged.

"Alright, I'll see what I can do," Marvin answered.

Thankfully, Marvin was high up enough in the military to get an emergency pass to temporarily leave his post again. Marvin caught the red eye to the city where Eric lived in America. When he came to Eric's house, Marvin was greeted by an older man he'd never met before, but who looked familiar to him for some reason.

"Hello Marvin," the man said with a kind smile as he stood up and held out his hand to shake. Marvin reluctantly shook the man's hand.

"Uh, hello, who are you?" Marvin asked frankly.

"I'm Otis Fisk, your father."

The shock to Marvin wasn't that he wasn't Jonah's son, but the fact that he was still related to him by blood.

"You're my father? How are you related to Jonah?"

"I'm his uncle, we both knew your ma when they still lived in U.S."

This conversation happened twenty years ago, but Otis told his estranged son everything, especially about Martha and Jonah. The affair he had with his mother, how Jonah got a boy he was messing with lynched, his great-grandmother sending Otis away up North shortly after her grandson and his wife left the country and why it took so long for Otis to contact Marvin.

"Yo ma didn't have any livin family in da U.S when you were born, so she didn't see any reason to contact me cause she figured I wouldn't care."

"Did Jonah know about you and mama?"

"Probably so, you and I have the same cheekbones and eyes."

He knew! That's why he never showed me any love or attention! Instead, he gave it all to Pete, Marvin thought in a rage.

After this conversation, Jonah and Marvin never spoke again, despite the urging from his mother to do so. He never confronted Martha with the truth either, even though she suspected he knew the truth, especially after he decided to go to Otis's funeral. Until the day Martha died, Marvin was disappointed in his mother staying with a man who only half loved her.

For some reason, Marvin always chose to be close to Natleaha, despite his hatred for her father. And he was greatly concerned when she disappeared out of public sight away from her parents.

But he knew her better than she suspected. Her motivation, her habits, through these things Marvin was able to track Natleaha down. The whole family knew she was pregnant, but the details about the father of the baby were vague and Marvin didn't want to ask Peter or Clearessa because he couldn't stand talking to either of them more than he had to.

So, he asked Natleaha herself when he found her. She then reluctantly told Marvin the whole story about how his grandnephew was conceived. Marvin understood why his niece couldn't be a mother to Ivan and he wondered why the boy drew breath in the first place.

He hated his brother and wife even more for practically forcing Natleaha into having the baby. To Marvin, Peter and Ivan were both blights on the family who needed to be dead in the ground like Jonah.

Him and his damn deal with Korcoff. Mama should've left his ass and headed back to the states as soon as Jonah took Korcoff up on his offer. Natleaha wouldn't have been in that situation where she got raped if not for Korcoff, Marvin thought with venom.

So, when somebody working for Oliver and Janet contacted him with an offer to join their makeshift cabal, he had to hear them out. And he was glad he did when he found out the group's main mission, to destroy his half-brother and grandson and those like them.

Ok so they mean mainly those like them in Russia, but as long as Peter and that white devil wound up dead it didn't matter, thought Marvin.

The group collectively may have come up with a plan that might work. Natleaha wasn't the only in the family with pacific habits. Though he's had lovers his own age, Ivan's always looked for a father figure in some, mainly in the special forces lieutenant.

Even in that pervert teacher that the group found out molested Ivan. The cabal was thorough, Marvin had to give them that. They believed in doing their homework. So, if they think they have the right bait for his freak nephew, Marvin was completely on board.

Chapter 11

"Yes, the village of Tanzenrowby is twenty miles east in that direction," the store merchant says pointing his finger in the direction he mentioned.

"Thank you, you've been a big help."

Natleaha answers with a friendly smile placing her hand on the merchant's shoulder. Minutes after she leaves his shop, he feels a sharp pain in his chest.

"Wh—what's happening, I can't breathe," he stutters, but before he can call for help from a nearby store, the man drops to the floor. Sadly, the man was dead as soon as he laid eyes on Natleaha. It was one of the main precautions she used to keep from being identified and probably caught.

As she is driving on the rough African terrain, Natleaha sends a text message on her cell phone.

"I have the location, sending it to you now. Leave the agreed package in a box there away from prying eyes. Make sure you're gone before I get there," Natleaha texts.

"Of course, like always," they respond back.

Natleaha first contacted this person through one of her old sources from the K.G.B ten years ago. They've never met face to face, only talked on the phone with the person on the other end using a voice distorter. So Natleaha doesn't know if the person she's talking to is a man or a woman. But however, they've played by her rules and given her proper currency and locations that are places to hide in exchange for intel on people and places.

The information Natleaha was giving up was unimportant to her, as long as the person known to her as Zee kept their end of the bargain. At first, she thought Zee was her uncle Marvin, especially after he was the only member of her family to find her. But she quickly realized Zee couldn't be him because Marvin wouldn't waste time with this type of subterfuge on her.

But he did give her a crypted warning when they last spoke a year ago.

"War is coming Leaha, a war to partially cleanse our family."

"Uncle Marvin what the hell are you talking about?"

"Some people in the Russian government want to bring things back to the way they were in Russia before people like Korcoff and your father corrupted it."

"Why, because they're gay? That makes no sense, I fuck other women as well as men. Does that make me a blight on Russia too?"

"I don't know, but that's why I want you to stay out of this. It's between me along with the people I work with and your father with your unwanted son that was forced on you."

This is crazy, my father still has connections in the government due to years of loyal service and Ivan is with the Bratva with a lover and friend in special forces and a computer tech. They can't hope to possibly win, even with my uncle's help, Natleaha carefully thought.

She didn't have a chance to further voice her concerns because Marvin ended the video chat. She was aware things were getting ugly when she received news of her mother's death, which prompted this months' long quest to help save her father.

Ivan was a lost cause to her, but in spite of everything, she didn't want to see the last person she loved in the world to die horribly. So, this intel in a box in a small village in Nigeria would be her best hope in helping save her father. Naturally, after she receives this package, Natleaha would probably need more help along with whatever that package was.

She arrived in Tanzenrowby within an hour and no one bothered Natleaha as she went to an old wooden building in the village. She quickly finds the box in the building, then wearing leather gloves she carefully lifts the box and tears it open with a knife. Inside is a small package wrapped in thick plastic.

"What are these?" Natleaha asks herself curiously when she rips open the plastic to find three DVD's. She didn't have a portable computer with a DVD player on it, Natleaha would have to wait until she was back at one of safe houses in another country.

"Naw I got a better idea. I know who could probably help move this along weather they realize it or not," she said out loud to herself as she left the building, then the village.

"We haven't heard from the Russians in months now. Maybe we did put a bigger dent in their operations than we thought."

"Not likely, they've been operating in secret and in full view of the public since before you and I were born. If anything, they gearin' up for sumthin' big, we jus' don't know what."

"Well, we better find out what it is and fast cause the Captain wants us to concentrate on other crime groups in the city. He considers the Russian problem dead, at least for the time being."

"I gotta gut feelin dat might be a mistake."

Just then, the phone rings on Sam Givens' desk at the 21st precinct.

"Hold on for a sec," Sam tells Repen as he picks up the phone.

"Yeah hello."

"We need to talk," the strong female voice says to Sam from the other end.

"Who is dis?" Sam demands in irritation.

"My Mr. Givens, don't tell me you've forgotten me, it hasn't been that long since we first met. I thought we had a connection when we saw each other in your apartment."

It takes Sam a minute to remember, but it eventually comes back to him.

"What tha fuck! Connection? You tried to fuckin kill me!"

"I didn't try anything, those shots were just warnings, if I wanted you dead we wouldn't be having this conversation. You're a pawn in a larger game, an important pawn, but a pawn nonetheless. And you're correct in assuming that the Russian mafia have something bigger in mind, it's just not with your city."

"How the fuck does she know what we're talkin bout? The place can't be bugged can it?" Sam wonders in shock. But he right away surmises that this woman knows a whole lot more about this situation than he'll ever guess.

"What do you want to talk about?"

"Not over the phone, I'm afraid our business will have to be done in person."

"You can come to my station. I could give you directions."

"I don't think so and I'm sure you're not comfortable with me coming to your place again."

"Where then?"

"A place where you met some people we both know, the bar called Lelha's. I'm sure you'll feel safe meeting there."

"The night after tomorrow at 9:30pm. I'm off then."

"Good, don't be late," she warns right before she clicks off.

"What was dat all about?" Repen quizzes his partner when Sam hangs up the phone.

"I'm not sure, but I think I've met a player who has more pieces to the puzzle and who's five moves ahead of me."

Sam gives Lelha a heads up about what type of company to expect the next night.

"A gang of 'em like last time?"

"No, supposedly just one person this time, but still be on your toes, dis chick is still dangerous," Sam advises.

Natleaha arrives on the appointed night an hour before her meeting with Sam at Lelha's. She finds the atmosphere more to her liking than she thought. Though she preferred to have men as long-term lovers, she also liked the physical company of other women, especially beautiful women like herself. And it appears to be plenty of all kinds of women here, besides the butch stereotype. And if Lelha's reputation is to be believed, Natleaha could find women of similar interests here.

"You seem miles away," someone says to Natleaha snapping her out of her thoughts. She turns to the direction of the voice and is staring at a cute redhead.

"What are you thinking about? It must be really serious to ignore all these gorgeous women here."

"Not that serious, I was only wondering about a little something that was on my mind. Killing time until the person I'm waiting on shows up," Natleaha answers back to the woman.

"She must be really special for you to think about her so much even when she's not around."

"I'm waiting for a man actually."

"Oh."

"No, no it's not like that, it's a business meeting. He's a friend of the owner," Natleaha reveals honestly. The redhead almost right away loses interest.

"Oh well good luck with your meeting," the woman says then walks away.

Natleaha chuckles over the exchange. She spends the next fifty minutes soaking up the ambiance of having two glasses of fruit juices. Several more minutes pass by when Sam walks in. Natleaha notices he doesn't appear uncomfortable or out of place in a lesbian bar, feeling he has to assert his manhood.

"So, what is it you need to talk about?" Sam asks Natleaha while sitting at her table.

"First, let's go to a backroom and ask your friend if she has a laptop we can use."

"What for?"

"You'll see. Now ask her to point out a back-room and loan us her laptop," Natleaha orders. Seeing is how he figures he has little choice. Sam convinces Lelha to let them use her computer in her office. When it looks like Sam is about to ask more questions when they're in the office, Natleaha cuts him off.

"All will be revealed in a moment," she states pulling out the DVD's she got in Africa.

She then slips the first of them in the disk playing section of the computer. An elderly woman comes across the screen and Natleaha knows who it is right away, Isha Vamitri, Korcoff's wife. Natleaha hadn't thought about her in years. The tape is dated five years ago and although Isha was fifteen years younger than Korcoff, she would still be pretty much up in age today.

"Who's this?" Sam asks.

"Somebody I thought I would never see again."

When the old woman sits in a comfortable chair she begins to talk.

"I'm not long for this world, which is why I instructed someone ahead of time to give these tapes to members of the Fisk family I trust. By the time, you get to view these you'll know all of you are in grave danger. My husband was quite busy before he met Jonah and his wife, but hardly any of his diversions panned out as well as the Fisks, which caused great resentment among his rivals. Chief among his enemies were Jainko Rinka and his half-brother Marko Quartz. Their mother happened to be descended from the last of the nobility that barely survived from being wiped out like most of the rest shortly before the beginning of communism.

"To her credit, she was a seductive beauty with a political savvy mind that rivaled any great leader. Through careful planning, she sought out two officers in the ruling Communist party. One of them, Rinka eventually becomes a powerful scientist and spy in the intelligence community and the other Quartz, quickly rose through the ranks of the military. The two men, for some reason or other, never crossed paths until years later when it was revealed that each of them had fathered a son by the same woman. Each boy had been given their father's last name. As the years passed, each boy followed in their father's footsteps in the military and secret service."

"The two young men became rising stars in the U.S.S.R during the reign of Stalin, but other men were gaining notice in Russia, namely my husband Korcoff. Not as popular as Marko and Jainko, but still becoming recognized for his radical ideas for intelligence gathering for Russia. However, Korcoff had one major Roadblock that stood in his way of advancing more publicly in Stalin era Russia. And you can probably guess what that block was. So, it was decided that officially Korcoff would wield modest power in the government, but unofficially he would have unlimited resources to realize his vision. Despite the official standing of Korcoff, many knew the truth, including Marko and Jainko."

The first DVD ends.

So, it wasn't an accident that my grandparents met Korcoff, Natleaha thinks.

"So, what does this have to do with what's goin' on in Chicago and other states dealin' with the Russian mob?" Sam asks anxiously while having no idea what he was watching.

"Shh, be patient it's getting to that part," Natleaha tells him as she takes out the first DVD and puts in the second. Pressing the mouse, the disk begins to play and continue the story.

"Korcoff's experiment was fully underway, but years went by and it yielded nothing of potential. His superiors were getting impatient and the vultures were circling as they say. Then in 1930, a few years before Korcoff even met the Fisks, he found a young foreigner. He saw a chance in this strapping young Amish man who had been shipwrecked and separated from his family."

"The young man had been visiting relatives in Europe with other members of his family and were returning to an Amish community in the state of Ohio when the ship he was traveling on got caught in a severe storm. One of the relief worker who happened to secretly work for Korcoff brought the strange looking young man to his attention."

"So, he arranged to have the Amish man brought to his office. The man spoke a strange Swiss German language, but fortunately Korcoff spoke a little German. Foremost in the man's mind was to go home to his family. Korcoff told him for that to happen he had to work for a time in Russia. The man realized he had little choice, but to agree. The man however was clever enough not to give Korcoff his real name, as a matter of fact, he didn't give him any name, so Korcoff named him Statin in mock honor of Stalin."

"Korcoff almost right away began training Statin as a honed weapon and spy to use against his enemies within his country. Korcoff knew Rinka's and Quartz's deep resentment of him and what he was and believed that they would strike against him given the proper chance. So, using Statin, Korcoff struck first. Statin gained sensitive information about Marko Quartz and Jainko Rinka by seducing Marko's wife and Jainko's daughter. No one's sure what the information was, but it had to be damning enough to all their superiors for Marko and Jainko to resign from their posts and go into exile.

"Rumor has it Statin left Jainko's daughter pregnant. Both families swore revenge no matter how long it took. But Korcoff was more patient than he seemed, he knew he would be ready for whatever the two families had to throw at him. Statin meanwhile within the few years he trained under Korcoff learned a great deal, for instance smuggling. How to smuggle oneself from different places to be exact. Korcoff was in the process of beginning his search for his rogue agent when he met the Fisks."

The second disk ends.

"Your name is Fisk. You're part of the family this woman keeps talking about?"

Natleaha doesn't answer Sam, she only unloads the disk and puts in the third. Shortly after, it begins playing Natleaha gets a shock.

"Natleaha, I know you're the one who's probably watching this and some years have passed since I've recorded this. Jainko and Marko's children are starting to gain momentum in the government. It's obvious what their ultimate goals are. I'm dying now, but I have to tell you this, your father and your young son are in grave danger as I mentioned."

"Be careful of who you trust and be careful of your uncle, his loyalties to your family are close to nil and he hates you deeply. Marvin might have affection for you, but your family as a whole, I wouldn't be sure. But I am sure you'll find out the identity of Rinka and Quartz's children, if you already haven't. Also, Korcoff eventually found Statin in the state of Ohio at another Amish community and he still has the information that could damage these two families."

"Find Statin, he can help you. Remember, Natleaha, stay strong, your family can weather anything if they put their minds to it. Jonah proved this fact decades ago."

As the disk ends, Natleaha suspects something about her unseen contact Zee.

"Could Zee have been working for Isha?" Natleaha asks herself.

"Hey are ya done yet? I got some paper work to do before I close!" a voice suddenly yells banging on the door.

"We'll be out in a minute!" Sam yells back. Just then, he takes a good look at Natleaha, he concentrates on her eyes. They look familiar to him for some reason. His cop instincts help him make the connection.

"Wait a minute, you're that guy's mother, the boy that woman on the disk was talking about. The man who pulled me into whatever your family's got goin on."

Natleaha shoots mental daggers at Sam when he confronts her with this.

"He's not my son and I suggest if you want to keep breathing you won't say that to me again, Mr. Givens." Sam remains silent as she gathers the disks and leaves the office. The cold rage he saw in her eyes at that moment was chilling.

Early the next morning, Sam's cell wakes him.

"Yeah?" he answers.

"Man, you gotta get in here, you've got several messages from the albino sayin he's got more tips fo us to act on."

"Does he now?" Sam answers Repen with an edge to his voice at the mention of the Russian albino.

"Don't pop a blood vessel. I'm on my way, I wanna talk to him too."

"Al'ight man. I'll holla at chu," Repen says then clicks off.

Rage didn't begin to describe how Sam felt at this minute. He didn't like being used like a pawn on a chess board and now more than ever he was determined to get straight answers. Arriving at the precinct, he called the number Ivan left with his messages.

"Oh hell! I've been trying to get in touch with you. Did you change your cell number?"

"No, it was outta minutes and I just got it filled yesterday. Look, never mind about that, we need to talk."

"That's why I've been trying to contact you. I was thinking we could do more business together so to speak, it would be greatly beneficial for you like last time, but there might be other unexpected things you might have to do. The climate is changing on my end, changes that might spill over into your part of the world."

Sam couldn't believe this guy. After all that's happen, he was asking in around about way to practically break the law.

"Naw, naw 'fore anything else happens we need to meet face to face, there's some things we gotta discuss that I found out."

"I don't feel comfortable coming to your job."

"That's fine we can meet at the same place as before."

"No, I think we ought to meet in a more open place. How about this evening by the warehouse waterfront?"

"We could do this, this afternoon if you want? My Captain can spare me for an hour during my shift as long as I keep my radio on."

"If you want, this afternoon at the waterfront it is."

"Good, 1:00pm," Sam hangs up after he sets the time. "Repen, get a couple of guys we both trust who are off duty to meet us at the waterfront at 1 and a sniper from swat too."

"Al'ight I'm on it."

Ivan is sitting in a fancy hotel suite looking out the window on a cool autumn day. Rosa is by the front door with 38. Caliber strapped to her thigh in a holster while three-foot soldiers of the mob stand strategically in different areas of the suite.

"Why did he suggest to meet you before you did? Do you think your enemies got to him?"

"I'm not sure, but we'll find out soon enough later on," Ivan answers back to Rosa.

As benefits of his rank in the organization as a lieutenant, Ivan was given men to work under him. But by the Bratva standards they're considered expendable rejects, which is the main reason they were given to Ivan to command because the Bratva kind of consider Ivan a renegade in their organization.

The men present know that working with Ivan is almost certain suicide at this moment, but these men are fierce fighters, which suits Ivan, the rest of his family and allies just fine. Unfortunately, none of these men can speak a lick of English, so Ivan or Rosa have to go through the trouble of translating for people who don't speak Russian.

"What should we do until then? 1:00pm is almost five hours away."

"What else, Rose, we wait and prepare. Our men are ready for anything."

"Let's hope so, it would be a shame if you got yourself killed in this conflict, I would feel I failed at my job of watching you," Rosa sincerely says.

Ivan could tell she was showing her feelings through her steely exterior. He felt a certain affection for her after all the time they've spent together. It wasn't love or attraction, more like a deep friendly respect.

Though Ivan was mostly an assignment for her, Rosa couldn't deny that she was starting to become attracted to Ivan in a way. She has never found black men attractive, especially albino, but it was something about his lack of inhibitions, about being naked in front of her or showing physical affection toward his male lovers. But for some reason, she couldn't see the attraction Ivan had for the midget Emmanuel, also Emmanuel still liked women too or so he believes and he made a pass at Rosa, which she didn't like.

"Oh, hey mami you guard Ivan? Si, what else do you?"

Emmanuel boldly asked one day when Ivan and his people were Emmanuel's home country for a drug exchange.

"You little cockroach. You dare try to touch me?" Rosa muttered in Russian mixed with Spanish.

Ivan had to break it up before she broke Emmanuel's neck. After that, Emmanuel didn't go near Rosa.

A half an hour before the meet, Ivan orders his three guards to get ready to leave. Two of them leave the suite to get the car while one stays behind with Rosa to watch Ivan's back as they exit the room. Sam and his people are already at the waterfront warehouse along with the sniper hidden at a safe distance ten minutes ahead of schedule.

Ivan and his men ride in two bullet proof cars. Three blocks away from the waterfront Rosa gets out of the car to scout the area for hidden gun men. Both of Ivan's cars pull up to Sam's position. One of Ivan's men walks with him as the other two stay with the vehicles. Ivan and Sam silently square off against each other with their stares for a minute when Ivan decides to be one to break the tension.

"It's good to see you again, Mr. Givens," Ivan says breaking the silence.

"Yeah, let's cut the bullshit pleasantries, shall we? I got a visit or should I say a call that led to a meeting with a person that left me in a bad way the last time we crossed paths."

"I'm sorry to hear that," Ivan half-heartedly responds.

"Are you now? Well, this person showed me some disks that had some answers about you and your family, also along with more questions. For instance, did you know that the person who shot me was your mother? She was the one who showed me the disks on the computer too."

Now it is Ivan's turn to be stunned this time.

"My mother?"

"The woman who happened to shoot me in my own apartment months back."

"What makes you think this woman you met was my mother?" Ivan asks in an attempt to sound coy and try to see how much the cop really knows.

"Natleaha, name sound familiar? An old woman on the disk said her name along with your great grandfather's, Jonah and an uncle named Marvin. Somebody's gunin' for your family for a twisted purity reason. I could tell Natleaha was your mother by the way she looked at me when I confronted her about it."

"There are those in my home country as you call it, who want to see me and people like me erased. But how did Natleaha contact you and why?"

"That I'm still not quite sure about. She just showed up in my apartment one day awhile back and only a little over a day ago she called me at my precinct. Is this thing with your family one of the reasons you're playin' fast and loose with your mob bosses?"

"Partially, but there are some in my organization that feel as my enemies do, which is why I've helped you thin the herd as it were of my superiors minor holdings to see if you were up to the task, a task Natleaha seems to believe you might be able to handle."

"What task? What the fuck are you talking about?"

"The task of being my family's ally. I've done research on you Mr. Givens, you hate racism and prejudice of any kind. You had a cousin who was gay bashed when you were a teenager, did you not?"

"And you watched the animals who did it go free. Well, these are the same type of animals my family is fighting, only they're more powerful and dangerous."

"And you think because you know about a relative of mine that I'll fight a private war with you? Naw, uh, uh, I don't think so. I'm an officer of the law, I uphold the law and punish those who break it. I don't go around breaking it, even if I don't always agree with how it works. You and people like your mother probably could never understand that."

"I understand revenge, which is what I'm sure you crave more than anything. In a way, you could get back at the type of people who killed your cousin, give you a sense of peace."

"Sense of peace? Shit, we wouldn't even be having this conversation if you had been more careful. You wouldn't have even bothered to even learn my name."

"Then why did Natleaha? She must have discovered what you secretly desired way before I did."

"You may have given me a few tips to action, but that doesn't mean you can twist me around like a pretzel. If you want pawns to sacrifice in your fight to save your own ass, then look someplace else cause I'm not the one."

"It's not about sacrifice, it's about stopping an evil before it gets too powerful. If what I suspect you've learned, you realize these people who are trying to destroy me and my family won't stop with us in Russia. They'll spread their ideals and beliefs in other parts of the world, namely right here in America. History has taught us people like this start world wars that kill millions. You can help me stop them now, which will serve as a warning to anybody else who believe being different makes you a weak abomination to be destroyed."

This guy is still full of shit, he just wants to save his own ass, but he does have a point, Sam thought. He saw the DVDs, he heard what the old woman was saying, these people the albino's family was facing were bent on revenge and destruction on a global scale if given half the chance.

"Give me a week. I'll have an answer for you then."

Sam says to Ivan's proposal.

"Til then," Ivan says and turns and walks back to his car. Sam's not sure yet, but he's tempted to throw his hat into the ring.

"How did it go?" Rosa asks during the ride back to the hotel.

"We have our ally in America," Ivan says with a broad smile.

They say anything can happen in New York, that people in the city are so jaded that they couldn't be surprised or shocked by anything they've heard about or seen. But some might disagree with that assumption if they witnessed what's been going on in this fancy brownstone apartment located in Park Avenue. Peter arranged to meet Patrick at the brownstone Patrick rents whenever he's in town.

After not seeing Peter for weeks, he was beginning to wonder if the old man had forgotten about him.

Tapella didn't seem to mind when Peter said he wanted to see Patrick alone for a personal talk. She was fully aware that her husband messed around with other people without her. The two men met the day after Peter called Patrick.

"So, what do ya wanna talk about?" Patrick casually asks once they're alone.

Peter responds by slamming the Irishman hard against the wall and deeply tongue kissing him, nearly cracking the wall with Patrick's head.

"I need a favor," Peter says in a deep seductive voice as he bites on Patrick's earlobe and reaching down his pants.

And just like that they're out of their clothes in record time. No place is untouched as Peter erotically wrestles Patrick all over the place, knocking over chairs, pictures on the wall and other things. Peter is fully medicated with his enhancements going toe to toe with his much younger lover.

"Mother of Christ! Yer fuckin' crazy amazin' is what chu are!" Patrick screams as Peter mounts him into several orgasms soiling out three condoms.

When Peter wasn't doing that, he was sucking Patrick off violently causing the man to grunt roughly. The experience was taxing on Peter, but he knew it would be worth it if he got what he wanted. By then, Patrick was practically foaming at the mouth and breathing heavily.

"So, will you help me? Help me fight a war? Your friends in the I.R.A will be taken care of financially," Peter manages to say in an exhausted breath.

"Bloody hell! I should've never told ya bout dat, no matter how good yer old ass and cock are. This is a private matter, the army would kill me whole family fer promisin' them fer matters dat don't concern them," Patrick expresses in frustration.

"It doesn't have to be you personally, maybe some members who are similar to you and me who would be sympathetic to my family's plight. Don't tell me you've never messed with some members who were closeted, especially when you were younger. None of the older Irish council members didn't have sense enough to make a pass at you?"

Patrick grows silent at Peter's words.

"Dis is jus fun fer me, not a lifestyle."

"I know they couldn't have been too pleased when you married a Latina woman."

"Who I marry has nuthin' to do wit the army, only being loyal to the fight."

"But in a way this a fight for people like us."

"Not us, you. I'm fine wit me life, nobody's tryin to kill me and my family, jus yers. Yer in a sorry state ole boy, but there's nuthin' I can do bout it."

Suddenly, without warning, Peter flips Patrick on his stomach on the hard Italian wood floor.

"What the fuck are ya doin?" Patrick exclaims in shock.

"Helping you change your position," Peter answers firmly.

Patrick is young and strong, but Peter has leverage over him. For ten minutes, Peter relentlessly plows into him causing Patrick to feel like he's being torn apart. But part of him is getting sick pleasure from being abused like this.

"Alright, alright!" Patrick screams as he manages to push Peter off him.

Asshole-blooded, Patrick speaks in a whimper tinged with a hint of excitement.

"I, I know who might can help ya, but he'll want payment."

"That's fine, I told you my family can pay whatever your men want."

"Are ya sure bout dat, dis guy's a sadist and a harden killer. He's busted outta two British prisons where he was servin' time fer acts he did fer the I.R.A., they can barely control 'em."

"What will he want to fight for my family?"

"Underaged boys," Patrick answers in a shaky voice.

Peter doesn't even know how to think about agreeing to terms of a man he's never met, but for his family's sake, he does.

"He'll get his payment after my family's war is done. When can I meet this man?"

"Next week at the earliest in Canada. He's paranoid bout comin' to the states or Britain."

Peter agrees to the meet.

The following week, Peter is introduced to the man that's supposed to help him in Quebec.

Peter gets the shock of his life when he sees the man is black like him. One of his eyes is missing and he has thick dreadlocks and a gold tooth he showed off when he smiled at Peter as he said hello.

"What skills do you have?" Peter asks the man in an effort to resist the urge to look at the hole where his missing eye used to be.

"Heh, heh I can blow mass shit up, I'm good wit guns and breakin' necks," he replies with an Irish drawl, but not as thick as Patrick's.

"Leave us."

"Why?" Patrick asks.

"Cause me and your Black Irish friend are gonna talk about stuff that could cause you to lose your career if you overheard," Peter explains. So, Patrick walks out of the room.

"Ay it must be nice and bonnie ta shag a lad young enough to be yer grandson. I bet he whimpers like a babe every time yer up in 'em," the man comments after Patrick left the room.

"We're not here to discuss that, we're here to discuss what you'll be doing for my family."

"Ay I'll help ya kill some Russians who are tryin to dead ya. Race and class wars are right rough, gets bloody on both sides. Me and me mates have been tryin to off da brits fer time on end. All sides round hate us fer what we are, but they sure do love usin us ta die in their fights."

"What do I call you?"

"The name's Jack O'Connor. Yer friend told ya bout me payment?"

"Yes he did."

"So ya know I won't put in a day's work til I'm properly paid."

"Don't worry your payment's here. You can come in now!" Peter says loudly prompting the door to the room to open again. A young boy who looks barely fifteen walks in looking clueless.

"Uh hi," the boy nervously says rubbing his arm. O'Connor can't take his eyes off the boy, licking his lips with a predator's stare.

"I'll expect you to be ready to leave with me in two hours after you've had your payment," Peter says before he steps out of the room.

O'Connor doesn't answer, instead he stays fixated on the boy. Peter hated that Jack firmly refused to be paid after his job for the Fisks was done, but these were desperate times and so Peter had to make a desperate decision.

Nonetheless, a smug grin forms on Peter's face. The boy Jack O'Connor is with is not a boy at all, but a twenty-three-year-old short actor who's shaved and waxed all over his body to give the illusion of a young teenage boy. It was a plus that the man has never been anally penetrated, unfortunately that's soon about to change, but for the five thousand dollars Peter paid him, the man can endure it. Peter had no qualms about the deception. Simply, there were some lines he wouldn't cross, even for family.

Chapter 12

"You've been working with the people out to destroy us Uncle. Don't bother trying to deny it, I have proof," Natleaha says in anger to Marvin while she was showing him a video of him with his partners meeting in Venice on an e-book device.

Marvin couldn't believe it. Janet and Oliver swore that the location was secure and no one was observing them. As if reading his mind, Natleaha explains.

"If you're wondering, my source hacked into the network of one of the guard's cell phone, causing it to click on and record. Later on, when the guard put down his phone to shower, my source had someone sneak into his room, download the video and transfer it to this. Why Uncle? You know people like this won't just stop at killing men like my father, your brother and my son. They'll kill me too, Uncle Eric and his family because people like this believe that they carry the defective gene of what made my grandfather and the rest."

"Why, you ask me why? Because people like Peter don't deserve to live and neither did Jonah. He never cared about my mother, messing around with that boy behind her back thinking that nobody knew. It was no wonder she went to Jonah's uncle for affection. And my so-called grandmother, shit, she let Jonah get away with it."

"Letting him drag my mother away from her home in America to a wasteland in Russia when she was pregnant with me by your grand uncle Otis. Look at how Peter treated you when you were raped? Forcing you to carry that monster, your own mother doing nothing, letting your father ruin your life. I didn't shed any tears when that bitch was killed and I notice you didn't either. You know I'm right. This has to be done."

"But they'll kill me too like I said, I like women too as well as men. Does that make me any different from my father?"

"You only acquired that habit of wanting other women to work better in the field. You never were really like that before then. Besides my allies don't even know you exist, you can stay steps ahead of them anyway," Marvin rationalizes. But Natleaha bursts his bubble.

"I've got news for you, Uncle. I've always been like this, even before I began working for the state, you just refused to see it. Though it's against my better judgement, I'm going to make contact with my family, all of them. Uncle Eric has to be warned if my father already hasn't warned him."

"You can't do that! It's not necessary, they only want Peter and Ivan."

"He's your brother and my father."

"Peter's not my brother! He never was, he's been dead to me for decades, my partners are only making it more official."

Natleaha stares deep into Marvin's eyes and her instincts tell her that Marvin doesn't really care what happens to his family, any of them, if he ever did.

"They may kill us all Uncle, but you won't live to see the results either." Then without warning or hesitation, before he can react, Natleaha pulls out a concealed Swiss army knife and slits his throat. She watches him fall to the floor of the abandoned building in Korea where she asked to meet him. It was a hundred miles away from the nearest town, no surveillance to speak of, no one followed them and unlike Venice, there was no chance of them being secretly recorded.

Natleaha's source Zee helps her find her cousin Ida whom she considers the weakest link in the family, a person her family's enemies would go after first to hurt the family due to Ida's drug addiction.

"She's in Louisville Kentucky at a shelter on the edge of town," Zee tells her over the phone while Natleaha is on a flight from Korea to the States.

"Find a way to get a message to her to let her know that I'm coming. It's important that she stay at this shelter, at least until I get there."

"That's gonna be kind of tricky. I can get a message to her, but I don't know if she'll stay and wait for you."

"Wire some money into a bank in town and tell her that she can have the money but only I can get it for her," Natleaha suggests.

"I'll see what I can do," Zee answers back.

Like most addicts, Ida perks up when she hears there's free money for her to use to get a fix.

"Can I go get it?" Ida anxiously asks the employee at the shelter who gave her the message.

"The money's in a fifth third bank, but your cousin Natleaha is the only one who can withdraw it for you," the employee says to Ida.

"Shit! Bitch ain't been heard from in over twenty-five years! Ain't called no damn body and the bitch have the nerve to make terms to somebody! This is bullshit!" Ida rages.

She's also frustrated because she's feeling for a hit of meth, heroin or coke. It doesn't matter to Ida as long as it numbs the pain and makes her feel good. Life has not been kind to Ida since she ran away from home when she was sixteen. Her body racked from drug-use and miscarriage after miscarriage due to the drugs and venereal diseases. At one time, Ida thought her life was turning a good corner when her cousin Natleaha agreed to move in with her in a two-bedroom apartment in the inner city of Chicago.

Things seemed to be going great, Natleaha appeared to be the first person in the family to believe in Ida despite her problems. Ida even managed to get off the drugs for a while, but of course Ida had a few relapses here and there, one of them almost killed her, but her cousin was there to save her. Afterwards, Ida pulled herself together a bit after that. She didn't even care if Natleaha was a dyke. Ida was finally beginning to think things were looking up, but then out of the blue, Natleaha disappeared from Ida's life for no reason without a trace.

Although Natleaha couldn't tell Ida the awful reason she had to suddenly leave Chicago. So, Ida was left to believe her cousin left her life and she didn't know why, only that she was gone. When many months passed and Natleaha hadn't returned to their apartment, Ida decided to get out of Chicago.

Using the money she has, she takes a bus to Cincinnati and stays there for a while, but grew tired of the place there, so she moved to Louisville. And she's been surviving on the streets ever since by prostitution, begging and panhandling, ducking into a shelter here and there every year or so.

"This bitch better have a good ass reason for darkening my doorstep after all dis time," Ida fumes when she gets word her cousin is in town.

When Natleaha arrives at the shelter, Ida screams and curses at her until her voice was practically raw.

"Why! Why da fuck did you bail on me, leavin me ass out? Why?"

"I had to Ida. I'd been raped," Natleaha calmly says as she begins to explain.

"What? Raped, how?" Ida mutters in confusion.

Natleaha then continues to recount her whole life story, being a Russian spy, an assassin, running a one woman hit squad for hire after she came to live in the United States, being bisexual and lastly how during her last hit, she was brutally raped by a man she soon after killed. Ida sits in a chair in the lobby of a shelter staring into space with her jaw drops.

"You're a spy?"

"Was."

"Is Natleaha even your real name?"

"Yeah, but I did have a call sign in the field though, the black spider, but I don't use it much nowadays."

"And you had a son from the muthafucka dat raped you?"

"Yeah, he was part of the Shower Posse, the name of the Jamaicans that tried to set up shop in our old neighborhood."

"On the news, those murders dey was talkin bout, dat was you? You did dat shit all by yo self?" Ida continues to ask in shock.

"Yes," Natleaha answers in her continued calm tone.

"Uncle Eric never told you most of our family is from Russia?" Natleaha asks in surprise.

"Uh no he and Mama said our people came from the South."

"Well yes and no."

"What the fuck does that mean?"

"Grandpa Jonah and his wife our grandma Martha were born in a small town in the state of Alabama, but they migrated to Russia before Uncle Eric and my father were born."

"Dat shit doesn't make any sense, Daddy, Uncle Peter and you don't even have a foreign accent."

"Our grandparents spoke English at home, we didn't have to speak Russian unless we were in school or talking to government officials. Uncle Eric never really had to learn that much because he moved back to America when he was old enough." Despite Natleaha's explanation Ida, is still not convinced.

"Dis shit is soundin' too far to the left, Nat. If you was born in Russia, say sumthin' in Russian."

"What would you like me to say to convince you, cousin?" Natleaha says in pristine Russian accuracy like a native born.

Ida is stunned.

"Oh my God, it's true, you really are from Russia. What chu told me bout bein' a spy is why you left town years ago, you got into some kinda trouble."

"That's what I've been telling you, but that's not the only thing, I've tracked you down to discuss something else."

"What?"

"There are people trying to eliminate our family."

"What, you mean kill us?"

"That's exactly what I mean. They may try to come after you, you need to be careful and lay low until me, my father and son can deal with them."

"Lay low? Shit girl, I've been lying low fo decades. I don't need ya to tell me dat."

"I'm serious Ida, this is no joke. These people are relentless and dangerous and dead set on destroying people like us."

"What, black?"

"No gay."

Ida is taken aback.

"Gay?"

"Yes my father and son are both gay and I just told you I'm bisexual."

"Dat's why dey wanna kill our family? Cause of dat shit? Dat's some homophobic racist bullshit Nat."

"Yeah it is."

It doesn't take much convincing for Ida to agree to go into hiding at a safe house set up by Zee in the Florida Keys. There also happen to be a drug tank located at the house for Ida to dry out in. It would be very difficult for Ida, but given the circumstances, this was no time to be gentle. As suspected, her father or somebody else already told her uncle Eric what was going on. Both Natleaha and Zee searched for him and her other cousins, but there was no sign of them. Now came the difficult task of reconnecting with her father and facing the son she did not want.

"I can find them for you very easily," Zee offered over the computer.

"No that won't be necessary, I know several places my family might be."

"You know the proper channels and conditions for reaching me if you change your mind."

"Of course," Natleaha replies, then logs off.

Natleaha thought, if her father was involved in helping build a powerbase it would be in Cuba, especially since her mother was killed, her father feels in some ways, he's still protecting her mother in a roundabout way. Also, Natleaha is aware that one of her son's lovers is from there and does business with Russia's special forces.

She also knows that Ivan is probably in Chicago due to his fondness for certain people there. And if they're not in these places, then Natleaha would try France where they also have allies working there. Natleaha thought about Russia, but figured that would be the last place her family would be, given that the enemy is most powerful there.

Natleaha then gets a surprise, which rarely happens. One of her older contacts from her K.G.B days leaves her a message telling her that her son was trying to find her. Naturally, she knows of his obsession in locating her, but gives it no mind. But still, she figures she would have to face him sooner or later, so she arranges to meet him for the first time at a casino in the city of Cincinnati.

So, a couple of weeks after taking care of Ida, Natleaha drove to Cincinnati. Halfway there, she parks her car in a private parking lot and takes a bus to the casino, opting to keep a lower profile this way. She notices that in her late forties, she still got looks of admiration. The bus ride takes almost an hour because one of the main freeway ramps into the city is under reconstruction, so the bus has to take detours through nearby Covington.

Natleaha doesn't need to ask for directions after she gets off the bus near the casino because she googles them before she leaves Louisville. From the bus stop, it was a short walk to the casino, which is located next to the court house in downtown Cincinnati.

"Hey how ya doin tonight?" an average height black man with sort of a pot belly ask her when Natleaha walked through the entrance facing the town court house. The guard has on a blue blazer with a name tag that says Tom with black pants, black socks and comfortable black shoes. He is standing at a podium facing the entrance.

"I'm fine. How about yourself?" Natleaha says back to the man.

"Good luck to ya, I hope you win big tonight."

"Yes, thank you, I hope I do," she says as she walks past him.

The casino is filled with various types of gambling and slot machines of different shapes and sizes. Natleaha also notices off to the far left and right were signs for the restrooms and by a computerized betting table was an entrance leading to a smoking area.

Whoever thought a city like Cincinnati would have a gambling casino, Natleaha thinks while remembering information from not long ago about the state of Ohio not being known for such things.

As she continues to stroll through the casino, Natleaha searches for Ivan, though she hasn't seen him since his birth she's fully aware that she could spot him anywhere given what he is. Suddenly, after ten minutes of browsing, a male voice calls out to her.

"Hello Natleaha," she hears from behind her. Her instincts on alert, she turns with her hands on a concealed weapon she picked up from a trash can that she had arranged to be put there by the bus station, before she left Louisville.

"Ivan?" she asks, although knowing the answer to her question.

"Yes, I saw you come in earlier. I didn't want to approach you right away in case you wanted to look around for a bit."

Natleaha wants to kick herself for not sensing his presence before he got this close to her.

"I take it you didn't come alone," Natleaha says making a good guess.

Ivan slightly nods to his left and Natleaha glances in that direction to see a dread locked one eyed black man playing on a slot machine, but she could tell that he had his eye on Ivan by the way his head was tilted. He quickly looks at her then back at the machine. There was something about the man that made Natleaha uneasy.

"Is your friend up for the task ahead?"

"He's not my friend but he has his uses. What do you know about the people who've declared war on us?" Ivan asks his mother getting down to business.

"I know it's a family that's had a vendetta against Korcoff and his like that goes back to before your great grandparents even came to Russia. It goes without saying that these people have connections and positions in the Russian government and other places as well."

"You think in the Bratva too?"

"Probably."

"Hmm, that's good to know but one problem at a time. What made you come out of hiding? From what I'm told, you could've let this play out without being discovered."

"It's not that simple, Ivan, despite what you might think, I do love my father, your grandfather."

"Even though he made you have me?" Natleaha had to think a second before she answered.

"Yes, even though. I don't wish to see my father to suffer a horrible death, not anymore anyway." Strangely enough Ivan believes her.

"Besides from what I've learned, these people wouldn't be just satisfied with your and my father's death, they want all Fisks dead, but I've personally denied them an important asset."

"Really, what?"

"That's not important anymore, just know it won't trouble us anymore."

"If you say so," Ivan says not quite wanting to take her word for it. Right in the middle of the conversation, Natleaha changes the subject briefly.

"Who is that you brought with you? An officer from your American ally in Chicago?"

Ivan is not surprised his mother knows about Sam Givens, she would have to be well informed to last this long on her own as well as manage to outwit the aggressive efforts on his part to locate her over the years.

"His name is Jack O'Connor, he works with the I.R.A. He was introduced to Grandpa by someone he's seeing."

"Really, who?"

"An U.F.C fighter who's Irish." Natleaha bursts out laughing.

"So now father's chasing after men younger than his grandson. See, I told you, he doesn't need anyone to kill him, he'll kill himself with his wild sex life. Maybe I should give this guard of yours a try before we get too caught up in this war."

"You're not his type," Natleaha arches her eyebrow.

"I see, one of your playthings."

"Afraid not, I'm too old for him." Natleaha is confused at first by Ivan's statement, but then it dawns on her.

"Then hopefully he'll die first if we're lucky," she bluntly states ending the discussion on Jack O'Connor.

"Have you seen Grandpa yet?"

"No, I don't want to risk giving our enemies a too easy target. I'm taking a big risk by meeting you out in the open like this as it is. Besides, isn't the man my father crossed paths with in Africa working with the people trying to destroy us?"

"Yeah, but Grandpa Pete has a few ideas on how to deal with this man."

"I'm sure he does," Natleaha says smugly, imagining the tortures her father has in store for the man who murdered her mother.

"Tell your grandfather I'll make contact soon."

"I will."

Natleaha then ends the meeting by walking away without so much as a goodbye.

As he watches his mother walk away, Ivan wonders if she could ever care for him, but realizes that'll probably never happen. Given the circumstances of his conception, he could hardly blame her.

"She contacted you!" Peter asks in shock from the computer skype screen from a safe house in Istanbul. He couldn't believe it when Ivan told him of the meeting.

"Yeah she said she wanted not to see you dead basically and that she believes these people would come for her next."

"Still, she was taking a big risk on her part, which is highly unlike her. I'm having a hard time believing she would come out of hiding after all this time even for her own sake. Your mother and I didn't part on good terms at all."

"I know, but I do believe she's worried about you in her own way."

"Rinka and Quartz must've gotten too close to Natleaha somehow for her to be so worried."

"She did say she got rid of an asset of theirs, but didn't tell me what it was."

"Knowing your mother, it probably was a person she killed that was valuable to Rinka and Quartz. And we probably never will find out who was working with them that she killed that was so important unless Natleaha wants us to."

"I found it strange that she asked about the man who was with me, Jack."

"Oh him," Peter says dismissively, openly showing his dislike for the man.

"She said she hopes he dies first."

"Unfortunately, he can't die too soon, not until we get our uses out of him first. Sometimes you have to work with people you don't like or who disgusts you to serve your means to an end."

Ivan understood what his grandfather was saying. He knew that many in the Bratva loathed him for being a homosexual, but he worked well with them anyway, although these same men greatly hoped he dies in this family war.

"Is your unofficial shadow and probation officer Rosa still watching every move you make even now?"

"Especially now, the Bratva want to make sure I keep my promises I made to them. Rosa is in the other room cleverly pretending not to monitor and listen to me," Ivan says with a sly crooked smile, his way letting Peter know that the woman is attracted to Ivan.

Ivan has headphones in on his end, so whomever happens to be listening to him from another room can't hear what Peter is saying to his grandson. They can only hear Ivan if they're at his location.

"Pussy is not all bad son, even for men like us who prefer other dicks. You should sleep with her anyway to ensure her loyalty to you."

"She's not an amateur Grandpa, she'd see through that attempt of seduction. It's not like when you were my age Grandpa, where a black man had to marry to hide what he was to stay alive. I can be with who I want without all the pretending you had to go through with Grandma."

"Well, it's not like you would be bad at it if you went that route. You've had the same training in that sort of thing as I got. What you seem to forget Ivan is that men like us in the type of world we come from use whatever weapons we have to stay several steps ahead. You're still young yet, but you're slowly learning how the underworld works for us. Which is probably why you're subtly stringing along your old classmate for your own ends."

"It's not like that with Eleanea, she knows nothing can happen between us."

"Your actions say otherwise. Being friendly and charming toward her whenever you want something. She reads into that like there might be a chance with you. They don't like to admit it, especially nowadays, but women are more in tuned with subtle messages than men, gay or straight are. Be careful Ivan, if you play with a woman's heart, any type of woman, even your mother's type, you might get hurt psychologically and physically. If you won't sleep with Eleanea, then don't make an enemy of her, we can't afford it."

Ivan doesn't agree with Peter, he is sure that Eleanea understood that all they could be was friends. The same could be said about Rosa, she is assigned to watch him and keep him in line, that's all. It isn't his fault that she catches feelings for a fag. Well, not exactly the same, Rosa has orders to kill him if he steps out of line, but still he is sure she knows where she stands on the prospects of a sexual relationship with him.

"How's everything going on your end?" Ivan asks in an attempt to change the subject.

"I've left the necessary bread crumbs for them to follow, namely my old friend Emmubahta. He's a wild card. I'm sure Quartz and Rinka have problems controlling. They're gonna have to do without him soon," Peter boasts to Ivan.

"So, you think the trap will work?"

"If not, it'll give that motherfucker something to think about. He murdered the love of my life, irreplaceable to me, I owe him," Peter says with bitterness.

"What do you mean they all got killed by unknown shooters from a distance!" Emmubahta shouts into the phone.

Janet and Oliver can only sit at the other end of the table staring with clueless expressions. Unfortunately, Emmubahta is shouting in a dialect they're not familiar with, which means he's not the type of African they thought.

"Emmubahta, Emmubahta what is it?" Janet asks interrupting his heated phone call.

"Something has happened to half my men, I just got word of it from a contact in Cape Town."

"I'm sure whatever's happened is tragic, but we have more important things to discuss," Janet calmly explains.

"This is fucking serious woman! Everything I've accomplished and built is on the verge of collapsing around me!"

"Yes everything you built, not we. We all still have a mission. With the combined resources at our group's disposal, you can rebuild your little army, especially after we've destroyed the Fisks."

"That's going to be harder to do now that we've lost Marvin Fisk, the renegade of the family," Oliver reminds them.

"That's not really a major threat in some ways."

"What do you mean?"

"True, he gave us valuable inside information about our enemies, but he was still on the outside with most of his family," Janet answers to Oliver's question.

"Our resources suspect it might've been his own niece who killed him."

"Probably, but like I said it's no major setback, especially this far into the game. We still have other assets to use against the Fisks and their allies."

"Yes, but are we sure that they're up to the tasks we set for them?" Oliver asks with concern.

"We'll see," Janet calmly says to him.

"Never mind all that. I want Peter Fisk dead! He should've died by my hands decades ago, but I foolishly let him live to plague me further down the road. I don't care what the rest of you say, this is my livelihood, my life's blood and reason for being! I will not let this stand. I don't care what you say. My contacts says he fled to Istanbul after the massacre of my men. He thinks he's safe, that I don't know the area, but he's wrong."

"Fine, finish him quickly and get back to one of our secured locations. We can't afford to lose you at this stage," Janet instructs Emmubahta.

"The one good thing is, with Peter Fisk dead, his grandson won't have anyone left to watch out for him," Oliver adds before Emmubahta walks out of the room.

Chapter 13

"Oh Jack, Jack god damn shit!" the woman screams as the black Irishman pounds her mercilessly from behind. Yanking her braids, squeezing her sweat covered breasts.

"Ooh dat's it, dat's it, hurt me oh hurt me! You tearin it up boy!" she continues, but Jack doesn't say anything, he only stares into space with a glazed look in his remaining eye. This is not any kind of pleasure for Jack O'Connor, it never has been.

It's a necessary chore for him to do to get what he really wants. Finding a black woman with a son in Cincinnati to seduce was easy. In the three weeks Jack has been in the city, Ivan has kept a tight leash on him, keeping Jack close, not letting him wander off to places where there might be children.

"I don't like small children." he adamantly denies to his temporary allies, but they all are weary because of Jack's reputation.

He knew he had to be careful around them. He was aware that the Fisks needed him, but he didn't want to take the chance of being castrated or killed before his use was over. So, he secretly met a woman in town who was waiting in a line outside the welfare building.

She was attractive enough with a nice shape with well-made braids down past the back of her neck, but what caught Jack's eye was the tall handsome young boy standing next to her. He looked to be barely over eleven, but was still very tall for his age.

"It's a nice day out, lucky ya picked today ta stand out here eh. Ya fella is mighty right laddie ta have a fine lass as yerself," Jack says in introduction or for what passes for one to him.

"Excuse me, what?" the woman asks put off by his accent.

"I don't mean to bother ya now, I was jus sayin' yer a beautiful lady and da tyer husband must be a lucky man."

"Oh, I'm not married," the woman says as she begins to understand what Jack is saying.

"So, dis is yer boyfriend now?" Jack asks staring straight at the boy. The woman chuckles.

"Heh, no this is my son."

"Well now, how old are ya lad?"

"I'm thirteen," the boy shyly answers.

"Wow thirteen, I would've guessed you were in ya twenties."

"Where are you from? I can't place your accent."

"I'm from Ireland in the town of Belfast."

"They got black people in Ireland? Dat shit's weird," the boy expresses.

"I done told you bout cussin at strangers boy," the woman chastises to her son.

"It's alright, I'm not offended, boys are gonna be boys no matter where they're from."

Jack was charming to the woman, like he always is whenever he wanted something.

"So ya been waitin' in dis line long lass?"

"Bout an hour, tryin to git a food stamp card," she casually admits.

"Well, now maybe after yer done, I could take you and yer boy for lunch, ta show dat der was no misunderstandings on anybody's part."

"I would like that. Could you give me your number? If I have time, I could call you later."

"Sure dat's fine," Jack answers with a heartfelt smile.

From that moment on, Jack knew he had her. He knew the type on sight, desperate to be desirable despite being a single mother, worried that having a child might scare a man off. Why else would she volunteer personal information about herself after first meeting a stranger and not training her son not to openly speak to strange men too quickly.

The woman calls Jack later that evening.

"So, it's good to hear from ya. Maybe we could have a breakfast one morin if ya not too busy dat is?" Jack asks subtly while thinking about her cute son.

"I'm free the day after tomorrow, we could have lunch."

"Dat's good lass, I could get away from me job for a while," Jack says lying through his teeth. Jack went to lunch.

Later on, Jack went to lunch with this woman with a man tailing nearby to make sure he didn't mess with any children. But when he saw Jack meeting a woman, the tail reported back to Ivan what Jack was up to.

"My name's Gladys," the woman says after they sat down to lunch.

"I'm Jack. What's your son's name?"

"His name is Gerald and Gerald's my pride and joy."

"He seems rough round the edges, but a good kid."

"From your lips to God's ear."

"Oh, don't be worried Gladys, Gerald jus needs da right guidance is all."

That was all Gladys needs to hear, within days, Jack is at her apartment steaming up the sheets. Jack causes her to reach orgasm when he uses his lips and tongue to massage the inner walls of her puffed up mound. She yelps when Jack bites the tip of one of her titties as he squeezed the nipple of the other. After they were done, Gladys rests on Jack's well-built chest.

The way he say things gently to her in his Irish drawl has her eating out of the palm of his hand. Jack manages to ditch his tail to be here at this moment. He calls and tells Ivan that him and the man that he was with got separated by accident, so he'll be back at the safe house as soon as he can. He figures he'd string Gladys along for the weeks he's in town until he could get close to Gerald. Jack isn't much in the face, but he has a nice body that women found pleasing.

"Can I use yer shower fore I go?" he asks hopping out of bed giving Gladys a clear view of his thick ass.

"Sure, it's down the hall to the left," she answers.

"Thanks, I won't be long."

Quickly finding the bathroom Jack steps into the shower, shuts the curtains, turns on the water and adjust it to near hot. He spots a bar of soap, letting the water run through his dreadlocks. Jack is so engulfed in his shower, he doesn't hear the bathroom door open and shut. Not until he hears the toilet flush, does he realize somebody else is in the bathroom. He peeks through the curtain and see it is Gerald. Jack then stops the water to speak to the boy.

"Hey lad what's up, can ya hand me a towel?" Jack kindly asks.

Gerald complies by handing Jack a towel off the rack across from the sink. Jack takes it and it's barely able to wrap around his waist. Jack smiles as he steps out of the shower.

"Thanks lad, appreciate it," he says while walking past the boy. Jack had to play it cool, he didn't want to spook the boy, he wanted to go slow and ease into it without scaring him.

Jack is invited a couple more times to Gladys' place and spends the night a few times. One of the times, he catches Gerald coming out of the bathroom wearing only his jockey underwear. Jack could tell Gerald is going to grow up to be a good-looking man.

I know some lads who'd pay good money for a boy like him, Jack thinks. What he doesn't know is Ivan was fully aware of what Jack is doing. He thinks he lost his tail the day he first met Gladys and her son and when he went to her apartment that first afternoon, but he is wrong. The man hid out of sight and slyly followed Jack from a greater distance Jack couldn't see. He then reported back to Ivan when he discovered what Jack was up to.

During the last week he would be in Cincinnati, Jack convinces Gladys to let him take her son to the Y.M.C.A.

"I'll drop 'em off at home when we're done, it's only gonna be bout an hour or two after school on Friday," Jack assures her.

"Well alright, but have him home before dinner, I don't want him out in the streets after dark," Gladys sternly says.

It's kind of warm out this fall Friday, so Gerald changes into a tank top and basketball shorts to work out in when him and Jack get to the Y.M.C.A. They start out their exercise by playing basketball with other members and their sons. Afterwards, they went to the nautilus room, lifting hand weights, running on the treadmill and working out on other nautilus machines.

Gerald feels like a grown up using the machines and weights. Gerald is still kind of shy when they took off their clothes to go sit in the steam room. The boy quickly wraps himself in an oversized towel. Jack still gets a good look at the boy's body, admiring the smooth hairless parts of the overgrown boy.

"Isn't this nice?" Jack asks as they inhale the steam and wet heat.

"I guess so, feels kinda weird," the boy responds.

About twelve minutes go by when Jack suggests that they take a shower. When him and Gerald come out of the steam room, Jack gets the shock of his life.

"Hey Jack, what's up?" Ivan asks when he greets him by the door of the steam room dressed in a pair of bicycle shorts and a white T-shirt.

"Uh, uh Ivan I didn't expect to see you here. I thought you'd be back at the house getting ready to leave tomorrow."

"I was, but I had a little time to kill after I finished packing, so I decided to work off some stress. I see we had the same idea. Who's your young friend?"

"Oh, uh dis is Gerald, a son of a friend of mine," Jack answers in a shaky voice, realizing he's been caught red handed.

"Hi Gerald, it's a pleasure to meet you. Where were you two gonna go after you left here?"

"We was gonna go to me and my mom's place fo dinner," Gerald says with a confused look on his face, not knowing what's happening now.

"That's nice, but I'm afraid Jack won't be able to make it, he has to do work for me right away. But don't worry there's a cab outside that's already been paid twenty dollars to take you home. You can go get dressed now, I'm sure your mother is anxious for you to get home."

The boy sees no recourse, but to obey the strange pale man. So, he walks back to his locker to get dressed. Within six minutes, Gerald is dressed and leaves the locker room. Jack attempts to mouth a feeble explanation, but Ivan holds up his hand to stop him.

"My grandfather wants you in Istanbul tomorrow, he wants you to set up a proper welcome for someone who's coming to see him soon," Ivan orders with his arms folded nudging his head in the direction he wants Jack to go.

Chapter 14

"He has eluded me for too long and made a fool of me in the process, but today the faggot dies," Emmubahta mumbles to himself as he makes his way through the countryside with a dozen men. They are five miles away from where his enemy is supposed to be, according to his contacts.

"Yeah he's here, about two blocks away in an abandoned building on the top floor," his lookout told Emmubahta by text message.

"Let me know if he changes position," he texts back to the lookout.

Him and his men approach the targeted position dressed as Istanbul natives riding on horseback. Fortunately, Emmubahta can speak Turkish and can explain his very dark skin by telling people he and his men are trade merchants from a country that has a trade agreement with Turkey.

The anticipation is almost choking to Emmubahta as he rides closer to where his enemy is. He senses that this is probably the last battle between him and the man he's hated for so long. When they're half a mile away from the position, Emmubahta orders his men to dismount and hide the horses in the hills by a watering hole. As him and his men move closer to the building where the target is, Emmubahta gets the feeling something is off.

"Where's the resistance? They've had to see us by now. Why has no one attempted to intercept us?" he wonders. His suspicions unfortunately come too late because when they're a block away from the building, Emmubahta and his men are set upon by hidden bombs. They don't even have time to react as the ground below them explodes.

"Everyone take cover! Get out of the open now!" Emmubahta yells while getting off the ground and heading to the nearest building in hopes that it's not rigged with explosives.

"Yeah, run you muthafucka, run," Peter says as he watches from an undisclosed location.

He knew someone was watching him ever since he enter the country, so he arranged to secretly trade places with a decoy.

"How far do the bombs go?" Peter asks a man next to him who helped the bomber plant the explosives.

"They're planted through half the neighborhood that's abandoned, including the building that he thinks you're in."

"Tell the decoy to remain in place long enough for Emmubahta to think I'm still there, then have the decoy lead him to me. Kill the rest of his men if you're able, but I want to face Emmubahta myself."

"Yes sir," the man next to him answers.

Through the carnage, Emmubahta manages to evade the bombs by realizing the spots where they might be planted. As his men are fighting for their lives, enemy combatants come from out of other buildings nearby to engage Emmubahta and his men. He seems to be the only one able to fight back, as his men are too busy being blown to pieces or at the very least too distracted by the bombs to escape enemy fire.

"You will not take me you jackals!" Emmubahta screams in his native tongue.

Out of the dozen who came with him, only two are left with him as they make it to the building he thinks Peter is in. The place is five stories with no elevator. There are men waiting for them on the last two floors. Emmubahta tosses several grenades at the men on the fourth floor as they make their way up the steps.

When the grenades knock them off their feet, Emmubahta's small party finishes them off with gunfire. On the last floor, they fight seven men hand to hand with fists and knives. Emmubahta's remaining men die in the fight, but he's able to kill the men that are left over from the skirmish, but not before he questions the decoy.

"Where is he? Where's that faggot at?" Emmubahta demands while holding a machine gun in the man's face.

"He's waiting for you on the outskirts near the plaza about a half an hour away," the decoy answers. For his trouble, his face is blown off by Emmubahta's gun.

He quickly finds the plaza on foot. When he arrives, he finds Peter sitting in a chair.

Emmubahta is fully on guard sensing another ambush.

"This is between us now, as it should be," Peter says as if sensing what Emmubahta is thinking.

"You killed my wife, you animal. She was not your enemy. She never did anything to you. Why? Because she was married to me?"

"Why not? Your wife was willingly married to you, you who's not even a real man, just some freak who lays with other men. Me and the people I work with won't tolerate your kind infecting proper society like Africa and Russia."

Peter laughs in his face.

"Proper society? Russia? They hate you and me for the color of our skin and Africa, shit the countries in that continent have among the worst race and class riots. The Arabs in Sudan raped and killed a black family for having a picnic on their grass they let cows graze on Rwanda was literally on fire for a couple of decades because some people there opposed apartheid. These Russians you call friends are using you. Once not long ago they would've killed you like the ignorant savage you are."

Emmubahta doesn't respond with words, he fires his gun at Peter. He dodges out of the way, but Peter catches two bullets in the shoulder. When he ducks from the hail of bullets, Peter reaches in his holster on his ankle and pulls out his own side arm. Firing back, he continues to move as Emmubahta steadily fires.

"You won't get the drop on me this time! This time, it'll go a different way!" Peter taunts.

Emmubahta notices that Peter is moving like a man half his age, instead of a man who's approaching eighty. He looks aged, but not as much as he should, considering how many years ago they first met.

Emmubahta is in his late fifties himself, but he's in fair shape, but not enough to pass for somebody in his twenties.

"You can't avoid me forever you old punk muthafucka. You might as well let me end this now, save yourself the agony!" Emmubahta shouts.

"I don't think so boy! But you are right, it's time to end this."

Then Peter does the unexpected and charges at Emmubahta who's still firing the machine gun at him. He takes three more bullets to the chest, but they aren't severe enough for Peter to stop.

Emmubahta is so busy trying to blow Peter's head off that he doesn't see the Swiss army knife hidden in the back of Peter's pants. By the time he realizes what his foe is up to, it's too late. Before he can react, Peter catches him in the side of the neck with the knife, quickly ending Emmubahta's life by giving him a deep bloody gash across the rest of his throat.

"I told you this would end today. It's done Clearessa, the animal who took your life is on his way to hell," Peter says in gasp breaths, collapsing to the ground due to his injuries.

Thankfully, Ivan had given strict instructions to Peter's men to have hidden medics where Emmubahta and his allies couldn't detect them. So, they were camped out in an underground bunker below radar.

"This is alpha 1 to gold leader, come in," one of the men who's seen Peter fall on the ground says in his com.

"I repeat this alpha 1 to gold leader, our care package is damaged, we need to repair it so we can ship it off on time."

"This is gold leader we read you, we'll have someone to repair the package, so we can mail it on time," they say in code in case the wrong people are listening.

Another factor that worked in the Fisks favor was that the medics resembled the Turkish people who lived in the country. So, they wore plain clothes not military uniforms, which helped them move better and faster through the area. Fortunately, the medics get to Peter in time to help him.

"Your grandfather will live, but he'll be out of commission for a while," a doctor whom works on mobsters says to Ivan over a skype screen the next day.

"Thank you doctor. I'll contact you again soon if I can," Ivan says with a heavy sigh.

It was good news in its own way. His grandfather was vulnerable, but still he was able to avenge his wife's death by killing the man responsible.

Peter was in far better shape than Ivan's best friend and former lover. Gregor was a victim of a biochemical attack by Rinka and Quartz. They had gotten the location of where Gregor would be along with other members of the Bratva. They were off-loading barrels of dangerous chemicals to sell to a Middle Eastern dictator, so he could make bio weapons to use against his enemies. But before the Bratva could finish unloading the barrels, some small drones carrying missiles attacked, dropping the missiles and igniting the chemicals.

Many of the men, including Gregor were doused in flame and exploding biohazard. As a result, the men got various forms of severe burns and incurable types of cancers. Gregor got intestinal cancer, which quickly spread to other parts of his body. Because of the aggressiveness of the cancer, the treatments for it didn't work. Now Gregor lays in a hospital bed in Berlin wasting away and waiting to die.

Gregor's wife asked Ivan to stay away for the sake of her and Gregor's children, but he couldn't, so he snuck into Gregor's hospital room late at night when his family wasn't there. It was easy to pay nurses and doctors to let Ivan know when Gregor's wife came and went.

"In spite of everything, you were my first love and I'll never forget you," Ivan says to Gregor's sleeping form in the dark room. His friend's I.V is pumping him so full of drugs to ease the pain and help him sleep that Ivan doesn't know if Gregor's aware he's there or not.

"Remember when we first met? You were the only person besides Eleanea who didn't see me as a freak. You were always there for me, even after we broke up. You taught me to survive the treacherous waters of the Bratva and thrive. I didn't mind that while we were together, you got married like you might've believed."

"I knew you liked women a little more than other men and that you wanted children someday. Eleanea admitted to me that she loves me. I don't know what I'm going to do about that and it's been months since she told me. You'd probably tell me to fuck her because you think that's what she really wants. And I'd disagree with you, knowing full well you'd hate that as you always did. I can see your likeness in your children, especially your oldest so. He's gonna have his pick of any beautiful girl he wants or maybe boys if that happens to be the case, you never know."

Just then Gregor coughs in his sleep and Ivan figures he might wake up, but that doesn't happen.

"Our war is going steady, we've dealt our enemies a severe blow, but it's still far from over, especially after what's happen to you and the other men that were with you. I swear to you, on your soul, we will make them pay, even if it kills us. On slightly positive note, I'm not sure yet, but anyway my mother whom I've met for the first time, weeks ago, has agreed to help us."

"Grandfather is glad she wants to help, but I'm not sure and I know you wouldn't be either. She just shows up out of nowhere after being out of my life all these years. It doesn't sit well with me even though I had searched for her nearly over half my life. But she says that our enemies are after her too."

"The Bratva are not pleased that you and a number of their men are dying slowly because of this attack. This conflict is spilling over to other people who didn't want to get involved and their patience with situation is growing short."

At that, Ivan leaves his friend's bedside after he's said all he can say.

Gregor's funeral has a large turnout. A number of his family members, friends and coworkers attend. Ivan sits in the back with the few well-wishers who barely knew Gregor. His wife breaks with tradition and opts to have her husband cremated. Ivan stands in line with the rest of the people who want to offer their condolences after the services are concluded.

"Your husband was greatly admired he will be missed," Ivan says to Mrs. Feldman when it's his turn to speak to her.

"Yes, I know and I also still remember what you were to him. I know you loved my husband as much as I did," she states surprising Ivan as she remains calm and dry eyed.

To say Ivan was caught off guard was putting it mildly. He did wonder why she didn't want him to visit Gregor when he was in the hospital, but he thought it was because of his appearance. He wasn't aware that Gregor's wife knew about the two of them. He doesn't say another word to her afterwards. He then watches her get into the black limousine along with her children, which then follows the hearse with Gregor's body to the crematorium.

Ivan realizes that his list of allies is growing short. With his grandfather in the hospital and Gregor gone, he has to tread more carefully. He decides not to reach out to Sam Givens in America just yet. He figures he'll use him for the end game if he can. But he does reach out to Ingramisck to discuss their next move.

Believing that with the death of Emmubahta their enemies don't have the firm hold they once had in Africa, they decide to meet in Kenya at an ocean side hotel in a suite. Naturally, the room is swept for listening devices and hidden cameras. The two men are alone in the room with their guards stationed outside and on the balcony. Rosa waits on the balcony with the guards stationed there.

"Quartz and Rinka are growing more desperate than we are."

"What do you mean?" Ivan asks Ingramisck.

"Your mother was right, she did get rid of an asset of theirs, it was your own uncle Marvin."

"What?"

"Yes, come to find out he had been working with Quartz and Rinka for quite some time."

"Are you sure?"

"I am, here see for yourself," Ingramisck says handing Ivan a holder.

He opens it up and sees pictures of his uncle with a man and a woman who he assumes is Rinka and Quartz. Also, there are pictures of Marvin with Emmubahta in Moscow and labeled tapes of their conversations on burner phones they thought nobody was listening to. Ivan plays the tapes on a player he's brought along. Right away, he recognizes his uncle's voice when he hears it.

"Is my no-good freak half-brother dead yet?" Marvin says with disgust.

"No, but he will be soon, be patient. Don't worry, he will die slower and more painful than his wife. What about his daughter, your niece?"

"She wants to remain above the fray, but she's slowly realizing that she has to pick the side that leads to survival, our side. I know for a fact that she wants her father and her son dead more than we do."

"And you're sure she can be trusted on this matter at least?"

"Of course."

The tape ends.

"This was recorded a week before your uncle's body was found in Korea."

"Then it's evident my mother can't be trusted, but I do think she's doing what she's doing for her own sake."

"Then we play her close to the vest?"

"Naturally, but we don't arouse her suspicions too much, if we do that she'll kill all of us, given her reputation."

"Yeah I've heard the stories about your mother too. Do you think she knows about what happened to your grandfather?"

"Given her resources, I'm sure she does."

"Maybe we wanna include her in our next move against our enemies."

"She has taken an interest in Sam Givens more than I have. She probably get up to speed way before he's notified of our plans. My mother has remained off the grid for more than twenty-five years undetected and suddenly she reappears to her family, the family she loathes. Somebody else has better information than us and Rinka and Quartz. That other person more than likely is talking to my mother, which explains her reappearance."

"But fortunately, she's not our biggest problem, I've been getting the feeling that some of the men under my command can't be fully trusted."

"Well, nobody can be really fully trusted in our line of work, Ingram."

"Still, I'm expecting a move, Ivan. Quartz and Rinka have people in Special Forces and the Bratva, that's a fact. The question now at this point is what are we gonna do about it now."

"We know about it that's the point. We can weed out who's disloyal easy enough."

"How?"

"Pay attention to the people who seem like they're your shadow, too loyal for no apparent reason. Trust me, they're there if you know how to look."

"Hmm, I see what you're saying. Do you think they might've gotten to any of your boys you mess with?"

"No, I don't think so, they're safely out of harm's way. Besides they wouldn't understand the situation if our enemies even tried to approach them."

"I don't know if I can say the same. There's this young soldier in this unit I'm training who's suspect. I'm not too open about liking other men, but this boy seems like he's interested in me, but when I show him any extra attention in front of the other soldiers he looks embarrassed, except when we're alone."

"You always did like the young boys, didn't you?" Ivan teases, making Ingramisck blush.

"Only when they're worth liking and this one seems to want me to get to know him better."

"Sounds like a good place to make our next move."

Three days after, the meeting Ingramisck is at a secret Russian troops training facility in Retalhuleu Guatemala. The soldier Ingramisck mentioned to Ivan is also there. Following the standard beginning exercises, Ingramisck orders his troops in formation.

"Alright, now, you will form up in pairs of two, waiting your turn to face off against the other man in your pair. You will have three minutes to race through the obstacle course, dodging land mines and hidden traps. Some of these traps are real, so I'd be very careful if I were you!" Ingramisck instructs.

The first four pairs of soldiers move through the course within the appointed time limit, but one of the men in the fifth pair fell into one of the pit falls that had razor sharp spikes in it. The spikes didn't penetrate the man's boot, but they got his legs good.

Meanwhile, the other man of the pair completed the course, which happen to be the man Ingramisck had his eye on.

"Medics, get that man outta the hole!" the lieutenant orders. They quickly remove the screaming man away. Strangely enough, the female soldiers scores on the course are better than their male counterpart.

"Did you think to go back for your injured partner?" Ingramisck asks the soldier in question later on in his office.

"He wasn't my partner, but my opposite number. We were in competition with each other sir," the soldier answers his superior officer while standing at attention.

"I see. What if the situation were reversed? Do you think he would've left you behind?"

"I cannot answer that sir. I can only concern myself with the task at hand, which was completing the mission."

"So, you think you're on a mission?" Ingramisck asks stepping closer to the man.

"I'm always on a mission sir, ever since I decided to join the military."

"So, you do whatever is required of you for the mission, is that it?"

"Isn't always, sir? I'm sure you've had to do things that you weren't always comfortable with to complete the mission."

"Of course, but I'm sure you realize it's not always prudent to leave a man behind. Sometimes, there are assignments where you may need backup, even on the field of battle."

The soldier has noticed by now by the way his superior officer is looking at him. He doesn't react when Ingramisck puts his hand on his shoulder. Ingramisck gets a good look into the man's eyes and after a minute it tells him what he suspects.

Despite his suspicions, Ingramisck continues with the seduction.

"You are a promising recruit soldier, very promising. Your name's Egriff, isn't it?"

"Yes sir, Egriff Spinor."

"Ah yes that's right Spinor. Your history is impressive, top marksman in your class, skilled at low-level infiltration according to your advanced training classes. You will do very well in espionage when your time comes and added to that you're good at languages. But all the training and roleplaying prep can never fully prepare you for the type of things you may have to do sexually to sometimes help you accomplish a mission."

"I think I'm up for anything on that front sir," he says to Ingramisck now standing practically nose to nose with him.

Ingramisck makes an aggressive move and kisses Egriff fully on the mouth. The man doesn't resist him, in fact he kisses Ingramisck back.

"You are up for anything," he says to Egriff as he struggles with his belt. Within seconds, Ingramisck has the soldier's pants down around his ankles and he's on his knees in front of him. As Ingramisck is servicing Egriff, Egriff produces a garret wire from the sleeve of his uniform.

"They said you had a sickening weakness for young men." Ingramisck is stunned for a moment by the statement.

"Who's they personally?" Ingramisck asks standing to his feet.

"Your pale friend's enemies." And he can react Egriff wraps the garret around his neck.

"Don't bother trying to call or expect help, I've sabotaged the surveillance cameras, they only see an empty office and no one saw me come in when you called me here, I made sure of that," Egriff taunts, but as he's strangling Ingramisck with the wire it snaps in his hands.

Then it was Egriff's turn to be stunned. Ingramisck uses the momentary distraction to turn around and seize Egriff in a gripping bear hug, spraining his back, causing him to fall to the floor in pain.

"Yes, I do like beautiful young men, a lot, but I'm not blinded by them. I had one of my men check your uniform while you were in the shower earlier today. That's how I knew about your little surprise and took the proper precautions. Ivan told me our enemies would try to play on our appetites, but unfortunately for you, we're gonna have fun of a different kind and see how much you know," Ingramisck says and then uses his boot to knock Egriff unconscious.

"You were right, he does work for Rinka and Quartz, for about six months now. They wanted me eliminated after Gregor to lower your ally pool even further," Ingramisck tells Ivan on the phone on a secure line.

"Was your boy saying anything else useful?"

"Only that Quartz likes to frequent a secret sex club located in London, which is where he met our boy along with a woman he happened to be with."

"That sounds interesting."

Ingramisck didn't see the significance of Ivan's statement.

"Why, you and I have might safely guess have been to clubs similar to the kind Oliver Quartz like to frequent."

"What I mean is it can't be your run of the mill type of sex club if your private told you this."

"You mean something illegal perhaps, immoral by most liberal standards?"

"Maybe?"

"If this is true then maybe it does warrant looking into."

"Well then first off we have to find out the name of the club and figure out how to get in."

"The boy gave me the name of the club. It's called Dante's 9th Wonder."

"Ok, but how do we get in?"

"I don't know, Egriff didn't tell me, he only said it's very expensive to even get invited as a guest. I couldn't find out the contact information because Egriff died on me before I could get it."

"I think there might be a way to get into the club. Between you and me along with other people we know, somebody has to at least heard of Dante's 9th Wonder."

So, Ivan, put the word out but nobody among his friends and contacts seemed to have heard of this club until Ivan found a source in the last place he would have thought to look. Against his better judgement Ivan had been feeling nostalgic since Gregor and him broke up, feelings made worse by his death.

So lately, he's been talking more to his old lovers, especially to Calhoun. During one of their skype conversations, the two men were talking about whom they were happening to be sleeping with.

"Yeah brah dis is freaky and she has da nerve to be phine as fuck. She's into threesomes and shit like doin da honeys wit us. I think she might've figured out dat I like dudes."

"Oh yeah, why do you say that?"

"I don't know man she's always askin how'd I feel bout watchin her fuck another dude."

"What did you say?"

"I couldn't say nuthin', I didn't want her askin too many questions if I talked too much bout it. You know how females are if they suspect you of some gay shit?"

"I guess," Ivan answers mildly not really understanding what Calhoun is so nervous about.

"Anyway, she said a friend of hers told her bout dis club somewhere in Britain or England, whateva dey call it, but it's like straight up freaky. So, my girl talked into takin her durin' one od da days of tha' off season from ball."

Calhoun pauses for a moment after he says this.

"So, what was it like?" Ivan anxiously asks. A shit eating grin forms all over Calhoun's face when he starts to talk again.

"Brah, dawg, da shit was off da chain! Everybody was gittin freaky wit everybody, man, woman, animal it didn't matter somebody was doin it. Some people was into pain and shit some rooms wit weird lookin harnesses connected to poles and posts. Da stuff was unreal. So, an hour in we catch da eye of dis cute white couple. Da woman of da two said her and her husband had a private room and asked did we wanna go der. Ole dude and his girl didn't seem to be bother by my looks."

"All I know is dat my girl and dat English white chick was really feelin each other from what I'd seen. When we got to da room and locked da door everybody was outta dey clothes. Honey had a bangin body and her husband was kinda thick fo a white boy. Da white chick took me to tha bed in da room and went down on her while me and her husband watched."

"So did you and the husband get into anything?"

"Hell naw! I told ya I wasn't tryin' ta out myself. We jus watched our females tang team each other as we stroked ourselves. And man, dey was goin' at it. The Englishman got so turned on he joined in. He fucked his wife, then he did my girl while his wife squeezed and smacked his ass. Dude was hittin' it hard. I didn't think white men could git down like dat."

Ivan could tell Calhoun was turned on by what he had saw by the way he was describing it.

"And you weren't tempted to do the white man? You already said he fucked good."

"Naw, but he wanted to do me cuse he looked up and back at me and smiled. He wanted me to come over to 'em."

"Why didn't you? Sounds like they would've liked that."

"I don't know man, I couldn't even bring myself to fuck his wife, I jus rubbed on her a little bit. My girl had a great time dough and she rode me sumthin' fierce after we got back to the hotel."

"So' what was the name of this club anyway?"

"Some shit called Dante's." A lightbulb went on in Ivan's head.

"Dante's 9th Wonder?"

"Yeah dat's it. How'd you guess?"

"I think I might've heard the name somewhere while I was in Europe. So have you thought about going back?"

"I don't know man, my girl wants to. She said the woman she was wit found out where we were stayin' at da time and left her card wit her number on it at da front desk fo us."

"Do you think you might want to go back by yourself or with somebody else?" Calhoun appears bashful at the suggestion, but he kind of already knew what Ivan is suggesting.

"I don't know, the people who run da place said I passed all da intros to be a Member and if I wanted to I could come back anytime."

"So, you have thought about it. Maybe during a Day or two away from the field we could go when your girl is too busy working?"

"I don't know Ivan da sounds kinda risky. She'll wonder why I went wit another dude, she ain't stupid man. We don't have to fly to London together, I could meet you there. Just find a phone store and buy a burner to use to call me and after you're done with it you can throw it away. And it sounds like this club is discreet, so nobody won't be calling your girl telling her who you came with."

Calhoun's face shows that he is considering the idea.

"Ok, I'm down. I'll let chu know when my next off day is."

"Sounds good, I can't wait to hear from you."

"Al'ight peace."

Calhoun then clicks off his computer screen.

Instead of turning off his computer, Ivan makes another skype call to Ingramisck on a secure channel.

"How'd it go?" Ingramisck asks right away when he sees Ivan's face.

"I've got my foot in the door. I'll let you know after I've successfully connected." Ingramisck's eyebrow arches slightly when he hears that.

"Anyway, tell me something how did you get an invite? This club is notoriously secretive with security that would be a problem for the best spies to get past."

"Getting an invite wasn't as hard as I thought it would be. I just caught a break from an unexpected source."

"If you say so, just let me know when we can move further."

At that, both men log off.

Chapter 15

It takes three weeks for Calhoun to call Ivan back, but when he does, Calhoun is excited.

"I got Friday off after practice, but I gotta report to the field Saturday to get ready for the Sunday game," Calhoun explains.

"What about your girl?" Ivan asks with concern.

"We'll have dinner Thursday night after practice followed by breakfast in da mornin' fore she goes to work."

"She won't be calling you while you're in London, will she? I don't want you to get caught in an awkward situation."

Ivan is being extra cautious. He doesn't want to have to kill this woman for being too nosy or Calhoun for that matter because of too many questions.

"Yo chill man, don't sweat it. She won't bother me, we've been together long enough to where she knows I like to have my quiet time by myself, it won't be a problem."

"I'll see you in London on Friday then."

"Al'ight, I'll holla at chu."

There is no turning back now, Ivan is dragging an innocent person he cared about into a dangerous situation. Hopefully, Calhoun's part wouldn't be too much longer than Ivan hopes it will be. As instructed, Calhoun contacts Ivan on a burner phone he bought from a cell phone store an hour away from the airport.

"I gace da people at da club my name and told 'em I'd be bringin' somebody wit me. Dey checked der records and remembered me. I told 'em we'd be comin' at 8:00pm tonight."

"Good. I'll meet you outside of your hotel," Ivan responds before he hangs up.

During the phone conversation, Calhoun also tells Ivan that the people who run the club like their customers to dress nice, so when Ivan meets Calhoun that night, he is dressed in a tailor made light brown suit with a matching tie and polished dress shoes. Calhoun has on a blue business suit and his dreadlocks are tied back showing off his goatee. Ivan has cut off his braids and is wearing his hair in a cut fade with waves.

"Damn brah, you lookin nice," Calhoun complements while looking Ivan up and down.

"Thanks, so do you, let's go."

From the hotel, they take a cab. Ivan figures it would be safe because he already has Rosa and one of his men steaked out a block away from the club. This is in case he'd have to make a fast get away. The outside of the club is not what Ivan expected. He was expecting to see a seedy building like most of the night clubs in the states or the larger cities in Russia.

But when the cab drops them off in front of an elegant mansion with properly dressed security with doormen opening car doors for guests. They also appear to have valets to park the customer's cars. To the left of the entrance is a podium with an Indian man dressed in a black suit standing at it. When he see Ivan and Calhoun, he looks at a laptop he had on top of the podium.

"Mr. Calhoun Williams and guest," Calhoun announce to the man at the podium.

"Ah yes here you are. Welcome back, Mr. Williams. And you are?" the man ask turning to Ivan.

"I'm Ivan Fisk," Ivan answer. "Welcome to Dante's 9th Wonder Mr. Fisk, I'm sure you'll enjoy yourself," the Indian man says to him with a proper British accent.

"Thank you," Ivan says to the man before he waves them in.

As he probably would have guessed, Ivan is scanned for hidden cameras and other devices with an electronic wand by security once he's inside. They do the same thing to Calhoun. The floor is a checkered black and white fashion with fancy Italian markings on the white sections of the floor. There is a long staircase with an elevator to the side wall, beautiful works of art on the walls and an antique crystal chandelier hanging from the ceiling.

"This shit looks more like a presidential palace than a kinky fetish house," Ivan says in amazement.

"I told ya dis place is dope, but don't be fooled da real freaky shit happens behind da closed rooms. And check dis out, in da basement, dey got a ring where muthafuckas have all kinds of fights. The prizes anything you want, man, woman or whateva."

"Even animals?" Ivan asks Calhoun with a skeptical tone.

"I don't know but probably. You can't have any of da employees dough, dat's dey rule, plus you can't kill nobody, of course."

"Well, ain't that a shame," Ivan says sarcastically.

As the two men walk through the spacious mansion like club Ivan notices there are guards dressed in dark suits strategically stationed and placed in different areas of the place and female guards dressed in business wear walking around pretending to be guests. But Ivan could tell by the way the women moved that they were ex-military of some kind.

Ivan wanted to move around more freely to check to see if his target was at the club, but by him being a guest of a potential member he had to stay at Calhoun's side for the time being. Ivan figured a man like Oliver Quartz would be prone to check out the fights in the basement, but Calhoun wanted to peek in the different rooms instead.

One room showed a white man dressed up like an old plantation owner from the old American South whipping naked black women while a dark complected man is chained to the wall. Another room featured men dressed in Nazi uniforms taking turns sodomizing a dark-haired woman in peasant rags screaming in Hebrew. Another room showed a woman dressed as a magician with a wand standing next to a giant top hat.

"Ladies and gentlemen, for my next trick, I'm going to pull a rabbit out of a hat. Abracadabra, presto!" the woman shouts.

Then in a puff of smoke a naked fat white man jumps out of the hat wearing bunny ears on his head and a puffy tail on his ass.

Calhoun thinks this all is funny, but to Ivan, this is stupid and the other scenes so far too degrading. Nothing seem to catch Ivan's eye until him and Calhoun come to a large room made to look like a courtroom.

There is a tall black man dressed as a bailiff standing to the side and in the middle of the room is a judge's bench podium. Also, there is a table with a white woman wearing nothing, but high heels, an office shirt with a tie and glasses. Calhoun wants to move on, but Ivan is intrigued.

"Hold on a minute, let's see how this plays out," Ivan urges Calhoun.

The makeshift bailiff then speaks, "All rise for his honor Judge Benjamin Mathios presiding!" the bailiff announces in a booming voice that filled the room.

Next, a well-built black man who appeared to be in his fifties with skin a nice shade of brown walks out of a door from the wall wearing dark pants, a judge's robe opened at the front showing off his chest, which was partially covered in graying nappy black hair. He was kind of tall, not like the bailiff, but still over six feet a bit.

His face was nicely framed with a well-trimmed goatee with sprinkles of gray in it. The top of his head was bald and the sides were closely cut. Despite his age, he was a good-looking man and Ivan took note. He never imagined a scene like this.

"You may be seated!" Benjamin says. "Prosecution, present your case," the judge orders.

Just then three naked white men are lead into the room in ankle chains and handcuffs with grand dragon tattoos and Nazi swastikas on their bare bubbly butts with Klu Klux Klan hoods on their heads.

"What are the charges?" the judge asks the prosecutor.

"These men are charged with being sexually suppressed bigoted faggots who have no regard for human life. The people move for immediate severe punishment," the prosecutor says while winking at the judge and blowing him kisses.

"How do the defendants plead?" the judge asks.

"We're innocent! We got a God-given right as Americans to express our beliefs and we got nuthin' but contempt fer dis nigger court!" one of the three men shouts in a Southern accent.

"Then, it's the judgement of this court that I find you guilty and I hereby sentence you to the severest punishment for men like you. Bailiff, prosecutor take them, but save the one who mouthed off for me."

Suddenly, the bailiff comes toward the men unzipping his pants.

The three white men have a look of terror, especially when they see the prosecutor slip on a strap on dildo with ticklers at the end of it. The judge steps down from the bench while noticing Ivan staring at him.

"So, you think this is a nigger court boy? This is a court of law and your out of order," the judge says sternly to the convict who spoke to him.

He knees the man hard in his bare groin and spits in his face when the man crumbles to the floor. All the while the other two are being ravished from behind, their screams filling the room.

"You're not even worth my time you piece of shit," the judge says in disgust walking away from the humiliated man. Judge Benjamin instead ignores the man on the floor and walks toward the defiant looking Ivan who can't seem to take his eyes off the older man in authority.

"Did you think my verdict was just, my ivory brother?" he asks Ivan while keeping in character.

Ivan is slightly put off by the question at first and due to the fact the man is standing so close to him that Ivan can smell his breath doesn't help, which reeks of bourbon and mint gum.

"This is your show, my opinion doesn't matter," Ivan answers back.

Benjamin then turns to Calhoun, who has an irritated look on his face.

"What about you, do you feel the same way as your cute friend?"

"Man, I don't give a fuck. Aw Ivan, let's git outta here, dis scene is borin'," Calhoun blurts out angerly.

"I'm afraid we have to go, but maybe we'll see you again sometime," Ivan then says with a smile.

"I hope so," the judge says with a similar type of smile.

"Aw Christ, mate whatta are ya doin wit dat pale wanka mate? Are ya gonna fuck me wit dat black cock of yours or not?" the man who spoke to the judge earlier in an American Southern drawl suddenly yells in his native British accent.

"It's fine, you'll get yours like always. It's my dime anyway," the judge responds as he walks back to the man who yelled at him, but steadily looking at Ivan over his shoulder.

"Man, what was dat shit? Dat mutha fucka was straight up tryin' to git in yo draws. Shit is sick, dude was old nuff to be yo gramps."

"He wasn't that old, Calhoun, he was just being friendly. Sides what do you care? You've got somebody to fuck on the daily basis, It shouldn't matter to you who I talk to. Now, if you're so annoyed let's go down to the basement. I wanna see the fights before we go," Ivan suggests, not feeling Calhoun's jealousy at all.

Relenting, Calhoun agrees to take Ivan to the basement of the club, even though he wanted to explore other scenes he had witnessed the last time he was there at the club. To get to the basement, they have to take a special elevator operated by one of the employees. He uses a key card to press a button to take them down.

The basement looks like a large banquet hall with rows of fancy tables and chairs. The fighting ring is far up in front of the hall encased in what looks like bullet proof glass. A movie screen size viewer is hanging over the ring for people to see who happened to be seated far away. Before they sit down, Ivan and Calhoun are checked again for hidden devices.

"This way if you please," another employee politely says to them as he escorts them to their table.

The fight hadn't started yet, but the hall was still half full with people, so Calhoun and Ivan are seated in the middle of the hall. They aren't in the front by the ring, but they can still see it even without the view screen.

"Man dis is some good seats we got brah. I hope it's a good ass fight," Calhoun comments.

A few minutes later, the view screen from above clicks on. A distinguished-looking gentleman appears on the screen wearing gold rimmed glasses and a top hat. From the upper part of him that's showing, it looks like he's wearing a black tuxedo. When he speaks, you can hear his voice all through the large hall.

"Ladies and gentlemen I hope you're enjoying your visit at Dante's 9th Wonder. Our establishment has many diversions to entertain it's guests, including what you are about to witness here this evening. As always we hope you enjoy this evenings matches and diversions as long as you obey our rules. Now to our first match, this is a handicap match, two against one. Presenting from the deepest parts of the continent of Africa, but educated here in Europe, able to speak six different languages, standing at six foot ten inches tall Karum Tishumby."

The near giant African native steps into the ring completely naked covered in tribal war paint, wearing a golden lion's mane on his head and holding a gleaming spear. From the distance they're sitting, Ivan and Calhoun could still tell the man was powerfully built and well-endowed in the middle.

I'll bet his wife is happy, Ivan thinks to himself.

"And his opponents hailing from Kyoto Japan, Mr. and Mrs. Hashimoto, educated in their native Japan and the United States where Mrs. Hashimoto hails from in Hawaii. Both can speak collectively seven languages."

The couple enters the ring with Mr. Hashimoto wearing only a red thong trimmed in black lining holding a Japanese samurai sword and his wife is dressed in a hula skirt, topless with a spear native to her homeland in her hand. Though the couple is smaller than their opponent, there's something dangerous that Ivan sees in their eyes.

The fight starts with Karum making the first move swinging his spear at the couple. They skillfully tumble out of the way and attempt to cut the larger African's tendons on the back of his feet, but he's much faster than he looks, leaping up in the air like a dance causing the blades to miss his feet.

But he's not the only one with acrobatic abilities, when he lands back on his feet Mrs. Hashimoto uses the ropes of the ring as leverage to leap up and knee Karum in the jaw and catches him on the side of his neck with her spear. Karum then back hands her across the face, sending her flying to the mat. Mr.

Hashimoto charges at Karum with his sword pointing straight at him. Karum kicks him away, but instead of falling to the mat Mr. Hashimoto back flips, throwing his sword up in the air and catching it when he's standing upright again. By then, his wife has recovered. It's clear the fighters are more than they seem.

This time, the battle is joined and the fighters come at each other with all weapons drawn. Though it appears both of the Hashimotos are moving in the same way at Karum, Mrs. Hashimoto suddenly changes her position leaping onto her husband's shoulders and flying at Karum's throat with her spear.

As she does this her husband goes after Karum's exposed genitalia, but as if expecting this Karum has his legs go into the splits, avoiding Mrs. Hashimoto's attack and guarding against Mr. Hashimoto's sword assault against his dick and balls. Before they can react, Karum uses his long legs as windmills, going on his back swinging them wildly, knocking the couple to the mat.

Mrs. Hashimoto crawls out of the way, but Karum gets a hold of her husband's sword and puts his neck in a scissor hold. Mrs. Hashimoto remains free with her weapon and she grabs Karum by the throat, but she won't be able to cut his head off before he snaps her husband's neck.

"This match is a draw!" the announcer on the monitor yells, but the fighters don't move from their positions.

"The match is a draw, it is over! Yield your weapons now!" the announcer orders. Some of the security comes to the ring armed. One of the security guards, aims his gun at Karum's kneecaps. Seeing this, he releases Mr. Hashimoto and his wife drops her spear.

Though it's against tradition, Mrs. Hashimoto helps her husband out of the ring. Meanwhile, Karum jumps up and down around the ring, shouting in his native tongue as if he won. Calhoun and Ivan are getting a kick out of watching Karum's penis swinging from side to side, twirling around as he moves.

Ivan tenses up when he senses someone is behind him. He turns around with a fork from the table in his hand. He's stunned to see Benjamin Mathios walking toward him wearing a yellow suit instead of the judge's garb he had on earlier when Ivan and Calhoun first met him.

"Shit's intense, ain't it? You know, some of the fighters are members who participate in these matches as part of a fantasy and win a prize, usually by another member who bet against them and lost. The Hashimotos are big on threesomes with different types of men and Karum likes to bottom and be disciplined, which is very unusual for a black man. I could introduce you to either of them, but I'd rather have you for myself. That is if your friend doesn't mind," Benjamin says to Ivan looking him up and down like a juicy steak.

"Naw yo honor we cool, but maybe my friend can check you out some other time playa."

Benjamin doesn't respond to Calhoun's sarcastic tone. He just stares at him with an arched eye brow. During the exchange, another match begins.

"Oh, you'll like this, it's between two men fighting over the same woman. One of the men is from India and the other from Spain. They've been going at it for a year now in the ring, the woman in question continues to sleep with both of them," Benjamin states to Ivan while ignoring Calhoun.

"What did you say your name was again?" Benjamin then asks out of the blue.

"I didn't."

"Then, in that case, can you tell me now?"

"Maybe, next time if I'm in town again."

"Then until next time," Benjamin says seductively with a wink.

No sooner than Benjamin leaves, another person approaches them about a half an hour later. This time, it's a beautiful tall shapely blonde woman.

"Hello, how are you? I was wondering would you be interested in playing a little game with me and my girlfriend?" the woman asks with a thick foreign accent.

"Sure, we'd love to play," Calhoun eagerly answers. But once again, he's ignored.

The woman focuses her attention on Ivan.

"You look like a Greek ivory statue. I would love to watch my girlfriend paint all over your body. Then we would make love to each other at your feet," the woman expresses.

"Uh, where are you from Mrs...."

"Olga, I'm from Sweden and my girlfriend is German."

"I'm sorry, Olga, but I don't like women sexually."

"That's fine, you can stand still naked while we make love in front of you to remind us when we first met at the history museum in France."

"That sounds nice, but I'm afraid I'll have to pass, but thank you for the offer though."

"Are you sure?"

"Yes I'm sure," Ivan answers with slight smile. The woman walks away with a disappointed look on her face. Calhoun can't hide his frustration.

"Man, what tha fuck? Am I invisible or some shit? You must've been tempted to try pussy da way I see da honeys hollin at chu."

"No not really, I've always been queer since I was a boy."

Deep down, Calhoun suspects the reason people are put off by him is because of his burned scarred skin, but he doesn't let it bother him too much. He of course, occasionally gets attention from women, though Ivan's the only man he's been with. But the way Ivan was outshining him without even trying was bothering.

The second match doesn't hold their attention that much, neither does the third, which is of two women dressed as Greek Amazons. Toward the end of the third match, Karum comes out of a room facing the back of the ring with his war paint washed off dressed in a tailor made tan colored dress pants, brown size thirteen alligator shoes and an oversized white button up polo shirt.

"You gentlemen enjoying the show?" he asks with a thick accent of his African country.

Ivan is rolling his eyes as he gears up for another person to make a pass at him, however Karum was intriguing like the judge. So, he decided he was going to make him work for it if he wanted to get in his draws. But suddenly Ivan is surprised. Karum's eyes shift from him to someone he didn't expect.

"And who might you be?" Karum inquires looking straight at Calhoun. He didn't expect to be the object of somebody's focus, so Calhoun doesn't answer right away.

"I think he's talking to you," Ivan whispers to Calhoun.

"Oh, uh Calhoun man. How you doin?"

"Well Calhoun. I'm Karum. Did you enjoy watching me fight?"

"Yeah it was good."

"What did you think of my body? You know, where I'm from, my people hardly wear clothing at all. When boys come of age in my village, they're taken to the local river and the men of my village use machetes to shave their bodies until they're bare as newborn babies. A tradition that's practiced throughout our lives with the men in my country's life. See?" Karum says unbuckling his pants revealing he's not wearing any underwear and a hairless pubic area.

Without warning, he takes one of Calhoun's hands and places it on his exposed area in full view of the other guests without shame.

"See, feel how smooth that is. We use special oils to keep our bodies from becoming infected and too bumpy."

"Th, dat's uh, uh is smooth brah," Calhoun stutters, letting his hand be guided by Karum's.

But nervousness of being watched by other people, especially a large group, causes Calhoun to pull his hand away.

"Don't be embarrassed, I don't mind being touched, in spite of our people's history. Men shouldn't be ashamed of touching each other, even black men. The men in my village touch each other all the time, as well as the women. You've had a rough life, haven't you? Too many people are unwilling to touch you because of how you look. I also bet you like feeling and giving pain as a result. I like that, a man who feels pain through rough pleasure. Healthy pain lets you know you're alive."

"I had a lover, an Apache Indian who's tribe had a ceremony to test a man's worth. They would tie hooks at the end of ropes and put them in a man's nipples, making him march as they stretched his chest with the hooks and ropes. Damn, did he have a lot of anger. I love a man who's full of anger, it makes sex great," Karum says through his heaving chest.

"Well, I don't know if I'm all dat, me and my girl get along ok. We git a little freaky sometimes obviously, but we ain't into pain shit."

"So, you like women too, you're bisexual as they call it. I have a wife too, a white woman with lots of money. Her father came to my village looking for undocumented labor. He took me and a little girl, I was sixteen at the time. The girl trained as a maid and I worked as a grounds keeper for five years. Surprisingly the man paid well and I used the money I saved to go to college and business school. I started my own business making it grow."

"My former owner was old fashioned, he wouldn't let his only daughter run his business, so she tracked me down and offered me a proposition, agree to marry her and she would give me a third of her family business."

Ivan and Calhoun realizes that Karum like to talk about himself.

"So, she doesn't mind your hobbies here?" Ivan asks interrupting Karum's recount to Calhoun.

"She doesn't care, we haven't seen each other in almost six years, I'm free to do what I want," Karum says proudly.

The more Ivan learns about Karum, the less he likes him. Ivan would never marry a woman for convenience to hide what he is. He couldn't stand that type of lie. Although Gregor was married, everybody knew he also liked men and about Ivan, Gregor didn't try to hide it. Sure, there are always going to be people who like men and women, but closet cases who hide what they are were unbelievable to Ivan. Although there were exceptions like Calhoun who just wanted affection from anybody.

Calhoun however is totally into the tall African. Rubbing his hand up and down his back, he whispers in Calhoun's ear.

"My room that I rent here is upstairs on the top floor. Why don't we go up there and you can show me how angry you really are."

"Damn dat sounds like a plan," Calhoun readily agrees.

"Don't worry about me, I'll find some way to keep myself busy while you're gone for a bit," Ivan insists while looking at the different people in the hall. Karum then guides Calhoun to a different elevator than the one him and Ivan rode on earlier.

"Where does dis go? It ain't da one we came on," Calhoun asks and says anxiously.

"This is for members who don't always want to play in public."

A strange statement given that Karum is clearly an exhibitionist.

Karum doesn't even wait until they get to his room before he unbuttons his shirt and lets it fly open as he takes off his pants leaving on his alligator shoes showing his matching brown dress socks.

"You always walk around wit no draws on?"

"I didn't know what underwear were until I was twenty-five and then found them too constraining, even boxers," Karum explains while flinging his pants over his shoulder.

Calhoun felt a tinge of envy for Karum, the same he already felt toward Ivan. He wished he could feel that confident about his body. He had added muscle mass from working out to play football, but part of his body was still burned.

Calhoun was sure Karum barely notice the stares they were getting on the floor with the private rooms from the other guests who happen to be walking past them in the hall. Once they're in Karum's room Karum removes what little clothing he has on and throws them to the floor along with his pants.

"Get undressed, I want to see you," Karum orders Calhoun. Reluctantly, Calhoun begins to come out of his suit. When he's done he stands naked before Karum feeling more vulnerable than he's ever felt in his life. Karum then kisses him passionately and deeply.

"Beautiful, so beautiful," Karum repeats as he runs his fingers across Calhoun's scarred part of his body down to his undamaged penis, which is sticking straight out.

He never thought he'd be with a man taller than him, but here he was looking up at Karum.

"Do you want to punish me for being beautiful?" Karum asks, walking over to the closet opening it up. Inside the door of the closet were different types of whips and paddles hanging on hooks. Seeing the tools for discipline Calhoun gets another idea.

"I wanna wrestle."

"What?"

"I wanna wrestle. I don't wanna whipya or some shit, I wanna feel yo body fore I take ya."

Before Karum can utter another word, Calhoun tackles him to the floor like a linebacker. Karum struggles back making his makeshift opponent grapple harder. Karum is stronger, but Calhoun has experience with this type of fighting from when he wrestled in high school. Feeling the other man's body struggle against his was the ultimate rush.

Calhoun never did anything like this with Ivan. For some reason, he never wanted to until now. Their playful battle leaves rug burns all over their bodies along with over turned furniture and broken objects. They take a moment to catch their breaths. They look at each other, chests heaving, eyeing the marks, foaming at the mouth.

"I'm ready," Calhoun announces, taking charge hoisting his larger lover on the bed with his powerful legs in the air.

"You got any rubbers?" Calhoun asks with caution.

"No, but I can have some brought up."

"Dat's cool, I'm really in da mood to smash right now."

As if they're psychic Karum presses a button on the night stand and less than a minute later, somebody knocks on the door.

Calhoun's feelings of inadequacy and embarrassment disappear when he walks to the door still naked, taking a second to get a tip for whomever is at the door.

"Yeah thanks," he says to a timid appearing woman holding a basket of various types of condoms.

She grins mischievously when she sees Calhoun's erect manhood. He hands her a twenty before shutting the door on her. He then retakes his position over Karum, he stands up on the bed because Karum is so tall. Lifting his legs up in the air once again, Calhoun slides his condom covered shaft inside him. Calhoun flinches when Karum's insides clamp around his manhood tightly.

"Is something wrong?" Karum asks looking up at him with a smirk.

"You feel funny, kinda strange."

"I exercise it with a cumber and ice, you'll get used to it, ease into it."

Calhoun listens and starts off slow inching in little by little picking up a steady pace. He goes a little faster with every thrust, picking up a comfortable rhythm until he's on his knees with Karum's legs pulled back by his head.

"Aw man, yo ass feels good! I bet chu fuck good too, shit! Aw, ah, ah shit god damn!" Calhoun screams as his liquid cream fills the rubber. Karum legs wrap around Calhoun's waist as he rests his head on his chest.

Minutes later, Calhoun slips on another condom and takes Karum from behind with him on all fours. The large man straddles Calhoun when he jumps up in the middle of it and pins him to the bed. He squats on Calhoun's dick and begins to ride him like his girlfriend sometimes does. Calhoun loves this position because he gets to lay back and relax this way.

"You like fucking me, don't you? It gives you a thrill to be with a man stronger than you, to use him, abuse him however you want?" Karum asks in a seductive tone.

"Y—yeah," is all Calhoun can utter at the moment.

"Oh, you're so beautiful. Does your pale friend know how lucky he is? Your girlfriend can't appreciate you enough if you have to search for real pleasure that truly satisfies you."

With an expert clinch of his ass muscles Karum milks another nut out of Calhoun.

"Do me, do me," Calhoun urges as he pat his quivering asshole.

"No, may be next time. Besides, you looked like you needed to let out your frustrations on somebody more powerful than you."

"When did ya realize you like bein fucked by other niggas?"

"I always knew, even when I was a boy playing in the water with other boys. It always felt right to me. I never felt ashamed of it like most men do who are like us. So, I became rich enough to where I could enjoy myself how I wanted without scrutiny from people who don't understand."

"I wish I could be dat free," Calhoun says as he stares into Karum's eyes, slowly he eventually falls asleep.

Back down in the basement of the club Ivan is still watching the fights and scanning the area in case his target shows up. Despite his strange color, Ivan is still very handsome. With his white skin people at the club find him exotic, gay or straight. This time the ones to approach him are the Hashimotos.

Up close, they are an attractive Asian couple and he wonders if this is a coincidence that they have approached him awhile after Karum did. The wife makes the introductions.

"I'm Khulonnie and this is my husband Arran. You already know our last name, we are pleased to make your acquaintance."

"I'm Ivan Fisk, please to meet you."

"We noticed you were pretty impressed with our fight, which leads us to believe you might be curious about other aspects of us," Khulonnie boldly surmises.

"Oh, do I?"

"We are not talking about sex. We realize you are not here for that. Your mind is on another task, one we cannot guess."

The wife continues to talk while the husband remains silent with his hands crossed over the front of his kimono, which is covered in Japanese lettering. Ivan could tell right away that the couple was intelligent as advertised, but the wife appeared to be more intelligent than her husband.

"We would be pleased to get to know you on an intellectual level, though if sex did occur we would not be adverse to that possibility."

Finally, it seems someone has caught Ivan's attention without making a pass at him. The Hashimotos were interesting enough for to take them up on their offer. Besides Ivan had a way of keeping in contact with his backup.

"I'd be honored to get to know you better. Would you like to talk here?"

"If it pleases you, we would rather speak in someplace more private," Arran says in a stern voice, finally speaking.

"Lead the way," Ivan urges.

Chapter 16

The Hashimotos were speaking the truth, they does want to get to know Ivan for who he is, not just what he could do for them in bed. Though he is having problems believing this when they all enter their personal suite and Khulonnie suggests he take a bath. They have personal attendants who helps Ivan undress and personally bath him. Ivan finds it strange that neither of the Hashimotos stays in the large bathroom to watch Ivan be soaped up and washed in the big built in round tub.

The attendants, who are both female, seem to enjoy themselves washing every crevice Ivan had and those he didn't know he had. After they were done, he feels itchy and raw.

As Ivan steps out of the tub, one of the attendants produces a bottle of lotion. It has a fragrant smell to it, relaxing Ivan's muscles and relieving the itchy feeling. All through the process they don't touch Ivan's penis, they barely wash it, only near and around it. When the women are done, a third attendant appears, a male dressed in a white business suit holding a black kimono.

"The Hashimotos are waiting for you in the main area," the male attendant says to Ivan while handing him the kimono.

"Your clothes will be taken care of and ready for you when you leave," the handsome Asian man states to Ivan as if reading his mind.

Ivan attempts to see if the man is turned on by his body or not, but he can't tell, his face is unreadable, as are the women. The Asian man holds his arm out for Ivan to follow him, after he puts on the kimono.

"How long have you been with the Russian mafia?" Arran asks right when Ivan walks into the room.

"What?"

"Your tattoos, they're the kind the Russians use," Arran points out. Ivan had almost forgot about them.

"In my business, I sometimes have to deal with men who are secretly with the yakuza. It peaked my interest in them, so I sometimes study up on them and other groups who are similarly inclined. You are in a very dangerous profession for yourself. The Yakuza tolerate men like you to a point, but the Bratva don't."

"I'm a special case, we've come to and understanding."

"Really interesting. So, they know you're gay?"

"Yes they do. Do your associates, all of them that is, know you entertain other men, ones you don't work with?"

"But we are not doing anything unseemly, we're just talking."

Arran was good. If he was attracted to Ivan, he didn't show it. His wife however was more forward in that regard. She couldn't take her eyes off Ivan.

"If you don't anything unseemly, then what are you doing in a place like this?"

"Because both me and my wife like to fight fiercely and this is one of the few places that let my wife participate with me and sadly she has a sexual appetite that I can't match. Such things are not permitted in my country by women who are married to prominent businessman. I told her it was a wasted effort with you, but she was determined to know you anyway. There is a mystery about you that we both find intriguing. If I were to guess, you have the duality in your family roots, loyalty only for a select few, mainly in your family."

"You may not like women sexually, but you have been with them before, probably out of duty for your country," Khulonnie says correctly deducing that fact about Ivan.

"Were these people spies?" Ivan closely asks himself. How else were they able to figure out these things about Ivan.

"You came to this club for a purpose having nothing to do with what goes on here, but yet you fit right in easily with the atmosphere here. Why is that?"

"Maybe, I just like to watch every once in a while."

"No, it's not that. Part of you probably feels you belong here. Everyone who comes here feels that way. Your friend certainly does, our opponent saw that right away."

"So, you were watching us together, seeing which one of us was to your taste."

"Unfortunately, you're not mine either. My wife may be liberal with her affections, but no offense, but the few times I've slept with other men it's been with my own nationality. European, African and western men are too boorish and socially primitive for my taste. But since I met you, I think you might be the exception."

This man has the nerve to be a snob and xenophobically racist as well as bisexual. Ivan couldn't wrap his head around it. Obviously his wife doesn't share his prejudice, at least not when it came to choosing her sexual partners that is. She also has another kink that Ivan slyly notice.

By the way, Ivan was inching closer to Arran and the way she is looking at them, Khulonnie liked seeing two men together. Ivan had heard rumors about this, but he doesn't believe them because he figures they were made up by horny men who were into women having sex with each other. As he inches closer, Ivan allows his kimono to open at the front.

"You've never found any other man the exception besides me?"

"No not really, I just allow them to please my wife. I don't even like to watch, it bores me."

"But I don't? That's why you gave me a bath first, so you wouldn't be bored by me?"

"I have all the men who come here cleaned, so they don't dirty up the linen we sleep on."

By now, Ivan is close to Arran to where he can feel his erection against his thigh, but he doesn't react.

"You are very sure of yourself, but composed despite your actions. You think we might work for a person you're really looking for, but I assure you we do not. So you might as well stop using your well-trained talents to seduce me."

The Hashimotos are well informed, Ivan has to give them that, but they still know too much for his taste. But before he could make a kill move on either of them, the two females who bathed him earlier appear out of nowhere and clip him to the floor. While trying to get up, Ivan gets another surprise by the third attendant who's standing over him with a samurai sword at his throat. Ivan didn't even hear them come in.

"Automatic weapons, other guns and listening devices are not allowed in this club, but certain metals and other materials are allowed when they are in pieces that look unassuming. But one can't fathom what they like put together.

So, I'm sure you have skill enough to kill us all before receiving a deadly blow from one of our guards, but you'd have to explain leaving a room of dead bodies. Many witnesses saw you enter."

"Don't worry, we won't mention this outburst to the owners, so you'll be permitted to return to the club to find your quarry. You can keep the kimono as a reminder of what might yet occur. We bid you good evening."

"Oh, by the way, you might have some difficulty getting your friend to leave, it's rumored that Karum has a habit of making his lovers emotionally spent as well as physically," Arran says with a partial smile.

Ivan had never been so frustrated and turned on at the same time. The only thing he could do was grab his clothes and walk out of the suite.

Thankfully, he had a hidden state-of-the-art listening device deep in his ear with special coding that prevents scanners from finding it and the women bathing him couldn't find it either when they were cleaning his ears. Due to the customs of the club, nobody notices Ivan walking at a swift pace with a robe fully open at the front with a full view of his swinging penis. Taking a gamble that Calhoun would remember he has a game tomorrow Ivan returns to the basement.

The gamble would pay off fortunately, Calhoun wakes up to the vibration of the bed shaking. Karum is on the floor doing a tribal warrior dance. Calhoun is getting turned on again at the sight of the tall naked African shaking and gyrating all over the place. Giving into animalistic instinct, Calhoun leaps from the bed and tackles his larger play foe once again, pinning him to the floor.

"I haven't even showed you how my people finish it!" Karum yells while laughing. Calhoun doesn't say anything, he just passionately kisses Karum on the lips. Near the beginning of a third round of male love making, Calhoun stops.

"Oh shit! I gotta go! I'm sorry man I got some place to be, I'm sorry," Calhoun says in a haste, running to the door, barely remembering to grab his clothes.

The guests are not amazed by a half-burned naked man, but by him running through the hall. He doesn't even put his underwear on first, instead he slips on his pants and shirt with his shoes. He puts on his jacket, but puts his tie in his pocket with his socks.

"Damn, you look like you're in a hurry," Ivan says in amusement when he sees Calhoun's disheveled appearance.

"Cut it out man, let's jus git outta here."

"Only if you agree to let me tuck you in again," Ivan playfully suggest, partially wanting to relieve some of the sexual tension he has built up.

"Whateva man, let's jus go al'ight."

Calhoun doesn't even ask why Ivan is wearing only a kimono instead of his clothes. A minute prior to Calhoun coming back the stairs to the basement, Ivan whispers into his ear piece for his backup to call it a night, telling he'll speak to them in the morning.

When Ivan wakes up in his hotel room the following morning, Calhoun is gone, so Ivan leaves the room shortly after.

"Uh excuse me sir, I think this is for you!" a woman working at the front desk screams as Ivan is walking past.

For me, but I didn't give my name out last night. How would they know to have anything for me? Ivan thinks.

"The messenger said to give this to a tall albino man," she explains while handing Ivan a bouquet of white roses. Ivan is stunned and at the same time, his cell phone rings.

"Hello."

"Your hunch was right, our boy does like to watch the fights in the basement of the club. I showed his description through text on the phone of the people we paid off from the decoder in your ear piece. I found out Oliver Quartz likes to watch them on Monday afternoon. The problem is the rest of the club is closed on Monday, so it's by special invitation. A high-ranking member has to bring through a more secretive entrance than the regular ones," the person on the other end informs Ivan.

He notices the bouquet of roses has a card attached to them. So, he pulls the card from the stems and reads it: "I still hoped you liked my judgement. Sign: Benjamin Mathios," Ivan reads.

"I don't think getting back in will be as hard as we figured Ingramisck," he answers in the cell.

Sitting in a safe house, fortified by the latest alarm systems and guards in Thailand, Oliver Quartz is preparing for his trip to Britain. As he's making preparations for a flight on a private airfield, his phone rings. It's on a secure line, so he knows it's important.

"Yes."

"Cancel your trip, it's too dangerous!" the voice on the other end yells.

"Janet? What the hell are you talking about?"

"Your man Egriff is missing and as far as we know Ingramisck is still breathing. He more than likely failed at his mission. The Fisks are onto you, they know who we are."

"Do you think Marvin might've told them?"

"No, I don't think so, he's dead. I think they found out some other way, I just don't know how. Our sources say Ivan Fisk was at Dante's 9th Wonder Friday, they've discovered you're a member there. I told you it was a bad idea to keep going to this mongrel filth palace."

"I only go to watch fights that are illegal in most parts of the world, besides you have to be a member to enter the club on Mondays."

"Then how did Ivan Fisk get in Friday?"

"He must have gotten close to a low-level member to bring him as a guest. You can't get in the club on Mondays unless you're a long-time high-level member and guests are not allowed. These fights are to the death and the people who watch these fights are very important and powerful with too much to lose to let some deviants like the Fisks come in."

"It would be wise to cancel your trip."

"No, I have a better idea, we'll set a trap for the Fisks in case they manage to show up. Let our spy in the Bratva know and to get closer to those who are the closest to the Fisk family."

"This better work, we've already lost two of our key assets, we can't afford to lag further behind in this secret war."

"Don't worry it'll work, but if we do manage to lose somehow we could always tell the Fisks the full truth of what their late benefactor was really up to. The truth would be far more damaging than anything we could ever do. I'll contact you when the plan succeeds," Oliver says then hangs up.

Though most of the organization don't believe it, Rosa believes Ivan will go far in the Bratva and parts of the government. His family already has ties in key cities in the states and special forces for Russia and Cuba. In her opinion, the Bratva have grown stagnant in their thinking, they've forgotten why they were born in the first place, in rebellion against the short-sighted, narrow-minded vision of Communist Russia. In Rosa's mind, Ivan could be one of the men to take them to the future.

"So, what if he's gay? It doesn't matter, he's a powerful man in spite of that. He's not the first to be so," Rosa reasons in her mind.

Her thoughts are disturbed by the man lying next to her. One of the rejects that the Bratva gave Ivan. He's slow-witted, but he managed to somehow find out one of the other rejects works for the enemy. He said the man had pretty shiny cufflinks and asked him where he got them because he wanted a pair. The guard said they were a family heirloom. But Rosa was curious because the other rejects said it was amazing because they knew the man came from a poor family that couldn't afford food, let alone expensive cufflinks.

So, she checked the man's finances and found he had a secret account not paid by the Bratva, but someone else. Of course, she let Ivan know a week before he went to the fetish club. The man who brought this to her attention wasn't attractive, but he was nice to her and treated her like she had intelligence, which was refreshing to Rosa. He wasn't an attentive lover, but he followed directions well.

Ivan stayed in Great Britain after his initial visit to Dante's 9th Wonder. He would give it until Sunday evening for the call he was waiting on. About 2:30pm in the afternoon is when he got a letter at his hotel. Being a black man who was an albino in London, he was kind of easy to track down.

The letter comes with one white rose this time.

"I hope you like the roses, I couldn't figure out what to get you, so I opted for something white and beautiful like you. I never thought I'd say that to a black man. I would really like to see you again. If you're feeling the same, here's my cell number 546-613-7636. Look forward to hearing from you Mr. Fisk sincerely; Benjamin Mathios," the letter says.

Ivan finds it curious that Benjamin knows his name.

"He's a powerful man, he must've did a background check on me somehow. If I really want to know how, I have ways of finding right now. I gotta make myself a date," Ivan says out loud to himself.

Picking up his cell phone, Ivan dials the number the Judge wrote in his letter. After three rings someone answers.

"Hello?" a female voice on the other end says. Ivan is puzzled, he's not sure he has the right number.

"Is there a Benjamin Mathios there?" Ivan asks uneasily.

"Yes, this is his wife Helen Mathios. What's this about?"

Thinking quick on his feet, Ivan makes up a believable lie.

"I have a message from his court clerk concerning a case he's hearing in the State Supreme court."

Ivan was taking a big chance. Benjamin could've been a regular lawyer living out a judge fantasy. But fortunately, his gamble paid off.

"Oh alright, just a minute. Ben, Ben there's somebody calling you about a case!" she yells in the background.

"Thanks baby," Ivan hears him say to his wife before she hands him the phone.

"Judge Mathios speaking."

"Hey Judge, I got the white roses you sent me, maybe I can send some to your wife," Ivan sarcastically says. But the judge doesn't break character. "Oh, mark I'm glad you called, I was wondering about the situation of the diamond case. When can you come to my office to discuss it further? I wouldn't want to have to go through tracking you down again," the judge slyly says adding a bit of truth in the last sentence. Ivan was beyond pissed.

If he didn't need this guy to get into the closed club on Monday, he would find him and kill him.

"Are you always in the habit of giving your home phone number to strange men you wanna fuck?"

"Don't worry, my marriage is good, my wife has always supported me on whatever case I'm hearing, as I support her on her job," the judge answers in a tone to suggest his wife might know of his extracurricular activities.

"Fuck this shit, I need you to get me into the fights at Dante's 9th Wonder tomorrow evening or I'll find you wherever you are and tell your wife what you think of my body. Afterwards I'll slit your throat in front of her."

"Is that all? Well, that's no problem, just call my bailiff Frank Waters, you probably spoke to him Friday when you spoke to my court clerk. He can get you anything you need, no matter how different or difficult. Now, I can't tie up this line, my wife is expecting her mother to call. I'll text you Frank's info from my cell. This is your number, I hope? Goodbye."

And the judge hangs up, not giving Ivan a chance to respond. Ivan figured Frank Waters is the guy who arranges the judge's secret field trips and keeps other secrets for a hefty fee probably.

An hour later, Ivan's phone beeps to let him know he has a text. He clicks it on and reads: "Sorry sexy, didn't mean to upset you. Was true about Frank Waters, he can arrange for you to be at the club on Monday. Meet him outside the club, he'll give my unique proxy for you to get in without me. Glad you got my roses, from what I heard, I'll bet you tear some shit up. I can't wait to wrap my legs round your strong body. You got my cell now, call that next time and we can get together," end of text.

The text also had Frank Waters' number and Ivan called it right away.

"Yeah I'm a heavyset white man, I'll be wearing a blue suit with a matching tie. Come alone or no deal. I'll have the judge's special proxy for you to get in the club. Meet me out front at 7:00pm," the male voice says without giving Ivan a chance to talk, then he clicks off without another word.

As soon as that one-sided conversation is over, Ivan calls Rosa.

"Yeah it's all setup, bring along our disloyal friend. Tell him the time, 7:00pm, but tell him I'll be coming inside with someone, but of course I'll really be alone, so leave that part out. I have something special for him. Inform Ingramisck of my plan."

"Understood," Rosa answers.

The main reason the fights on Monday at Dante's 9th Wonder are illegal is because they are always to the death fought by prison inmates on death row from various prisons from around the world.

The winners have their sentences regulated to life, but there's always the possibility that they have to fight again. Also, before and after a fight, any prisoner can be used by a guest for whatever they like for the right price. This is what Frank Waters tells Ivan when he arrives the next evening at the club. But Ivan is surprised by the judge's proxy. It's a wedding band with the initials H.M carved into it.

"It's the judge's wife's wedding ring. He tells her he likes to take it to be cleaned every month, but sometimes it gets lost in the strangest places, but the judge always finds it. It also has a very small diamond inside it, so it can be scanned by the people here. The club knows anyone who wears it is a close associate of his honor," Frank Waters explains.

"Hmm, you must be a crazy fuck for the judge to give you this honor," Frank Waters adds before he walks away.

Like the other time, Rosa and the bodyguards are sitting in a van with tinted windows a block away from the club. Rosa brought the spy as instructed along with her slow-witted lover. The man is playing a video game on T.V in the van while the double agent is ever alert. A light blinks on his phone.

He thinks Rosa isn't watching him from the back where he's seated because she is up front. He quickly glances at his phone with a message telling him the trap is set for Ivan but Rosa is fully aware of him.

Oliver is seated at his regular spot waiting for the first fight to begin. However, the anticipation of killing one of his most irksome enemies has him feeling antsy. But the fight starts and his people stationed around the hall report not seeing Ivan. Another hour passes and Ivan is nowhere to be seen.

Oliver waves over one of his people to see what's the matter. The man is disguised as a waiter handing out drinks, so no one would question him talking to a guest too long.

"Where the fuck is that freak?" Oliver asks out of the side of his mouth.

"I don't know sir, our man reported to us saying that Ivan Fisk met with a man before he enter the club. It appeared the man he was talking to had given him something. Then he came in. He went by the elevator, but afterwards, they lost track of him," the waiter explains.

"Then find him now!" Oliver orders in an irritated tone. In spite of what's happening in the ring, Oliver is not concerned. He barely notices who kills who because he's so distracted by Ivan not being there.

Eventually, preparations for the beginning of the third match is underway. The announcer appears on the large video screen.

"Tonight, we have a special treat for you. A mini street fight type of grudge match, three men of the Aryan national gang from the prison of Pelican Bay from the state of California versus three laborers from the diamond mines of Botswana."

All the men are large and imposing, but there was something about the Botswana slave laborers that is deadly fierce. The announcer continues his pitch.

"This is a bareknuckle fight, all the prisoners have been thoroughly checked for hidden weapons. The rules are the other side wins when every member of the opposing team is dead. Let the grudge match begin."

Though all the Africans are wearing coveralls, one of them looks darker than the others. The Aryans draw first blood when one of them breaks the jaw of one of the Botswanans. They retaliate back by one of them grabbing an Aryan and tearing out part of his throat with his teeth. The match is brutal with each side receiving broken bones.

After two rounds, the darkest of the Botswanans is the only one left alive while a half-beaten Aryan is barely standing. Giving a moment to square off the two men then charge at each other. Suddenly in mid-charge the dark man dodges the Aryan's attack and in a split second raises his arm aiming it at Oliver's direction.

Oliver is puzzled until a dart shoots out of the dark man's sleeve. The dart goes through Oliver's neck sticking out the back. The dark man then quickly jumps out of the ring, running past the guards. Without warning smoke bombs fill the hall. As Oliver is choking to death the dark man is standing over his dying body.

"Who's the freak now bitch?" the man says with cold venom in his voice.

Oliver doesn't realize who the man is until he wipes off some of the darkness from his face, revealing pale white skin under then paint.

"You mother fu—fuc—" Oliver can't get the words out, instead he chokes on his blood and dies.

The smoke and confusion are perfect cover for Ivan to slip out unseen on his way back up to the entrance of the club. On the way, he ditches the coveralls in a trash can and wipes off the rest of the black makeup on his face and cleans his hands with 90% strength alcohol. When he reaches the exit, he calmly walks past the guards stationed there as they are called to inside of the club to help contain the chaos. In one breath, Ivan talks into his ear piece and at the same time talks to Frank Waters.

"Tell the judge I said thanks, I had a great do it," Ivan says while giving back the wedding ring to Waters.

Meanwhile, Rosa receives the order, turns around and shoots the double agent in the head.

"Remove this body," she coldly says to her slow-witted lover.

He obeys, opening up the sliding van door and tossing the dead man's body out like trash.

Janet Rinka is furious when she gets the news of her cousin's death.

"The time has become desperate, they'll be coming for me next, I have to prepare a welcome for them," Janet reasons.

The search for her takes five months, even with the help of the members of the help of the yakuza allied with Ingramisck and the police the Fisks knew in Chicago were no help in this regard at all. When they do finally track down Janet, she is sitting in an underground installation. All three generations of the Fisk family were on her trail, but when they found her only the oldest goes underground to where she is encase, it's a deathtrap. There are no armed guards waiting for Peter, which he figures the place had other pitfalls besides kill crazy henchmen.

Further and further, he went with no resistance. After walking down another long hall, Peter sees someone sitting at a table, getting closer, he can tell it's a woman. Her hair is dark and straight tied back in a ponytail.

"Welcome Peter, so you finally found me, but the game is gonna take a turn you didn't expect. Your daughter, I suspect knows a bit more than you and hasn't shared. So, I'm going to fill in the blanks. Your father wasn't the first to have Korcoff Vamitri as a benefactor of sorts. Haven't you ever wonder why you age so well? A body of a man half your age, it's not good genes, I can tell you. Your father was a well-cared for guinea pig, like the man before him."

"What the fuck are you talking about? I don't look that much younger than my age. Shit, my father's been dead for fifteen years," Peter sternly says.

"Has he?" Janet sharply asks.

"Are you familiar with Statin? No? Neither were we until ten years ago when me and Oliver stumbled across some redacted files hidden in a buried safe under piles of snow in Siberia. Someone who worked for Korcoff for a long time put them there after his death due to the instructions Korcoff gave them."

"The files had interesting information, especially about genetic testing and chemical manipulation on the human body. You see, Korcoff also employed a geneticist to assist him in his work to make the perfect spy. The work didn't pan out as he hoped, but the treatments did have unexpected side effects, which weren't discovered until years later."

"What side effects?" Peter asks with growing interest, though part of him was still apprehensive.

"Korcoff managed to track down and observe his agent in the rural area of the state of Ohio, cleverly without Statin's knowledge. Though he tried to hide it, he looked to be a man only in his mid-forties even though he had grown grandchildren well past their twenties. That's the effect! In certain genes, it slows the aging process in people with the y chromosome."

"This only works on the initial recipient and maybe some of their descendants, though the effects wouldn't be as strong. We were sure that wasn't only side effect, but that was the part that was redacted for some reason."

"But my father never took no chemical for nothing like that."

"Oh, not to his knowledge. The geneticist would hide the formula in Statin's and your father's food, inject it through the air of the room they happen to be in. Checking the results in the blood they'd given at physical exams. But another drawback to the formula was this effect almost never worked, except in Statin and your family. But the general public doesn't know that, all they are going to know is your family and Statin's supposedly have the secret to supposed eternal youth."

"What are you talking about?"

"I've leaked information about your family on the web all over the world. Even if I die here today, my revenge for my family's humiliation and disgrace by Korcoff and his pet rats will be fulfilled. There won't be any place you or any member of your family can go without being hunted, well the men that is, if you can call yourselves men."

"You mean the message I carefully intercepted before it was sent out?" a male voice suddenly says from the background behind Janet.

The man mutters something in German as he comes closer to the two people. Peter and Janet can pretty much guess who this man is.

"Statin?" Janet asks in alarm.

"Yes, I answered to that name once long ago, but my true name is John Cutter. I was fully aware I was being watched by Korcoff. He never could realize he taught me too well during the time he trained me. Fortunately, I kept in touch with my great-grandson who left our family's faith to live in the outside world. He taught me about computers, so I was able to monitor certain things from time to time."

Peter couldn't get over it. If this man was born in the early twentieth century, he definitely doesn't look it. Statin appeared to be a man only in his fifties. Sensing her life was at end, Janet asks a nagging question in hopes that someone still loyal to her family will act on it if the answer is positive.

"Is the geneticist still alive?" Janet asks in an almost pleading tone.

"Sadly, no and thankfully, he had the foresight to have all his research destroyed prior to his death. The secret dies with the Fisks and Cutters. Too bad, if your grandfather and his brother hadn't been so greedy and jealous, they might have been the benefactors of the formula instead of being slowly destroyed by its subjects."

After Statin says that, Peter lifts his gun and blows a hole in Janet's head with a bullet.

Turning to face Statin, Peter's head is full of questions.

"Is my father alive?"

"I'm not sure, we age slower, but I don't think we're immune to diseases like cancer or others."

"But me and my family saw the body, the medical examiner did an autopsy on him after he died."

"If he did fake his death to avoid detection by the Rinkas and Quartz and also manage not to be detected by the Russians and Americans, then he's every bit the agent Korcoff had hoped. I don't need to tell you the importance of keeping this secret. Where I come from, they laugh this condition off as being blessed by God but I worry about the men in my family who are not part of the Amish Community. The gene might still be active in them and other people would notice a man that doesn't age like them. It's the same in your family."

"Don't worry the gene is not that strong in my family like it is in yours. I don't look that good for my age."

"Don't be so sure," Statin wisely responds.

Peter then turns his head away for a moment in thought, but when he looks back around, Statin is gone. Taking out power high yield explosives from a bag he brought with, Peter places them all around the underground base. Reaching the exit, he detonates them with a remote. His daughter and grandson are still waiting for him outside.

"It's over, our greatest enemies are dead," Peter says to them with relief in his voice when he sees them.

"It's never over, our family will always have enemies, especially because of who we are," Natleaha comments.

"We can worry about that later, but for right now, we don't have to hide who we are."

"I don't know Grandpa, Mom is right, there's always going to be somebody who will always want to get at us."

"Let them try Ivan, we've proven that we're up to the challenge of anyone who opposes us," Peter states proudly.

So, the three of them leave the sight and take flight in different directions to get on with their lives.

Chapter 17

Two more years have passed and the Fisk family are steadily moving about with their lives. Peter still on occasion goes to UFC matches of his favorite ultimate fighter and the sex is still amazing between them. Patrick's wife doesn't join them as much since she's had a baby. Tapella is a doting mother more concerned with her baby daughter than participating in her husband's sexual antics.

"I'm a father. Can ya believe dat now?" Patrick brags with pride.

He happens to be out of town doing a fight when Tapella goes into labor. Patrick is going to arrange to see Peter after his fight, but he calls and tells Peter something came up.

Peter isn't too surprised because he knows Tapella is pregnant, it is all Patrick ever talk about when they are together. But having a baby to take care of doesn't slow down Patrick's time with Peter that much, if anything they talk more instead of mostly only fucking.

They are both fathers now.

"What was it like when ya had yer own lass mate?"

"It changes everything for the better," Peter proudly told his young lover and friend.

Natleaha, in a fit of remorse, tracks down her uncle Marvin's family. Of course, she doesn't tell his wife and children who killed him, only that he was a good man and that she was glad to know him. She settles back in a regular routine in Chicago working as a manager with a private security firm, only taking a hit job every once in a while to keep her skills sharp. Her cousin Ida has a rough road ahead, rehab twice since her cousin's return to Chicago.

The heroin and coke habit is hard to kick because each time Ida gets out of rehab, she relapse within five months. So, Natleaha and her uncle Eric decides to put Ida in very strict program that has a stay of nearly seven months with three of the first mandatory detox. Ida is released from the facility a few months ago and she seems to be doing ok so far. Natleaha is keeping a close eye on her.

Another reason Natleaha is eager to return to Chicago, well it is more like two reasons in a way. She goes back to the bar Lelha's and waited to see the red head she spoke to briefly all those months ago. The woman is stunned to see Natleaha again.

"What brings you here?" the woman asks her with a pleasant surprise.

"The right reason this time," Natleaha answers while taking the woman by the hand and leading her out to the dance floor where they bump and grind to various fast beat songs. Afterwards, they make passionate love when Natleaha pleasantly assaults the woman's body with her tongue on the tips of her breasts and the edges of her pussy with the help of a vibrator.

Then the next thing, Natleaha satisfied an itch that nagged her curiosity for the longest.

Another day ends at the 21th precinct and all the uniformed police and detectives are filing out sluggishly after having completed crazy hours.

"I'll see ya tomorrow Sam," Repen Stello says to his partner in passing.

"Yeah take care man," Sam answers back as he walks down the stairs.

When he's outside, he heads to the parking lot. Locating his 2009 model Lexus, he climbs in on the driver's side and starts the engine. It's a twenty-minute drive to his apartment from the precinct. His day as far as being a policeman goes was pretty uneventful.

He's so jaded that nothing could possibly surprise him. But detective Sam Givens would be wrong in that regard. When he enters his apartment, he's greeted by a sight in his living room. Laying across his couch is Natleaha, completely naked, eating an apple dripping with honey.

Sam's mouth nearly falls off his face at the surprise. Inching closer to fifty, Natleaha's body is still flawless, curves like an old seventies nude African woman painting.

"I was wondering when you were going to come home. You really should get better locks for your place. So, are you gonna fuck me senseless or did I waste a trip?" Natleaha asks seductively while licking her honey covered fingers.

Sam doesn't respond with words, instead he takes her in his arms and kisses her passionately. Within a minute, his clothes are on the floor. He's a little shorter than her, but he grips her tightly and firm around her waist. Taking a moment to get a condom from the bathroom, Natleaha slips it on herself as her mouth engulfs his now stiff penis. Minutes later, Sam returns the favor by kissing, pulling and sucking on her mound with his lips and tongue. Reaching up as they lay on the couch, Sam plays with her erect nipples using his fingers tips.

He enters her roughly and slowly with steady thrusts. Natleaha doesn't make a sound, she takes in the moment with her legs behind her head, then without warning, she flips Sam onto the floor so she could ride on top of him intensely. They ravish each other more than the first time, going through three condoms. It had been nearly three decades since Natleaha had been with a man. The rape would always be with her, but eventually her body and mind would have to heal, this was the first step.

Though time has passed, Eleanea's feelings has not changed concerning Ivan, nor did Rosa's. Though Eleanea eventually marries a man who loved her deeply and Ivan is a guest at the wedding, she is still steadfast on how she feels.

"You'll always be my first love, that'll never change," she tells Ivan the night before she gets married. Rosa just accept the situation with Ivan. Choosing to continue to sleep with the slow-witted semi-retarded bodyguard every once in a while to satisfy her sexual needs.

Over the following months, the lovers Ivan has, the situation changes with each of them in different ways. Him and Ingramisck are more on professional terms now, only having sex with each other if they're really bored.

Ingramisck has taken more of a liking at being an instructor at various black sites training young soldiers, pushing them past their limits of endurance and mentality. All Calhoun can talk about nowadays is his other lover Karum, openly inviting him to his games, spending more time with him instead of his girlfriend and having Karum at his family house for the holidays.

"I'm glad we met awhile back, dat's my boy!" Calhoun boldly says to Ivan after they were together. It is clear that Ivan had serious competition for Calhoun's affections. The midget Emmanuel simply wants something more serious and exclusive.

"I've never been with anyone who's more comfortable and accepting of me as I am. I know you have to feel the same way. So what bout it hommes?" Emmanuel expressed to Ivan a year ago.

Ivan doesn't speak inner city American slang like most black people, given the fact he isn't born or raised in America. But he usually gets the meaning of what Emmanuel is saying to him. Though he doesn't know how to really handle another man admitting they are having serious feelings for, not even Gregor fully did that. So, Ivan would just say distractive things to drag out the question until the man forgot about it. Ivan figures it worked with Calhoun, why not with Emmanuel.

Oddly enough, a few months prior to Emmanuel's declaration, they both get into serious trouble with the law. Emmanuel is doing a shipping and loading of a product for the cartel in New York and Ivan happens to be over seeing the transaction because the Bratva has purchased a quarter of the product in advance. But Emmanuel doesn't take the proper precautions like he was supposed to.

So, while he is helping move the product to the off-loading area, he gets made by some state trooper who reports it up the proper chain to where the D.E.A is called. Because of Emmanuel's screw up the Bratva doesn't know to find out about the D.E.A watching. So, everyone is arrested at the site during a combined surprise New York police and D.E.A agents sting operation.

Emmanuel has a lawyer on retainer by the cartel and all the men belonging to the Bratva are bailed out the next day after the arrests, except Ivan for some reason.

"It's stated on record that you have an attempted murder charge here in this city and they say there's a witness," his lawyer informs him.

"What charge? What the fuck are they talking about?" Ivan yells at him in a rage.

"Shot in the chest close to his heart outside a bar in the Bronx. The witness said to the police that they saw a pale faced man running away from the scene afterwards fitting your description."

"That's impossible, I was nowhere near the Bronx when they said I was, I was in Harlem with some of my men getting ready to go monitor the shipment."

"Uh, I wouldn't say that too loudly here, no telling who might be listening," the lawyer advises.

"What? You're my lawyer, we're alone in a closed room. What I say to you is privileged. Somebody is setting me up. Find out who and kill them, I don't have time for this," Ivan orders rashly.

"Ok, ok, but that'll take time. You might have to sit here in Rikers for a while."

"For your sake, it better not be too long," Ivan warns his lawyer in stern tone.

Ivan discovers his lover Emmanuel was far tougher than he appear to be. While at Rikers in the mess hall when him and Emmanuel make the mistake of talking to each other too long when three other inmates approach them.

"What tha fuck is this freakshow? Is Rikers cagin' circus acts now?" one of the inmates says making the other two laugh loudly.

"Ay fuck off ya prick," Emmanuel says bravely stepping to the inmates. The one who made the comments sucker punches Emmanuel in the face causing him to fall to the floor.

"Yeah you shouldn't fuck outta ya weight class little man!" one of the other inmates warns. Ivan was about to break the guy's nose with his fist when the man who hit Emmanuel screams. Blood is gushing out of the man's foot.

Emmanuel stabs him with a hidden shank and before he could react, Emmanuel gets him again in the neck by climbing on the table and leaping off it. Ivan easily lays out the other two inmates with several decisive blows and kicks. While the man who insulted them is laying on the ground, Emmanuel stands over him.

"Yeah the circus is in town and you a clown bitch!" he screams, spitting in the man's face and stomping hard on his nose, breaking it. After that, Ivan had a new-found respect for Emmanuel and took him far more seriously.

The two men were taken to isolation while the three other inmates were taken to the infirmary. They spent three days in isolation when following the third day Ivan and Emmanuel were dressed in clean prison uniforms and shackled.

"Where are we going?" Ivan asked one of the guards.

"Someones wants to see you about you and your friend's case," the guard answers.

Then a black hood is put over Ivan's head. From that moment, Ivan can't see where he's going. He can tell him and Emmanuel are moving in a van when they're thrown in the seats and hears the engine start up. He doesn't have on his watch, so he can't tell how much time it's taking to get to their destination. After they are unloaded from the van, they're taken inside a building.

Ivan hears a click and then a buzz sound followed by another click more louder than the first. So, Ivan guesses they're going through a locked door. He then hears the ding sound, which is probably the opening of an elevator. By the movements, they're going up.

They step off when they reach the desired floor. Seconds later are more clicking and buzzing sounds.

The hoods are taken off Ivan and Emmanuel when they are inside an office with carpeting, an American flag on a pole hanging inside a holder in the corner against the wall. Ivan notices a black robe hanging from a coat pole. Different law degrees are hanging on a section on the walls in the office. A photo of an attractive black woman is sitting on the desk, which is located in the middle of the office with a large fancy chair with a comfortable back to it.

Across from the wall of degrees, the woman from the photo on the desk appears again in a portrait picture with a handsome black man and two young boys who have familiar traits of both their parents. Ivan knows whom the man in the picture is right away. The realization gives him an uneasy feeling.

"Yo where tha hell we at hommes?" Emmanuel asks in puzzlement.

"In a judge's chambers."

A boom of excitement swells in Emmanuel at Ivan's answer.

"A Judge? No fuckin way man, our people got da juice! We gittin out today, I feel it."

"I'm not so sure about that. Just be cool," Ivan advises.

Suddenly, the door opens, startling the two men. A tall sort of heavyset white man comes in with a buzz cut wearing glasses and a gray suit, scratching his belly.

"Hue wee, you sumthin, jus like he said!" the man says with a broad smile on his face. The man then walks over to the desk and sits in one of the two less fancy chairs in front of the desk.

"So how you guys doin? Dey treatin ya al'ight at da place?" he asks casually. Ivan and Emmanuel don't answer, but the man still continues to talk.

"Well not dat it matters, but I like to ask jus in case, however ya ask it can make the difference in defusing da situation or makin' it worse. No matter da circumstances you have to know how to say the right thing. I'm sure I don't have to tell you gentlemen that." Ivan then presents a bold question.

"What are you into?"

"Why, what are ya offerin? I'm a pussy lovin southern boy, but I'm up fer anything from time to time," he answers back in the same brazen tone. Ivan is aware that the man's statement could mean anything, not necessarily gay or sexual.

Although Ivan couldn't get a read off him, gay, straight, bi or otherwise. He just acted like your run of the mill educated hillbilly, which made him dangerous in the legal profession.

"Why have we been brought here?" Ivan asks next.

"My colleague is might curious bout you and wanted to learn more bout ya. It seems you're a hard man to figure out and pin down. You're all he talks about on our off hours. You must've really peaked his interest when he met ya awhile back in London," the man says with emphasis in a southern drawl.

Emmanuel remains silent, but Ivan is still full of questions.

"Who are you?"

"I told ya I work with yer friend."

"That's not an answer and Benjamin Mathios is not my friend."

In that, Ivan was believing he was telling the truth. Benjamin kept trying to get Ivan to meet him in undisclosed locations off the grid, out of town or in London at Dante's 9th Wonder, ever since Ivan made the mistake of going out with him one time.

He also kept trying to get Ivan to meet his wife, hinting at inviting him into their bed. That bi closet stuff was played out to Ivan, though he put up with it from Gregor and Calhoun they never tried to drag their wife or girlfriend into the lie and it was evident to Ivan that Benjamin just wanted a secret side piece to hide whom he really was.

This guy is probably a paid flunky to keep the judge's secrets from the public and his family, Ivan thought. Thankfully, Ivan didn't tell Benjamin Mathios that much was himself during their encounters, but what does he think he knows now?

"Take us back to our cells," Ivan orders.

"Now, now all in good time, let's see how dis pans out."

"Man fuck all dat! We ain't playin dis shit!" Ivan shouts, surprising himself speaking in slang.

Emmanuel grabs Ivan by the arm.

"Man what are ya doin? We could be outta here today. Don't fuck dis up," Emmanuel whispers to him.

The white man just laughs at Ivan. He then takes off his suit jacket and lays it across the arm of one of the chairs.

"Hmm yer a feisty one ain't cha? Tha judge said you were into physical play. You wanna wrestle, would dat make ya feel better?" the man jokes.

It was taking every ounce of self-control to keep him from charging at this man and breaking his neck and also the fact that Ivan can hear the armed guards outside the door that stays his hand. It's just macho posturing pretty much until the man in question walked in.

"Is everybody behaving themselves?" is the first thing out of the Judge Benjamin Mathios' mouth.

"You aren't scaring our boys off, are ya, Ed?" are his next words.

Ivan was a little glad he found out the white man's name.

"Naw Judge we're jus tryin to git to know each other better is all," Ed says with a snide laugh.

Despite his faults, Ivan had to admit the Judge was still handsome. He had grown a full beard since the last time he saw him months ago. The conversation wasn't pleasant, but Ivan told him he didn't want to fuck his wife in a threesome.

"I'm not into women," Ivan adamantly told the Judge on more than one occasion. He thought after the last time he told him that Benjamin would take a hint. Obviously not.

"Leave it to you to find interesting playmates," the Judge says to Ivan while eyeing Emmanuel.

"I'll bet you boys have wild fun, the kind you only hear about in science fiction books. I hear you boys are into some shady stuff. The Russian mafia huh? I never would have guessed that about you Ivan."

"There's a lot you don't know about me, Judge," Ivan states in defiant tone.

"Well, I think that's gonna change soon."

"I doubt it."

"But you haven't heard my offer yet."

"If it doesn't involve taking us back to our cells, then we're not interested."

"I can make the attempted murder charge go away and help yo little friend out too."

"How?" Emmanuel anxiously asks.

"I'm giving a get together at my house for some people close to me and I'd like Ivan to be my guest this evening."

Oh, I see where this shit is headed, a damn swingers party where everybody fucks everybody, switching partners male or female. Some confused bullshit, Ivan thought with a tinge of annoyance.

"If you agree to this, I'll see to it that the witness in your case recants their statement. As for your little friend, I'll put in a good word so that he's eligible for bail tomorrow."

"And if I don't agree to your terms?"

"Then you go back to jail and take your chances with our legal system. Your friend's lawyer could file a motion to suppress the evidence against him, claiming entrapment, but I don't like your chances," the judge says with a smirk.

"Go out wit 'em ese he jus wants ta git in ya grill man. What could it hurt? I'd fuck 'em if he wanted me to," Emmanuel urges.

The Bratva's lawyer is good, Ivan knows this and he could probably get him off eventually, but if the lawyer takes too long, Ivan superiors may cut their losses and have him killed no matter what he promise them.

But something about the judge's offer isn't right. Ivan has the nagging suspicion that the judge has something to do with the charges against him. However, Ivan needs to be out soon, so against his better judgement he is going to accept the judge's offer.

"Fine, I'll do it, but I want everything you promised typed up in writing. And I call my lawyer and Emmanuel's so they can review and sign off on it. Now, take us back to our cells so we can be released and get this part of the deal over."

A smug expression forms on Ed's face, who witness the entire conversation with amusement.

"God damn boy you are smart jus like Ben said ya were."

"I don't suffer fools Ed, in any aspect of my life. I'll agree to your terms Ivan, but your friend has to go back to his cell until morning. He'll get out then. Your attorneys will be contacted and faxed copies of the agreement. I'll type out in a minute."

"You won't need to go back to Rikers, your personal items have already come when you were brought over. I had the feeling you might agree with my offer, but I didn't ask for your clothes though. I have an outfit I bought for you in your size, it should fit you nicely."

Ivan couldn't argue if he want this to go without a hitch.

"Bring them in," the judge orders as he goes over to his desk to write out the agreement.

One of the guards come into the office holding a name brand designer maroon wool sweater and tan slacks with a pair of Mike Jordan gym shoes. The judge lets Ivan make a call to his attorney.

"Yeah, you'll be getting a fax to look over and contact Emmanuel's lawyer to tell him he'll be getting the same thing," Ivan informs the lawyer. After he hangs up the phone, he holds out his hands.

"Give me the clothes and point me to the bathroom, so I can change," Ivan orders, but everyone only smiles at him.

"What's so funny?" Ivan asks.

"Now, you don't think I'd be stupid enough to let you out of my sight so you could hide a weapon on you to kill me, do you?" the judge asks with a grin.

"Sides I know yer not shy," Ed taunts.

"Modesty shouldn't matter, we're all men here and I've got a pair of jockey underwear here. Don't want your stuff peeking out through your boxers and scaring the women who'll be present at the get together," the judge adds.

Ivan just stares at him, but then reluctantly he begins to take off his jail uniform. He throws the pants and shirt on the floor revealing a tank top, boxers and white socks.

Ivan could tell the men present, except for Emmanuel were sort of fascinated by seeing a naked albino, especially when he removed his boxers fully showing his nappy blond pubic hair. The judge looks him up and down with relish while rubbing his chin.

"You are as beautiful as I imagined you'd be. Your hair is kind of nappy, but we can't do anything about it except comb it out. Fortunately, it's not long, so it'll be a small afro," the judge states before motioning the guard with the clothes to give them to Ivan.

"I'll see you soon," Ivan says to Emmanuel as the midget has a hood put back on his head, shackled and taken out of the office while Ivan remains behind.

"They're gonna love you bruh, I told 'em all bout chu," the judge brags to Ivan as a driver chauffeurs them to the judge's house in a black Lincoln town car. Ivan doesn't say much, but the judge continues talking.

"My wife can't wait to meet you, ever since she briefly spoke to you that Sunday. She said you had a nice and intelligent voice."

Is this mutha fuck a for real? What does he think this is? Ivan thinks in a rage. But the surprises aren't over.

When they reach the judge's home and he unlocks the front door, Ivan is greeted by the sight of black people of various ages standing and sitting around laughing and talking with small children running around. They are African Americans of different shades, very light, cinnamon brown and very dark.

Though Ivan has been to the states many times before, he has never seen so many blacks of different hues in one place. And the men are gorgeous of all ages, even the ones who appear older than Benjamin.

"My father's side of the family came from the deep south too. His mother, my grandmother was lovers with Mabel Hampton," the judge openly admits.

"How do you know where my family came from and who's Mabel Hampton?"

"The members of Dante's 9th Wonder have vast resources, especially when combined, we can find out anything no matter how well hidden. And to answer your next question, Mabel Hampton was a dancer and activist during the Harlem Renaissance."

"The Harlem what?"

"The Harlem Renaissance, a time in the 1920s and 30s where black people in America were musicians, singers, writers, actors and dancers who were very popular in New York, especially in the sector called Harlem. Even men and women like us played a key part. Although they wouldn't know what to make of you, a lieutenant in an all-white criminal organization with a grandfather who's a spy for Russia. You probably wouldn't have been recognized by the talented tenth."

"What?"

"Never mind it's a long story, here let's introduce you to everybody. You and your grandfather are more unique than you know," the judge says as he introduces Ivan to various members of his family.

The judge is true to his word, the charges against Ivan are dropped and Emmanuel is granted bail the next day. Although his bosses aren't pleased that he got pinched with a number of his other coworkers, seeing as how they paid crooked cops to avoid incidents that happen like that, they decide to let him live.

During the family get together, Ivan finds out more about Benjamin Mathios' family. His wife is fully aware of the judge's appetite for other men, especially younger ones. Helen only agreed to marry him to please her father who is a major shipping magnet. The two boys produced by the sham marriage is just another thing to please Helen's parents. She is however pleased to meet Ivan face to face.

"You're a lot more intelligent and mature than my husband's other usual boys," Helen comments.

Come to find out, Benjamin's grandmother was forced into a similar type of marriage to a man she didn't love. Her family also forced her to give up her female lover when they discovered she ran away from home to be with her. So, the Mathios considers Benjamin having what they call his grandmother's ways. Having gay relatives from long ago isn't the only thing the judge and Ivan has in common, they are both introduced to sex at a very young age.

The judge's older male cousin who Ivan met at the gathering started paying his cousin at the age of ten, five dollars so he could suck the judge's dick in secret. This went on for four years until his grandmother found out about it and made the older cousin stop. Ivan couldn't believe it. He didn't think that type of thing happens in African American families.

Another thing occurs that takes Ivan off-guard as he is reluctantly spending more casual time with the judge and his family, he realizes he is growing attached. He even goes against his judgement and breaks his own rule about dating a married man and starts to become intimate with the judge.

At first, the judge is an aggressive top in bed with Ivan, but as time goes on, Ivan and Benjamin are more equally giving to each other. Ivan is frightened about what is happening and the consequences that would follow, but he couldn't help it. He thought, after Gregor, it would never happen again, but it did. Here he is—Ivan Fisk, brutal and dangerous lieutenant of the Bratva falling in love with an American State Supreme Court judge.

To be continued. Find out what happens next in book 2…